SNOW FALLEN

Alex Walters

ALSO BY ALEX WALTERS:

Trust No One
Nowhere to Hide
Late Checkout
Murrain's Truth (short stories)
Dark Corners
Candles and Roses
Death Parts Us
Their Final Act

ALEX WALTERS WRITING AS MICHAEL WALTERS:

The Shadow Walker
The Adversary
The Outcast

SNOW FALLEN

Copyright © Michael Walters 2018

Michael Walters has asserted his right to be identified as the author of this Work in accordance with the Copyright, Designs and Patents Act 1988.

This is a work of fiction. Names, characters, places and incidents are a product of the author's imagination. Locales and public names are sometimes used for atmospheric purposes.

Any resemblance to actual people, living or dead, or to businesses, companies, events, institutions or locales is completely coincidental.

CHAPTER ONE

How long since he'd last been here?

Twenty years, he thought, or even more.

For many of those years, he'd accepted he was unlikely ever to return. Why would he? There was nothing for him here, and nobody wanted him, even if he'd had a choice in the matter.

Yet here he was. He still didn't even quite know why. His first instinct had been to ignore the letter. He had no intention of accepting the invitation, after all. But it had been a prompt to take the step he'd been considering for so long.

He'd arrived by train earlier that afternoon, travelling first to Piccadilly and then catching the local service out here. He'd had all that carefully planned, checking the timetables in advance to ensure he could make the connections.

But his train to Manchester had been delayed by some signalling problems south of Stoke, so he'd missed the local train. He'd had to wait forty minutes for the next service, whiling the time away over a stewed tea in an over-priced sandwich bar just down from the station. Perhaps it had been a sign, he thought. A last opportunity for him to change his mind. But he knew now it was already too late.

So he'd arrived later than he'd intended, and the walk from the local station had been further than the map had suggested. By the time he'd found the footpath and begun the slow trek up the hillside, the sun was already setting. When he reached his destination, the night would have long fallen.

That wasn't a problem. He'd never wanted to arrive in daylight. His only concern was whether he'd be able to navigate the final stretch of the journey in darkness, rather than in the twilight he'd expected. Even after all these years, though, he was sure he could find his way.

As he reached the top of the line of trees, he turned to look at the landscape behind. From these lower slopes, the land fell away sharply towards the Mersey valley and the wide Cheshire plain. It was a clear, cold day, and in the late afternoon the view was as spectacular as he remembered. Past the dark cluster of houses below, the countryside opened up once more. In the distance, he could see the squat towers of Manchester, and to its left the railway viaduct through Stockport. Otherwise the landscape was largely green pastureland stretching into the distance, the Welsh hills a faint dark haze on the horizon. The sun was poised above the horizon, half lost in strands of crimson cloud.

It was the last time he would see this vista and he allowed himself a few moment's respite, watching as the sun slowly dipped below the circle of the earth. Then he turned abruptly and resumed his journey, not pausing to look back a second time.

It was another thirty minutes, the twilight thickening, before he finally recognised the landscape. The footpath had joined a narrow metalled road. This was the route he'd generally have taken in the old days. He had rarely used the footpath, except for the occasional weekend stroll. He'd take the main road up from the town and turn off towards the village , finally ending up on this narrow track that led to the house.

The road was barely wide enough to accommodate two lanes, although in those days the chances of encountering other traffic up here were low. He wondered whether that had changed over the years, whether there was more housing up here now. New builds for families seeking to escape the urban sprawl. Somehow he doubted it.

By the time he reached the first house the darkness had fallen completely. The place looked largely unchanged from his time here. It could hardly even be called a village. It was little more than a cluster of houses surrounding the tiny church. It had been a much larger community once, farm buildings and workers' cottages serving the local farms and the long abandoned cotton mill down in the valley. Some of the houses had fallen into ruin, now barely discernible in the surrounding landscape. The few remaining cottages had gradually been renovated over the years, often being combined to create larger buildings. Some were now weekend or holiday homes, with a few occupied by couples and families commuting into Manchester or Stockport.

He could understand why. The views up here were spectacular, and the sense of remoteness belied the proximity to the suburban housing a mile or so below. That had been what had brought the family up here when the children were small. All of that, though, was something that had happened to another man. A man he no longer knew or understood.

The house itself seemed as unaltered as everything else. The road behind had been unlit, but by the houses and church there was a scattering of streetlights. As he passed, he could see that the front garden was overgrown, the paintwork needed attention. They'd been proud of the place when they'd first moved in, spending weekends decorating, working on the garden. Creating a family home. They were still a family, he supposed, those that remained.

He paused for a moment as he passed, making sure he stayed in the shadows. There were lights showing in a couple of the windows but no other signs of life. He imagined they were all in there, but would never know for sure.

Finally, he continued past the house to the gateway to the churchyard. When he'd first moved here, the church had already felt half-abandoned, with services held only once a month and on church holidays, the vicar traipsing up here from the larger church in the valley.

He'd half expected that by now the church would have been deconsecrated, sold off, perhaps turned into another gentrified residence. But he'd checked before setting off and discovered that this was unchanged too. A different vicar, but the same monthly services, presumably attended by the same or a similar handful of people.

He turned for one last look at the view. It was fully dark now, the final dregs of crimson drained from the western sky. Manchester was a haze of light, the relative dark of the Cheshire plain stretching away to the south. As the forecast had predicted, clouds were moving in from the west, obscuring the few visible stars.

It took him only a few moments, searching in the darkness, to find the grave. The church was no longer used for burials, and this had been one of the last bodies interred here at the far end of the graveyard, along with two or three others from the same year.

He read the inscription on the black marble. Just the name and the brief years of life. Nothing about the person. Nothing about the death or what had followed. He looked around for any other signs, but the overgrown churchyard was giving nothing away. This was as close as he could get.

This end of the churchyard was at the edge of the moorland, more exposed to the elements. He could feel the wind rising as the clouds thickened in the sky, a new dampness in the air.

He had almost nothing with him. He'd spent the last of his cash on the train ticket, scraping together a few remaining coins to buy the tea at Piccadilly. He had brought no credit cards, no wallet, no other documentation. It didn't matter. They would soon know who he was.

He pulled the small metal flask from his pocket, then removed his thin waterproof jacket and spread it across the grave. He lay down, facing upwards. The clouds were heavy now, the weather beginning to turn. The earth was cold.

Closing his eyes, he unscrewed the top of the flask and poured the cold liquid into his mouth. It would not be pleasant but he hoped it would work.

In those last few minutes, as he lay there, the first flakes of snow began to fall. By the morning, his body would be lost in a thickening blanket of white.

CHAPTER TWO

Murrain woke once in the night, his usually sound sleep disturbed by a dream he couldn't at first recall.

He lay in the darkness, listening to Eloise's rhythmic breathing. After a few moments, he eased himself from under the duvet, taking care not to wake her. He knew he'd get no thanks if he disturbed her at this time of the night. There was enough light through the curtains from the streetlight outside for him to slip on his dressing gown and find his way across the room. He silently stepped out on to the landing.

It was a cold night, the heating long turned off. He pulled his dressing gown tightly around him and made his way downstairs.

The dream had left him troubled, its forgotten content still resonating in his mind like the echoes of an unheard sound. In the kitchen, he poured himself a glass of water and stood sipping it, staring out of the kitchen window into the darkness of the back garden.

The predicted change in the weather had arrived. The last few days had been clear, bright and cold, but Murrain had already been tasting snow in the air. Now it had come, thick flakes billowing down. The garden was already under a thick white covering.

He sat at the kitchen table and closed his eyes. There was no point in forcing it. If he tried to remember, his mind would most likely remain blank. Instead, he sat silently, trying to think of nothing, hoping the memories would return.

It had been as if he'd been inside another man's head. Seeing through another man's eyes. Thinking, if that were possible, another man's thoughts.

Somehow, though he could recall few details, he was sure it had been a man. Not a woman. A man trudging up a seemingly endless hillside, wind and empty spaces at his back. A man with a destination. A man with a goal.

Had that been it? Had that been what he had dreamed? As soon as he tried to rationalise it, the memories fled away, scattered like the snowflakes tossed against the window.

He had been walking and walking. Then, finally, he'd reached his objective. There was—what? A house that looked like a child's drawing of a house. Four windows, a pitched roof. Smoke curling from a single chimney. Three faces in those four windows, staring back out at him. At the man.

Why three faces? Why had there been that one empty window?

Then he—the man—had passed by the house. His destination lay elsewhere. There was a church, Murrain thought. Again, a church from a child's drawing, with a steeple and arched windows. There's the church, and there's the steeple. Open the doors and there are the people.

Except there were no people. The man was alone. He had walked into the churchyard and there, as if waiting for him, had been an open grave. A blank dark space, perhaps empty, perhaps not.

Murrain opened his eyes, blinking at the bright kitchen lights.

The dream was already fading again. A man. A house. An open grave. Murrain hung on to those three images. A man. A house. Three faces. And an open grave.

He could recall nothing more. He rose and fumbled in one of the kitchen drawers for the pad and pen they used for making shopping lists. Carefully, in block letters, he wrote out the words.

A man. Walking. A house. Three faces. An open waiting grave.

Almost certainly it didn't matter. Almost certainly it could be forgotten. Even for Murrain, sometimes dreams were nothing more than dreams.

But there had been an intensity to this that had left him troubled. The sense of being in another man's mind. The details were now lost to him, but he had felt a depth of emotion that still clouded his mind like a slowly clearing mist. He couldn't have begun to describe that emotion—sorrow, anger, despair?—but it had been sufficient to rob him of sleep and drive him to try to capture at least something of the experience.

He was unlikely to sleep again that night. He rose to fill the kettle. Coffee, a book. Something to calm his mind as he waited for the night to pass. Tomorrow would no doubt reveal whether the dream was something or nothing at all.

As he stood by the kitchen window waiting for the kettle to boil, he watched the snowflakes endlessly tumbling in the darkness.

The snow had been a surprise. These days, she always retired early. Mainly, she thought, because there was little else to do. Even in the old days, they hadn't had much to say to each other. Now, of course, there was just silence. She wasn't keen on the television. Sometimes she listened to the radio, but mostly she simply sat reading until she decided it was time for bed. Then she had to go through all the usual routine before she could retire to bed herself, to continue reading, more comfortably and alone.

The others didn't wake particularly early, generally sleeping till after nine. Anne had always been an early riser. It had been one of the things—one of the many things—that had made her feel different from her sisters. As a child, she'd generally been up before the rest of the family, even before her father. When she was older she'd sometimes prepare breakfast for him – just toast or cereal – before he went off to work. She'd already be washed and dressed. After he'd gone, she'd sit reading by herself in what became an increasingly precious hour of solitude before school.

When she was grown up and living by herself, her sleeping patterns had barely changed. She'd be up before six, eating her meagre breakfast of toast and jam, the time stretching out until it was time for her to go to work. That was one reason she'd bought Dougie. Partly for company but partly to give herself something to do in those dead early morning hours. If she'd gone out walking by herself at that time of day, the neighbours would have thought her even odder than they did already. But nobody thought it strange to take a dog for a walk.

Her sisters had never wanted a dog, even a well-behaved labrador like Dougie. That had nearly been a sticking point when she'd moved back in here. But in the end they'd accepted Dougie's presence as long as he was excluded from the kitchen and the main living room. That suited Anne perfectly well. It gave her an excuse to seek Dougie's company on those evenings when she found the silence of the living room more oppressive than companionable. Now, of course, she could do what she liked.

That morning, she'd woken even earlier than usual, though still tired after a restless night. She'd felt the cold as soon as she'd pulled back the sheets. The central heating would not yet have come on, and her bedroom always seemed chillier than the rest of the house. She imagined this was why the room had been allocated to her in the first place. She could move now if she chose, but there seemed little point.

Despite the cold, the snow was unexpected, though she'd guessed as soon as she'd climbed out of bed. The room seemed brighter than usual in the first light creeping through the thin curtains. She'd felt a girlish thrill as she gazed out at the unsullied white blanket across the garden. Middle-aged as she might be, the sight of the snow took her straight back to childhood in this same place. Sledging down the hill opposite the house. Snowball fights with her sisters, always slightly more vehement than she would have liked. Returning home, soaked and chilled, trying to make herself warm as they all crowded round the tiny front room fire.

And, just sometimes, their father there, watching them indulgently, one of the few real memories she had of him from those days. The days before everything changed.

It seemed a world away now, all of that, to the point where she scarcely knew if the memories were real or imagined. It felt as if all childhood winters had been like that, snow-filled and joyous. But that couldn't have been the case. Even up here, even then, snow had been relatively uncommon, typically falling no more than once or twice each winter and then lying only for a day or so before melting into grey slush, lingering only in the darker corners further up the hillsides.

There must have been many darker days, when their mother was first gone, when their father had vented his anger on them. Even sometimes on her. All that seemed even more remote, like a story she had read rather than anything that had happened to her. It was as if she had buried the reality somewhere in the furthest recesses of her mind, never wanting to dredge any of it back up in the light.

She dressed quickly and made her way downstairs. She'd grab a shower later once she'd completed the morning routine. In the kitchen, Dougie greeted her as enthusiastically as ever, keen to be outside. She spooned some food into his bowl and topped up his water, while she went to pull on her heavy walking boots and waterproof.

The snow was already thicker than she'd expected. Perhaps nothing would happen today then, she thought. No visitor after all. That didn't trouble her. She hadn't really expected he would come. Despite the letters and the calls. Despite the supposed desperation. She'd called his bluff, knowing it would resolve things one way or another. Most probably, she'd hear nothing more.

Outside, Dougie responded to his first encounter with snow much as she'd expected. She was amused by his evident bafflement at the changed landscape, the way he tentatively placed one paw into the drift piled by the door and then hastily withdrew it. Within minutes, though, he had reconciled himself to the new world and was eagerly pulling her out into the garden.

She allowed him to tug her along the path and out into the street. Her usual routine was to take one of the footpaths down the hillside and then follow a looping route that eventually brought her back to the road a half mile or so from the house.

Today, she expected that the steep slope of the footpath would be treacherous and, if the snow had drifted, perhaps impassable in places. Dougie was normally keen to head into the woodland in search of non-existent rabbits, but today was too fascinated by the snow to care much about that. She decided to take a shorter and simpler walk around the perimeter of the churchyard. If Dougie was still restless after that, they could walk further up the road. But by then the dog might have tired of the damp and cold.

She tramped through the snow after Dougie, unfastening the lead so he could run free. Normally, she kept an eye on him at least till they were off the road, although few vehicles passed up here even in normal weather. Today, there seemed little likelihood that anyone but their immediate neighbours would venture on to these hilltop roads.

The snow had fallen to a depth of perhaps three or four inches, although much had drifted against the stone walls and hedgerows. She closed the garden gate behind her and followed Dougie along the road. It was growing fully light now, but the sky was leaden.

This was always a quiet spot, her walks generally accompanied only by birdsong and the brush of the wind in the surrounding trees. Today, the silence felt eerie. The houses were all still in darkness, and, other than Dougie skittering playfully through the snow, there was no sign of life.

Dougie had already passed the entrance to the churchyard. She hurried to the gate and called out to him, summoning him back. He was an obedient animal and immediately came running, scattering snow in his wake. She entered the churchyard knowing the dog would follow.

Her plan had been to walk around the perimeter of the church grounds, detouring through the rear gate into the woodlands behind where the paths were relatively flat and more sheltered from the worst of the snow. Dougie had different ideas. Instead of running towards her as she'd expected, he scurried off in the opposite direction towards the far end of the churchyard. She peered after him, wondering what had caught his interest. Some bird or animal, she assumed, though she wouldn't have expected much to be about in this weather.

She called to the dog again, but he paid her no attention, continuing to run in a tight circle near the perimeter hedgerow. It took her a moment to register where Dougie's interest lay. Then, puzzled, she strode through the snow towards him.

At that end of the churchyard, the ground was largely sheltered by the thicket of trees that ultimately merged with the woodland behind the church, and the snow was relatively thin on the hard earth. Dougie's curiosity, though, had been piqued by something in the far corner where the snow lay more thickly.

She knew that corner of the churchyard only too well, although it was many years since she'd last visited it.

At first, on her father's instructions, they'd made a point of visiting at least once a month, carefully removing the old bunch of cheap supermarket flowers and replacing it with the new, tidying the grave when it was needed. Within a year or two, their visits had become less frequent and eventually, even before their father had been taken away, they had ceased entirely. She couldn't recall the last time she'd even looked at the grave.

Dougie was still turning and turning in a tight circle, disturbed by something. He'd begun to bark too, something she really didn't want at this time in the morning. One of the neighbours had complained once about being woken by Dougie's barking. It had been a light-hearted complaint, at least on the surface, but she hadn't known how to take it. It was something she'd never really come to grips with, even after all these years. Making something into a joke because you meant it seriously.

She finally caught up with Dougie and slipped the lead back on him, telling him to be quiet. He obeyed as he always did, but the nervous energy of his movements didn't lessen. Something was troubling him.

It took her a moment, in the morning's half-light, to work out exactly what it was. Certainly, all the graves were different from usual, smoothed by the drifted snow angling into the hedgerow. The line of gravestones was half-concealed. Even so, she could already see something lying on the grave.

She moved closer. It was difficult to be sure at first because the drifted snow had smoothed the shape into an abstract form. It reminded her of a tomb you might find in a cathedral, a burial place for the local nobility topped by a full-sized likeness of the deceased, rendered here as if by an elemental Henry Moore. Then the full significance of that thought hit her. It was a human form, laid out on the grave as if in parody of the body buried beneath.

At first, she thought she must be mistaken. This must be some kind of joke. A left-over Bonfire Night guy, covered by the snow to fool the credulous. But no-one made guys these days. That was just another memory lingering from her childhood.

She took another step forward, Dougie barking anxiously beside her. She had no doubt now. It was a human body. Her first instinct was to flee back to the house, call the police or an ambulance. But the person lying in front of her might well still be living, despite the night's cold temperatures. Perhaps it was some down-and-out, or someone who had been taken ill. Perhaps even one of their neighbours. How would it look if she failed to check?

'Let's keep an open mind, shall we, Will? At least until we've had a look.' She'd had a similar conversation with their boss, DCI Kenny Murrain, before they'd set off. The report had come in early that morning, dealt with initially by a couple of uniformed officers out dealing with stranded vehicles on the hilltop roads. A body had been found by a dog-walker in a churchyard up in the tiny hamlet of Merestone. The initial assumption had been that it had been someone who, for whatever reason, had become stranded in the snow and had died from exposure in the freezing small hours.

'There's something odd about it, apparently. The original call was garbled and the uniforms haven't made much progress.'

'No change there, then.' Sparrow had been a uniformed officer himself until a couple of years previously but had quickly adopted the CID's familiar disdain for their operational colleagues. 'Probably just means they haven't tried.'

'I couldn't quite make sense of it,' Donovan went on, ignoring him. 'There was some story about the deceased being the elderly father of the woman who called it in. But she was shocked by the fact that he'd turned up. Not just that he was dead, I mean, but that he was there at all. Uniforms reckoned she wasn't very coherent.'

Sparrow was silent for a moment, negotiating a particularly tight bend in the road. Donovan caught a glimpse of the drop to their right and looked away rapidly. In fairness, Sparrow seemed to be doing okay now he was getting the hang of it. 'What is it, then?' he said, finally, once the road had straightened. 'Some sort of dementia case?'

'I dare say we'll find out. Kenny seemed to think it was worth checking it out, anyway.'

'One of his feelings, was it?'

She glanced across at him. 'I'm not keen on people taking the piss on that front, you know? Kenny saved my life.'

Sparrow made no response, clearly recognising he'd stepped over a line. That was the thing about Kenny Murrain, she thought. Everyone knew about the way he worked, and everyone had an opinion about it. But they all knew that, once or twice, when it had really mattered, he'd made the difference. In her own case, the difference between life and death.

In fact, though Murrain had said nothing explicitly, she suspected Sparrow was right. Murrain had some sense this case was worth following up, that it was more than simply an accidental death from hypothermia. He had offered no reason why he might think that, but he'd left her in no doubt he wanted her to follow up the incident as a matter of priority. Fair enough, she thought. Any unexplained death had to be treated as potentially suspicious, at least until they knew the circumstances, so their presence was required. Even if that meant tolerating Will Sparrow's driving.

They finally reached the top of the incline and the road levelled. They had seen only one set of tyre tracks ahead of them in the otherwise pristine snow – presumably the patrol vehicle that had preceded them. It was clear no other traffic had ascended or descended the road that morning. At the top of the hill, the road angled left into the village, the first houses visible ahead of them.

It was scarcely more than a hamlet—a scattering of period houses, a couple of newer-builds and, incongruously at the far end, a church that looked too large for its setting. Ahead of them, parked at the roadside, was a marked four-by-four, its blue light silently pulsing.

Sparrow pulled up behind it and the two of them climbed out. After the heated interior of the car, the chill of the morning was startling. The snow was falling gently, but the sky was heavy with the threat of much more.

'This the place?' Sparrow pulled his heavy waterproof more tightly around his shoulders.

'Looks like it.' Donovan regarded the house with interest. It looked as if it had once been two small cottages, long since knocked into a single sizeable dwelling. She couldn't immediately guess its age, but she thought it must be eighteenth century or earlier. It looked older than most of the surrounding houses which she thought to be Victorian, perhaps built to serve the Mill further down the valley.

There was a small overgrown front garden, and the cottage itself looked in need of some renovation. A new coat of paint, Donovan thought, and some of the roof tiles replacing. Not exactly neglected, but in need of more attention. Well, she thought, I know that feeling well enough.

She turned and looked behind her. On a clear day, the view would be spectacular, out over the valley and woodland towards the breadth of the Cheshire plain. To the north, she could just make out the dark blur of Manchester, its lights still visible in the gloomy morning, the silhouettes of the Beetham and CIS towers.

'Nice location.'

'It'd fetch a bob or two,' Sparrow agreed. 'Even up here.'

She walked past the house towards the churchyard gate. Over the low perimeter hedge, towards the far end of the grounds, one of the uniformed officers was pacing slowly up and down beside a line of graves. A chilly piece of sentry duty, she thought.

He looked up as she approached, clearly ready to send her away. Behind him, a line of police tape had been stretched across the area, and a small self-erecting tent had been placed over one of the graves. And, presumably, the body. It looked as if everything had been done according to the book.

'Morning. DS Donovan,' she called. 'Marie. How are you doing?'

'I'm freezing, mainly.' The man held out a gloved hand for her to shake. 'Relieved to see you. PC Tony Wadham.'

He looked vaguely familiar, though probably only because she'd seen him around in the canteen or the corridors. 'Good to meet you. Where's your colleague?'

'In the warm. Lucky bugger. He's with the woman who found the body. She's in a bit of a state.'

'What's the story exactly?'

'She was out here walking her dog, first thing. Dog started barking at something over here so she came to look. Found the body, lying on one of the graves, covered in snow. She was brave enough to check the pulse and realised he was dead.'

'We're sure he really is dead?' She knew it wasn't impossible for someone with severe hypothermia to have no discernible signs of life.

'We double checked. I'm as sure as I can be. I think he's been dead for some hours.'

'Not much else we can do. There's supposedly an ambulance on its way but I've no idea how long it'll take. They've a couple of all-terrain vehicles but I imagine there's a lot of pressure on them this morning. We've got to get the CSIs up here as well as soon as we can.' She paused. 'What's this about it being the woman's father?'

'That's the weird bit. To be honest, she wasn't making a lot of sense. But she says she'd looked at the face and reckoned it was her father.'

'Did the father live with them?'

'No, that's the thing. Like I say, she wasn't making much sense, but my impression was she hadn't seen the father for a long time. That she hadn't expected to see him, let alone like this.'

'Maybe she's mistaken. Shock can make people think strange things.'

'That's what I thought. She was a bit—well, almost hysterical. She might have just imagined the likeness.'

'You haven't checked to see if there's any ID on the body?'

'Thought it better not to touch it any more than we had to.'

'Quite right.' Uniformed officers weren't always so punctilious about contamination of a potential crime scene. 'Anything else you can tell me about the body?'

'Male. White. Quite elderly. I'd have guessed at least sixties, maybe older, though difficult to be sure without moving the snow. Looked to be dressed in walking clothes but again I couldn't really see much.'

'Could be some hiker who got stranded up here, I suppose. The weather wasn't expected to close in like it did.'

'But why would you just sit there? Or lie there. There are plenty of houses around. He could have found shelter easily enough, you'd have thought.'

'You'd have thought,' she agreed. 'But hypothermia can do strange things. Or maybe he was taken ill or collapsed for some reason.' She looked round at the dark clusters of houses beside the churchyard. 'Or maybe they're not as hospitable round here as you might think.'

CHAPTER FOUR

Sparrow had been waiting for her by the car. She suspected he was mainly keen not to be tasked with nursemaiding the body. They might have no choice but to volunteer for that duty, though, until the CSIs turned up. Operational resources would be under pressure on a morning like this. While it wasn't as if CID had time to spare, their demands tended to be less immediate. But they could deal with that once they'd had a chance to take a witness statement from the woman who'd found the body.

The door to the cottage was opened almost immediately by a middle-aged PC who was unfortunately all too well known to Donovan. He was a cocky Liverpudlian called Mick Delaney who'd shown himself adept at irritating his colleagues, uniforms and CID alike, in most circumstances and generally in record time. 'About bleedin' time,' he said, by way of greeting. He was chewing ostentatiously on a piece of gum which Donovan expected to fly in her direction at any moment.

'Morning, Mick. Always good to see your cheery face.'

'Can we get going now then, like? Seeing as how you lot have finally bothered to turn up.'

'Not just yet, Mick. We need your reassuring presence. Why don't you go and join your mate outside?' She imagined Delaney had pulled rank, or at least relative age, in forcing Wadham to stand outside in the cold.

'You don't need me in here, then?' He looked reluctantly past her through the open front door.

'I think we'll cope, Mick. Which way?'

He gestured to a door on the left of the hallway. 'She's in there.'

'She?'

'Anne Tilston. One of the three bleedin' witches, apparently.'

Before she could offer any response, he'd already exited and closed the front door behind him. From what she knew of his habits, he'd be lighting a cigarette before he reached the garden gate. She raised an eyebrow at Sparrow and pushed open the door Delaney had indicated.

The room inside was large, but with a gloom that made it feel claustrophobic. It was decorated in dark, Victorian-style colours – a green wallpaper, crimson carpets, similarly deep-red furnishings. The overall effect might once have seemed impressive, but now the room seemed shabby and depressing. Apart from the presence of a small flat-screen television in the corner, there was little to suggest that the room had changed since the house was built.

A woman was sitting by herself in an armchair at the far end of the room. The room felt almost abnormally silent. Although quite possibly Mick Delaney would have been able to do enough talking to compensate.

Donovan looked around the room, trying to quell her own discomfort. 'Detective Sergeant Marie Donovan. My colleague, DC Sparrow.'

The woman pushed herself to her feet. Her eyes were red, her skin raw from crying. She was dressed in plain black trousers and a black sweater. Practical, Donovan thought, but not inexpensive. Clothes that had seen better days. 'I found him—'

'Do you feel up to talking to us about it?'

'Yes, of course. Let's go through to the kitchen. It's more comfortable than this place.' The woman bustled past her, seemingly keen to leave the room. Bemused, Donovan followed her down the hallway into the kitchen, Sparrow trailing behind them. This area also looked as if it had barely been altered in recent years. There was a battered-looking Aga on the side wall, earthenware tiles on the floor, and an ancient oak table in the centre of the room. A dog was spread out on the floor in front of the Aga, barely bothering to raise its head as they entered.

'Can I get you some tea? Coffee?' There was a slightly manic edge to the woman's voice.

Donovan exchanged a glance with Sparrow. 'Yes, why not? If it's no trouble. Thank you.' The woman might benefit from the chance to busy herself with something mundane as they talked.

The woman filled an old-fashioned kettle and placed it on the Aga, before turning back to them. 'I'm sorry. I'm still in a bit of a state.'

'Don't worry,' Donovan said. 'Take your time.' Sparrow had sat down at the table beside her and taken out his notebook. 'First things first. We'll need your name.'

'Tilston. Anne Tilston.'

'And you live here with...?'

'My sisters. Charlotte and Emily.' She caught Donovan's expression. 'My mother. A Bronte fan. Luckily there was never a Branwell.' She stopped, as if about to say something else, but instead turned her attention back to the kettle. 'They're having a lie down at the moment. They're neither of them in the best of health. Tea or coffee?'

'Tea, please,' Donovan said. Beside her, Sparrow indicated the same. Anne Tilston busied herself finding teabags in one of the cupboards, then went through what was clearly a well-established ritual of warming the teapot, waiting for the kettle to finish boiling and making the pot of tea. By the end of the process, she looked calmer, as if a normal order had been restored.

When they were all finally seated, Donovan said: 'So tell me about this morning.'

Anne Tilston slowly talked through the events of the morning – the surprise of the snow, taking Dougie for his walk, the decision to visit the churchyard rather than take their usual route. Then, finally, the discovery of the body.

'I didn't know whether I should touch it. But I thought—'

'You did the right thing,' Donovan said. 'If he was suffering from hypothermia, there was a possibility he might have been still alive.'

'But you're sure—?'

'We are. Obviously, the paramedics will confirm once they get here. But, yes.' Donovan paused. 'You thought you knew the identity of the deceased?'

'I did know. It was my father.' There was no hesitation, no equivocation.

'You're sure of that? I'm sorry to press you, but in this kind of situation...'

Anne Tilston nodded. 'I know. That's what I told myself. You can't be sure. You haven't seen him for years. But I kept staring at the face. I'm sure.'

'You hadn't seen your father for a long time?'

'No.'

'Can I ask—?'

Donovan hadn't even been sure what it was she wanted to ask, but clearly Anne Tilston was ahead of her. 'He was Robert Tilston.'

There was a moment's silence while Donovan struggled to recall why the name seemed familiar. Then she realised. 'I see. I'm sorry.' Her first thought was that, in gaining an answer to that first question, she had raised many more.

'So you can see,' Anne Tilston went on, 'why we wouldn't have been in contact.'

'You haven't been in contact since he was released?'

'He made no effort to contact us. We had no desire to try to contact him.' It sounded like a well-rehearsed response. Perhaps, Donovan thought, they had already had to use it in dealing with the media.

'No, well—'

'He served his sentence. That's all. It changed nothing.'

'I understand. But why would he have come here now?'

'Perhaps he came home to die. Perhaps he wanted to see us.'

Donovan nodded, unsure how to respond. 'This had been his home? Before, I mean.'

'We've always lived here. All our lives. Me and my sisters, I mean. He and my mother bought the place a couple of years before Charlotte was born.'

Donovan wanted to ask why, despite everything, the three sisters had decided to stay on here. They no doubt had had their reasons—financial, most likely. 'We'll need you or one of your sisters to confirm the identity formally in due course. You've presumably told your sisters about this?'

Anne Tilston seemed to hesitate. 'Of course. They were still asleep when I came back to the house. But I woke them and told them.'

'They didn't know any reason why he might have returned here either?'

'I'm sure they were as surprised as I was.'

There was a shortness in her response that made Donovan wonder whether Anne Tilston was telling the whole truth. 'We'll need to speak to them in due course. Just in case they can offer any insights.'

'Surely there's nothing for you to investigate? Assuming he died of exposure.'

'We don't know the cause of death yet. I'm afraid we have an obligation to investigate any unexplained death. At least until we can ascertain the precise circumstances.'

Anne Tilston nodded, looking unconvinced. 'But in this case—'

'You're concerned about the media?'

'That's one of my concerns. Our concerns. Yes. We've had to deal with that before.'

'I appreciate that. We'll do our best to handle the matter discreetly, but I can't promise—'

'No, you can never promise anything, can you? I remember that from before. We were just left to twist in the wind.' Anne Tilston's previous meekness had been replaced, with an unexpected suddenness, by something that seemed close to genuine anger.

Donovan nodded, unable to offer any meaningful reply. The police couldn't be responsible for how the media might behave, and their ability to intervene was limited unless there was genuine harassment. Some of her colleagues undoubtedly had cosier relationships with journalists than was healthy, but most tried to handle these matters responsibly. Once the news was in the public domain, though, there was little they could do. She didn't doubt the Tilstons had been through some tough times, and there might well be another media storm once this new story was aired. 'We've got the Crime Scene people on their way. Again, that's just routine now with any unexplained death. And an ambulance to follow. I hope we'll be able to complete this straightforwardly.' It wasn't exactly a lie, but she spoke without much confidence. If Anne Tilston was correct about the identity of the body outside, it would be difficult to keep the news under wraps. 'Is there anything else relevant you can tell us, Ms Tilston?'

'I don't think so. What else would there be?'

What else indeed? There would probably be a need to take a more formal statement from Anne Tilston and her sisters, but now didn't seem the time to push matters further. 'In that case, we won't disturb you any more for the moment. We'll ensure everything's dealt with outside. We will need to talk to you all again, but that can wait.' Donovan pushed herself to her feet. Sparrow, looking slightly surprised by the curtailment of the interview, closed his notebook and stood up also.

Anne Tilston led them back through the gloomy hallway. She was clearly eager to have them out of the house and, after the most cursory of goodbyes, she closed the front door firmly behind them.

'That was an interesting set-up,' Sparrow said, as they walked back towards the churchyard.

'Very,' Donovan agreed. 'Like something from Chekhov.'

'If you say so. Place gave me the creeps to be honest.' He said nothing more until they reached the entrance to the churchyard. Delaney and Wadham were standing by the line of police tape, Delaney ostentatiously puffing on a cigarette and holding forth in his usual way.

Sparrow stopped outside the gate, just out of earshot of the two uniformed officers. 'So,' he said to Donovan, 'are you going to tell me? Who the hell is Robert Tilston?'

CHAPTER FIVE

'You okay, boss?'

For a moment, Kenny Murrain felt as if his vision was blurred, the mundane outlines of the office overlain with something else, some other image he couldn't quite capture. DI Joe Milton was standing in front of the desk holding two mugs of coffee. 'Brought you one. Thought you looked as if you needed it.'

'Thanks, Joe. You're the perfect support, as always. One step ahead.'

Milton sat down opposite Murrain's desk and slid one of the mugs over. 'I aim to please.' He took a sip of his own drink. 'What's the problem?'

'Just the usual. All the usual. You know.' Murrain couldn't bring himself to say that Milton himself was part of the problem, albeit only a minor part. He hadn't worked out how to broach that one yet. 'Too much on. Too much admin. Too little resource.' He gestured round at the unusually quiet office. 'And today we've even got people stuck at home or in the traffic because the bloody Council didn't get round to gritting the roads.'

'They'll be in.' Milton said. 'And any that are stuck at home have the facilities to work remotely. They can get on with all that admin.'

'You're right, obviously. You generally are.'

'Is any of this the usual...?' Milton trailed off, showing as always some discomfort in raising the question of Murrain's – well, who knew what they were. Premonitions? Feelings? Intuition? Murrain was never able satisfactorily to describe them, and Milton would never want to delve too deeply. It was some sort of ability that Murrain possessed. A form of second sight perhaps, that sometimes provided him with insights unavailable to others. On occasions it had proved to be a gift, but to Murrain it felt too often like a curse.

'Maybe. Who knows?' He rubbed his temples as if that might physically provide the answer. 'I've not been sleeping well. Things bubbling away in the back of my brain.'

'Anything in particular?'

'Not that I can recall.' Murrain shrugged. 'If it's important, it'll surface eventually. That's usually how it works. If it works at all.' He stifled a yawn, still struggling to overcome his tiredness, and tried to focus. 'How are we doing with these missing person cases? Anything new?'

'Not really. I've just been ploughing through the interview data for the latest Stockport one. Lots of potential witnesses but nobody seems able to cast any real light.'

'So often the way, isn't it? Doesn't matter how many people there are around. Nobody sees anything.' It was a familiar complaint among police officers, although Murrain knew that he and his colleagues would prove no more observant in their daily lives.

'It could well be there was just nothing much to see.'

That was true enough, Murrain thought. They still didn't know how seriously to take this one. The missing woman, Kirsty Bennett, was an adult, albeit a young one, who'd been living with her parents in Bramhall. She'd finished at university the previous summer and, unable to find a permanent job, had been working for a local temping agency, taking on various clerical roles. She'd last been seen two weeks earlier, on her final day in a short-term contract with the local authority. Her colleagues had understood she was heading off after work to meet up with some friends in the city centre. Her parents, on the other hand, had been under the impression she was spending the weekend away with a couple of friends from university. In Leeds, they thought, but they knew no more than that. 'She doesn't share much with us,' her mother had said.

The upshot was it wasn't until the Sunday evening that her parents had become concerned. Even then, on the basis of past experience, they'd assumed that, with no work scheduled for the following week she'd probably just decided to stay over another night. They'd texted her and later tried to call her mobile, but there'd been no response. Again, apparently, that was not particularly unusual. Her mother had said Kirsty often forgot to charge her phone. More likely, Murrain thought, she just avoided taking calls from her parents.

It hadn't really been until the Tuesday that her parents had become genuinely worried. Even then, their initial call to the non-emergency number had been embarrassed and apologetic. The initial police response had been equally half-hearted. Bennett's parents seemed to know little about her private life. As far as they knew she hadn't had a regular boyfriend since she'd split up with some fellow student in her final year at university. They didn't know anything about that last boyfriend except that his name had been Greg and he'd lived somewhere down south. She had some friends locally and she went out on the town, usually into Manchester, most weekends. But, no, they didn't really know who any of those friends were. The middle-aged PC who'd interviewed the parents came away shaking his head at the behaviour of young people today. But the truth was, Murrain thought, most parents would be in the same position once their children reached their late teens.

The initial assumption was that Kirsty Bennett had most likely extended her stay with her unknown friend or friends, and had simply neglected to inform her parents. It had happened once or twice before, though never for so long without her calling or texting to let them know where she was.

It was only as the week passed, with no word from Bennett and no response on her mobile, that the police had taken her disappearance more seriously. Even then, it proved surprisingly difficult to identify any clues to her possible whereabouts. Her parents could offer little information beyond a few half-remembered first names. Her past work colleagues knew almost nothing about her life outside work. Her sporadic social media activity provided a few contact names, most of whom were old school or university contacts who hadn't heard from her for months.

As time passed, they explored other lines of enquiry. Bennett had used her debit card to withdraw £100 in cash from an ATM a few hundred metres from her former workplace. There was no record of her using her debit or credit card to buy a railway ticket, and no further use of the card or her bank account after that point. They'd checked CCTV in Stockport and Piccadilly Stations but could find no sightings of her. Her mobile phone had been turned off shortly after she'd left work, and they had been unable to trace its location after that point. In short, they were drawing a blank.

Murrain's team had taken over the case because it was going nowhere. In the absence of other leads, Murrain had found himself re-examining apparently similar missing persons cases stretching back over the previous couple of years. All were young adults, mainly but not exclusively female, with ages ranging from eighteen to mid-twenties. Most were either living alone or renting rooms in shared houses. All were either in education or some form of work. All had seemed happy enough prior to their disappearance, according to family or friends – although Murrain knew enough to treat such opinions with a degree of scepticism. All had vanished apparently without trace – failing to meet up with friends as planned, not coming home at the end of the working day, not returning from a night out. As with Bennett, their bank accounts had remained unused, their mobile phones had been untraceable, and it had proved impossible to track their movements following their last contacts with friends or colleagues.

They now had half a dozen cases that followed this broad pattern from the previous two years. There was nothing to link the individuals involved, other than that they had lived in central or south Manchester. They were liaising with their colleagues in the north of the region to identify any similar cases. There were a couple that broadly fitted the bill but it was difficult to judge whether those were coincidental. People went missing every day, and for a wide range of reasons. They had no evidence of foul play in any of these cases, and no substantive reason to suspect it, except that the disappearances had seemed out of character and so complete.

'You think we're wasting our time?' Murrain asked now.

Milton shrugged. 'Not at all. I mean, it's not like we're overwhelmed with other leads, is it?'

'No. Though I don't want to stir the pot again on these older cases unless there's something useful we can add.' Some of the cases had been relatively high-profile news stories at the time of the initial investigation. As so often, the cases that had received the most coverage were those involving the more prosperous, middle-class individuals. A couple of students, in particular, had fitted that description, with parents who had done their utmost to keep the case in the public eye. Some of the other cases, particularly those involving individuals whose background didn't match the media's expectation of the conventional nuclear family, had received much less coverage. As far as Murrain was aware, no-one else had thought to link the various cases. All were notionally still 'open' but they'd inevitably slipped down the priority list pending the emergence of any new information or lines of enquiry.

As so often, Murrain was driven by little more than his own intuition. Somewhere in the back of his head he'd felt the discordant buzzing that told him this was a line worth pursuing. There was something here. But, as always, he had no idea what that something might be.

'What baffles me,' Milton said, 'is that people are always going on about how we're under constant surveillance. You know, someone's watching you, wherever you go, whatever you do. How come these people can just step off the grid and disappear?'

'I think it's surprisingly easy if you really want to do it. The question with all these cases is why the individuals would want to.'

'People often have reasons they don't share with those around them.'

'Is that your cry for help, Joe?' Murrain shook his head, immediately regretting his flippancy. 'Sorry, I didn't mean—'

'I'm not planning to disappear, Kenny. And, for what it's worth, things really aren't that bad. I'm getting through it now.'

'Handled with my usual sensitivity, eh?' Murrain knew he should have had this conversation with Milton weeks before. Or rather, he added to himself, not this conversation but a considered and constructive one. 'How are things actually going? Now I've stuck my size nines so clumsily in.'

'We're on to the practicalities now. The main one being what we do with the house. She's entitled to her share.'

Milton and his former partner had not been married, but had had a joint mortgage on their house. They'd parted on largely amicable terms – or, at least, as amicable as possible in the circumstances – and so far seemed to be dealing with the split in what seemed to Murrain a remarkably civilised way. No doubt there'd be pitfalls before they were done.

'What does she say?' Murrain asked.

'She says she doesn't want it. She's earning a decent tax-free wedge out there, and her rental's pretty low by UK standards. She reckons she's happy just to forego it.'

'Why not take her at her word, then? She's the one who chose to go.'

'And, more importantly, not to come back. I know, that's what everyone keeps saying to me. But it doesn't seem right. This isn't anyone's fault.'

More than a year before, Milton had told Murrain that his partner, Gill, was taking up a temporary job with the OECD in Paris. It was too good an opportunity to miss, he'd said, and it was only for six months. Even at the time, Murrain had wondered whether Milton was deceiving himself. In the event, six months had stretched to nine months, and then to a year. The couple's initially frequent visits back and forth had tailed off and they'd grown increasingly distant. Finally, Gill had broken the news, by then not entirely unexpected, that she didn't want to return to the UK. She hadn't offered Milton the option of going out to join her.

That had been a month or so back. Milton had said nothing at first, but it hadn't taken Murrain's distinctive sensitivity to detect that something was wrong. The truth had emerged when Milton had requested a few days' leave for a trip to Paris. Murrain hadn't enquired into what had been said during that visit but it had been clear on Milton's return that the relationship was over.

'So what's the alternative?' Murrain asked. 'Sell the place?'

'I might want to do that anyway. Not enjoying living there much any more.'

'I can imagine. Well, your decision.'

'Just want to end it on the right note, you know. I don't want any acrimony.'

'Take your time. Don't rush into anything. If you need more time off, let me know.'

'I think that's the last thing I need. Just want to throw myself into work at the moment.' He paused. 'By the way, what's this job that Marie's gone out to?'

That was the other part of the story, Murrain thought. He'd noticed a growing closeness between Milton and Marie Donovan. Paul Wanstead, the seasoned Detective Sergeant who never missed much happening in the team, was convinced there was already something between the two. Murrain had so far seen little evidence of anything beyond the occasional after-work drink, but he suspected things were becoming more serious. In due course, that might raise questions about whether they could continue working in the same team. Murrain's own wife was a senior officer in the force, but they'd always kept their careers very separate.

'Something and nothing, probably,' Murrain said in response to Milton's question. 'Body found in some churchyard up in the hills, apparently. Don't know the details yet. Some walker caught out by the snow, I imagine.'

'Poor bugger. It's miserable out there.'

'Sooner the snow goes the better,' Murrain agreed. 'It's a pain in the backside.'

'Sounds like you're the one who needs a break. So what do you want us to do with the missing persons?'

'I don't know. Kirsty Bennett's our case now, so we need to push on with that as best we can. As for the others...'

'Boss?'

'I don't know. We can't afford the resource to spend too much time on them. And there's unlikely to be a link.'

'Unless we've got some real multiple killer out there.'

Murrain rubbed his temples again, conscious of the nagging ache behind his eyes. 'Jesus, Joe. That doesn't even approach being funny.'

CHAPTER SIX

'Robert Tilston?' Sparrow prompted again.

Marie Donovan ignored him and walked into the churchyard. Delaney and Wadham looked up as they approached. Wadham looked awkward, as if caught out in some minor misdemeanour. Delaney continued talking, apparently about nothing much.

'Okay, boys, I think you might as well head off. We'll hold the fort here.'

Delaney was already heading for the gate, but Wadham hesitated. 'Are you sure? I mean, if you're—'

'No worries, Tony. I want to be here when the CSIs arrive, anyway. There's no point in all of us being stuck up here. There must be plenty of other stuff you can be getting on with on a morning like this.'

'Too right,' Wadham agreed. 'Everything's backing up down there.'

She watched the two officers until they were back in their car, then turned back to Sparrow.

'Robert Tilston?' he said.

'Didn't want any risk of them overhearing. Delaney's got a mouth as big as the Mersey Tunnel. The story'll get out soon enough, but Kenny would want us to be in control of it.'

'So what is the story?'

'Don't you remember Tilston? God, I must be getting old.'

'The name rang a vague bell,' Sparrow said. 'But I've been struggling to place it.'

There were a couple of benches at the end of the churchyard where Tilston's body was still lying. Donovan brushed the snow off one of the seats. 'Dedicated to Aggie Wentworth,' a plaque read, 'who loved the peace and tranquility of this place.' Rather you than me, Aggie, Donovan thought, glancing round the tree-sheltered gloom. Perhaps it was more attractive in the summer.

She gestured for Sparrow to join her. 'Might as well sit down while we can. You see, fifteen years ago, in your job, you'd have known exactly who Robert Tilston was.'
'Would I?'
'He'd have put the fear of God into you. Quite literally, probably.'
'Go on.'
'Assistant Chief Constable Robert Tilston. God's own representative in the force.'
Sparrow nodded. 'Right. I remember him on the news. Always pontificating. Had a beard.' He paused, thinking. 'Of course, fifteen years ago, I was only ten.'
'Don't rub it in, sunshine. I wasn't much older myself. But I was at Uni up here, and we heard more than enough about Robert bloody Tilston and his Christian values. He used to strut about like some Old Testament prophet expounding the word of God.'
'Don't get so much of that from the senior officers these days.'
'Thank Christ. He disapproved of almost everything. Young people. Protesters. The homeless. Students. God, he hated students. But mostly homosexuals, though of course he wasn't allowed to say so openly. Even we'd moved on from that. But he made life as difficult as possible for anyone who didn't fit into his conservative idea of normality. Constant clampdowns on clubs and bars, especially in the Gay Village, usually on some spurious pretext. Drugs raids. Raids on supposed brothels. Public order offences.'
'Maybe he was right. There's plenty of unpleasant stuff out there.'
Donovan glanced across at Sparrow. He was a pleasant enough young man and undoubtedly good at his job – if without the spark that some of his colleagues displayed – but he was already part of the establishment. As far as he was concerned, the force was always right and senior officers were beyond criticism. She could see Sparrow making Chief Officer rank himself one day.

'I'm sure some of it was legit,' she conceded. 'And I'm not really in a position to comment. I was just a student myself. But that was how it was perceived among those communities. Tilston the fascist.'

'That's how all the lefties see us, though. Part of the fascist state. Tool of the oppressors. All bollocks, isn't it?'

'Some of it is. Mostly we're just trying to do a job. Anyway, that wasn't the full story about Tilston. Remember?'

'There was some scandal, wasn't there? I remember seeing it on the news. Didn't he end up in prison for something?'

'Convicted of one count of manslaughter and several of grievous bodily harm.'

'Blimey,' Sparrow said. 'Why didn't I know that?'

'Because you're too bloody young, that's why. Stop reminding me.'

'I suppose.'

'It was all over the news. All of us lefty students hated the bastard, so we were glued to it.'

'But how does an ACC come to commit manslaughter?'

'In this case, by beating up an underage male prostitute to the point where he falls in a canal, smashes his head and is dead before he hits the water.'

There was silence while Sparrow absorbed this. 'An underage male prostitute?'

'Exactly. I'm not sure the full story ever emerged. Tilston had been caught on CCTV hitting the victim. He claimed at the trial he didn't know the individual concerned. It all happened in some backstreet in central Manchester. Tilston reckoned he'd just been walking back to Piccadilly after a night in the pub with some mates, and that it was an attempted mugging. He'd fought back in self-defence, thought he'd just used reasonable force, hadn't realised how much damage he must have done to the victim, had no idea how the victim might have ended up in the canal. Blah, blah, blah.'

'Sounds a reasonable story.'

44

'Except the investigation had already uncovered phone evidence that Tilston had had previous contact with the victim. He was telling the truth about going to the pub, but he'd left over an hour earlier and couldn't account for his movements between then and the CCTV footage. When the story hit the media, others began to come forward to say they'd had contact with Tilston. Turned out he had a reputation. Making approaches to men in public lavatories and the like. If he got a response he'd go off with them for, well, an assignation, let's say. When it was done, he'd beat the crap out of them. Not just that. It turned out he was an equal opportunities bastard. He'd done the same with some young female prostitutes around Piccadilly and Cheetham Hill. Picked them up, back seat of the car job, then slapped them around and dumped them in some back street. Not quite as brutal with the women, apparently. He was a real gentleman, our Mr Tilston.'

'Jesus. None of them had reported this?'

'One or two had, though it's not the easiest thing to report, especially as some of the individuals were underage. I'm not sure our lot had taken the reports very seriously. The victims didn't know Tilston's identity, probably couldn't offer much in the way of a description, and it most likely wasn't a priority for us. You can imagine.'

'I suppose. But why did Tilston do it?'

'I don't know. Some compulsion. Self-loathing. In court, as I recall, Tilston initially tried to stick with the self-defence claim. But that was never going to hold water. In the end, he went for diminished responsibility. Tried to suggest it was part of his religious calling. That he'd thought he was on a mission from God. Cleansing the world.'

'But if he—'

Donovan raised her hands. 'Don't ask me to explain it. I've no idea how that kind of mind thinks. But I don't think that argument helped him in court. It was clear from the CCTV and the witness accounts that the beatings had been genuinely savage. Tilston was a large man. Even if he hadn't deliberately killed any of his victims, he'd been capable of doing them a hell of a lot of damage. And, of course, there was the fact that he was a senior police officer – position of trust, all that. There was a suggestion he might get a life sentence, as a danger to society. In the end, he was given twenty years.'

'But he didn't serve all that?'

'Released on parole after about ten. He supposedly turned over a new leaf in prison. Was in isolation for most of the time, given his background. Kept his nose clean. Funnily enough, I read he continued with all the religious stuff. But in a much more genteel Church of England kind of way.'

'Tea with the vicar?' Sparrow gestured towards the looming church behind them.

'Something like that. Maybe that's why he came back up here. Or part of the reason.'

'When was he released?'

'Four, five years ago? Something like that. It made a bit of a splash in the papers at the time. But not so much. The story made the headlines originally because of who Tilston was. Ten years on, he'd been largely forgotten.'

'What happened to him?'

'Haven't a clue. I followed the story originally just because we all detested the bugger. We were delighted to see him get his comeuppance. But I never saw anything about what happened to him after he was released. He obviously didn't come back here.'

'Until now.'

'Until now. He was probably off doing good Christian works somewhere. Like Profumo.'

'Like who?'

'Jesus, you really are a youngster, aren't you? Never mind.' She was trying to think back to those student days, the eagerness with which she and her friends had followed this high profile case. 'There were all kinds of rumours at the time, as I recall.'

Sparrow had stood up and was stamping his feet on the snowy ground, trying to ward off the cold. 'What kind of rumours?'

'I think we wanted to turn him into a real pantomime villain. It was satisfying to see this sanctimonious pillar of the establishment brought down, you know?' Sparrow's expression suggested he really didn't know, so she went on. 'There were claims that the individuals who came forward weren't the only victims. That he'd been responsible for killings, but the bodies had never been found. Stuff like that.'

'Sounds like bollocks.'

'I'm sure it was. Nothing came out in court, anyway. All just our fevered imaginations. We wanted to turn him into some unholy cross between Dennis Nilsen and Peter Sutcliffe.'

'Who?'

'Oh, for Christ's sake, you can't mean—' She caught Sparrow's expression and realised that, this time at least, he was laughing at her. She found that, in this bizarre setting, a snow-covered corpse lying only metres away from them, she was finally laughing too. 'Oh, just bugger off, Will, you – you child!'

CHAPTER SEVEN

'They still out there?'

'Seem to be. One of the police cars has gone but the other's still there. There's another van now, too.'

'Maybe we should go and see if there's anything we can do.'

'They're the police, Liz. I'm guessing they don't really need our help.'

'Yes, but—'

'I know you want to find out what's going on. So do I. But it's probably nothing like as interesting as it looks. I was watching them when I went out for a smoke earlier, and they all seemed calm enough.'

'Maybe someone's been taken ill.'

'In which case, they definitely won't want you under their feet. Anyway, we'll find out soon enough.' Rob Carter was still peering out of the kitchen window. His wife was at the kitchen table, sipping at a mug of coffee.

'Why would they need the police, though?' Liz Carter said.

'I don't know. Surprised they could get up here. That road's lethal.'

'Yes, I heard you make that very clear. Was Tom really expecting you to come in?'

'You know what he's like.'

'He's an arsehole. That's what he's like.'

'That's a fair summary of his character. Was keen to let me know he'd been in since seven-thirty.'

'That's because he's a five minute walk from the office. Probably made a point of being there first so he could look smug.'

'Boss's privilege, I suppose. It's his company. But he knows full well I can work just as effectively from home. Most of us can. It's just that he likes to keep us where he can see us.'

'But he was okay about it?'

'He may be an arsehole but he's not a complete idiot. He could see there was no sense in trying to get into the office today. Even if I manage to get down the hill, the traffic'll be a nightmare. I'd probably arrive in time to start heading home again.' He paused to take a mouthful of coffee. 'What about you? What are your plans?'

'I'm free as a bird given they've decided to close the school anyway. Benefits of working in the public sector. Thought I might take the kids sledging.'

'Good idea. About time we got some value from that sledge.'

'Might be our only chance this year. Never seems to snow properly any more. Do you reckon I can risk taking the boys out now? Didn't want to do it earlier in case there was something going on I wouldn't want them to see.'

'Like what?'

'I don't know. If someone had died or something.'

'I imagine the police are pretty discreet. I'd take your chance while you can. Looks to me like we might be in for more snow before long.' He looked up at her, his expression suddenly concerned. 'You're not planning to go too far, are you?'

She smiled at him indulgently. 'We're not planning to get lost, if that's what you mean. Thought we'd just go in the field over the road. There's enough of a slope there for them to get going properly. But it levels off at the bottom so they ought to be all right.'

'Don't let them go mad, will you? You know what they're like when they get over-excited.'

'Nearly as bad as you are.'

'And make sure you come in if it starts coming down again.'

'Come and join us if you're so worried.'

'I've got to put in some decent hours today, or I'll have Tom the arsehole on my back.'

'Lucky you. Okay, I'll round up the boys.' She was still smiling. 'And you think your life is hard.'

In the end, it took her another half-hour to drag the two boys from their Playstation and get them suitably dressed in winter coats and wellingtons. Then she had to dig out the plastic sledges from the cluttered shed in the back garden. They'd bought the sledges in a fit of optimism during a brief snowfall the previous winter, but the snow had barely lasted long enough for them to be used. That was how it was these days, even right up here. They had one or two snowfalls each year at most, and the snow rarely seemed to linger more than a day.

As they left the house, she saw the police car and other vehicles were still stationed outside the churchyard. A strip of police tape had been stretched across the gate. Something more than just someone being taken ill, then.

'Why's that police car there, mum?' Ben asked, inevitably and immediately. The boys were eight and nine years old, and there was little they missed.

'I don't know. Maybe someone's been burgled.'

'They've sealed off the graveyard,' Jack said, his eyes wide. 'Maybe somebody's been stealing the *bodies*.' He uttered the final word in a doom-laden tone that made Liz wonder whether she ought to be more careful about his television watching.

'I don't think so, Jack.'

'Maybe someone's been *murdered*,' Ben added. Both boys collapsed into giggles, as if this was the funniest idea they'd ever encountered.

'I don't think that'll be it either. Are we going sledging or what?' She ushered the boys towards the gate leading into the field opposite. The field belonged to a farmer further up the valley, but he was happy for them to use it if there were no livestock present. She led the two boys through the gate, closing it carefully behind her.

'What do we do, mum?' Ben asked.

She gestured down the slope. 'I thought you could sledge down there. You should be able to get going properly down there, but it's still safe at the bottom.'

'What if we crash into the hedge?' Jack said.

'You won't. You'll slow down when you get to the level bit.'

The two boys looked disappointed that they were in no danger of careering into the hedge at the far end of the field. Liz helped each of them mount their plastic sledges, then pushed them to the edge of the slope. 'Hold on to the string carefully. And try to stay on until you get to the bottom.' She gave each sledge a gentle push to send it on its way.

The first attempt was largely a success. Both boys whooped loudly as their acceleration increased. Jack made it all the way to the bottom of the slope, more or less in a straight line, gradually skidding to a halt as he reached the level ground. Ben was less successful, veering off to the left in the middle of the slope before the sledge toppled over, depositing the boy in the snow.

Liz trudged down the slope, hoping Ben was unhurt. It soon became clear that, not only was Ben unhurt by the fall, he'd found the whole incident hilarious. Jack was now looking enviously up at his brother, and she knew he'd now try to engineer a similar accident for himself. The chances were that the two boys would now spend the rest of the morning falling off their sledges. She just hoped they could manage it without injury.

She dusted the snow off Jack's coat and helped the two boys drag their sledges back up the slope. 'Next time you both do this yourselves. I'm too old to be your servant.'

The remainder of the morning passed as she'd expected. In their next descents, both boys contrived to topple off their respective sledges, much to their joint amusement. This was repeated a couple more times until the boys became bored with that game, and instead began to focus on racing each other.

The sky was darkening with the threat of more snow. Rob had been right, she thought. Perhaps this time they really were due some serious snow. They'd never been genuinely stranded up here but another heavy fall would render the road impassible. Even the police four-by-four might struggle if the snow grew any deeper.

There was a hedge between the field and the road, and on the lower ground she was unable to see whether the police and other vehicles had departed. She'd heard the sound of a vehicle starting up earlier, but the boys' shouting would have drowned any further sounds.

As the boys' sledging skills had improved, they were increasingly travelling in a straight line and ending up further and further beyond the bottom of the slope. On his latest attempt, Jack had halted only a few yards from the far side of the field. She couldn't really believe they'd be capable of colliding with the hedge, but she'd been a mother long enough to know the boys could always surprise her. Particularly when it came to finding innovative ways to injure themselves.

She'd persuaded them they were capable of dragging the sledges back up the hill without her assistance, but she could see now that they were growing tired, finding the slow trek back up the slope increasingly difficult. Once or twice more, then they'd be more than willing to head back for a hot drink and some lunch.

Ben was dutifully trudging his way back, pulling his sledge behind him. Jack had stopped by the hedge, his attention caught by something in the next field.

'You okay, Jack?' she called.

He squinted back up at her. 'Mum, what's that?' He was pointing into the depth of the undergrowth.

'Probably nothing.' It would be typical of Jack to spot some dead animal. 'Why don't you bring your sledge back up for another go?'

'Mum, you ought to come and have a look.' He was sounding tearful now, his tiredness rising to the surface.

'It won't be anything important, Jack. Shall we all go to get something to eat?' She heard a cry of protest from Ben who had been preparing himself for at least one further trip down the hillside. 'Okay, you go down again, Ben, and I'll have a look at whatever it is Jack's found.'

She made her way cautiously down the hill, keeping well away from Ben's path. Jack was still motionless by the hedge, his eyes glued to whatever he'd seen. She reached out to take his soggy gloved hand in hers. 'There, mum. What is it?'

At first she assumed it must be some trick of the increasingly gloomy light. Something white was visible through the tangled bare thicket. Something which, from this angle, looked disconcertingly like a human hand.

She peered into the gloomy base of the hedge, then took a breath and, barely thinking, dragged Jack behind her. She heard the crunch of snow as Ben's sledge reached the foot of the slope.

She was already ushering Jack up the hill as she reached out and grabbed Ben's hand. 'Come on, we're going inside now. We'll get you a drink.'

'But mum—'

'No arguments. We need to get inside. I've some things I need to do.'

CHAPTER EIGHT

They were still laughing when the Scene of Crime Officer arrived. Neil Ferbrache had looked at them curiously, but Donovan knew he'd been in the job too long to be surprised by the behaviour of detectives at a crime scene. SOCOs had their own brand of graveyard humour, and everyone recognised that an over-serious approach to this job was one of the surest ways to burn-out.

'This a particularly hilarious corpse, then?'

'Not so's you'd notice,' Donovan acknowledged. 'But you know how it is.'

'Only too well. Sorry I'm a bit late. No point in trying to bring the trusty old van up here on a day like this.' He gestured towards the all-terrain vehicle from which he'd just disembarked. 'Had to wait till that monstrosity was available and then shift my gear over. Bloody traffic in town was a nightmare. Ambulance shouldn't be far away, but they're even more stretched than we are. What's the story?'

'Not much on the face of it. Elderly white male. Looks like hypothermia. Probably died overnight. No particular reason to suspect foul play, though obviously that'll depend on what you find and what the doc has to say.'

'But?'

She knew Ferbrache didn't miss much. 'But the elderly white male in question happens to be the estranged father of the three sisters who live in the cottage over there. He also happens to be Robert Tilston.'

Ferbrache peered at her with the expression she imagined he used when looking at a particularly interesting crime-scene exhibit. '*That* Robert Tilston?'

'The very same.'

'Christ. I sometimes wondered what had happened to him. How long's he been out now?'

'Four or five years.'

'You said estranged. Not in the habit of visiting his daughters, then?'

'Anne Tilston reckons they haven't seen him since he was sent down. We'll have to check that out, but I don't know why they'd lie about it.'

Ferbrache turned back to where Tilston's body was lying on the gravestone. 'You lot certainly give me some interesting ones.'

'We aim to please.'

Ferbrache looked up at the lowering sky. 'And you pick your times. Looks to me like we could get another hefty dump before too long. I'll get the protective gear set up and then we can get on with things. I'll let you know when I'm done.'

'We'll make sure you're not disturbed, Neil.' She led Sparrow back towards the churchyard gate. 'Don't take too long, though. It's bloody cold out here.'

There was nothing much else she and Sparrow could do for the moment. Earlier they'd heard the sound of children shouting from somewhere nearby. There were lights showing in a couple of the neighbouring houses, but little other sign of life.

'Who do you reckon lives up here?' Sparrow asked. 'Apart from the three witches, I mean.' He caught her disapproving expression and shrugged. 'Literary reference. I did *Macbeth* for GCSE.'

'Stick with Chekhov if you're going to resort to literature. To answer your question, I don't know. Some of these places look like holiday lets or weekend places. Other than that, I'd imagine it's mostly commuters into Manchester or Stockport. Maybe the odd working farmer clinging on.'

'Not much chance of anyone commuting in today.'

'Don't suppose they worry too much. How many days a year do we get weather like this? They probably just work from home or take a day's leave.' She looked back at the churchyard and the small squat church behind them. 'To be honest, place gives me the creeps. No wonder our friend chose it as the place to die. Let's go out on to the road.'

She ducked under the police tape stretched across the gateway, Sparrow clumsily following behind her. Once they were out on the road, she could hear the shouting children again from down the hillside ahead of them. That small addition of noise, she thought, made the place seem less desolate.

'Wouldn't suit me, that's for sure,' Sparrow said. He'd recently bought his first house, a small new-build house on an estate in Hazel Grove. He was, Donovan thought, the sort of person who used phrases like 'the property ladder' with a straight face.

'Not sure I'd fancy it much either, though imagine the views can be spectacular on a clear day.' She stepped across the snow-covered road, intending to look over the metal gate into the field beyond, where the land fell away towards the valley.

As she reached the gateway, she found herself face-to-face with a harassed looking young woman fumbling with the catch, two small children bouncing impatiently behind her. The woman looked up, startled. 'Oh, you made me jump.'

'Let me help you.' Donovan noticed the woman's fingers were trembling as she struggled with the gate, though her hands were wrapped in warm-looking gloves. Donovan took hold of the catch and slid it back, pushing the gate open. 'Are you all right?'

The woman looked momentarily confused, as if the question had been too difficult. She was looking past Donovan to where the police vehicle was parked. 'Do you know where the police are?'

'We're the police. DS Donovan and DC Sparrow. What can we do for you?' The last thing she wanted was to be fending off curious neighbours, but she was already forming the impression there was something different on this woman's mind.

'You're the police?'

'CID,' Donovan said patiently.

The woman turned to the two children and gestured towards one of the cottages at the far side of the churchyard. 'Go and get daddy to let you in. I'll be over in a minute.' She turned back to Donovan. 'I'm sorry. I've been a bit – well, shaken.'

'What's the problem?'

The woman pointed into the field behind her. 'Down there. At first I just thought – I didn't expect—' She stopped, as if she'd run out of words.

Donovan exchanged a glance with Sparrow. 'Take a few breaths. Then tell us what you can.'

'It was down there. In the hedge at the bottom of the field. I didn't think—'

'What was down there?'

'The hand— I mean, I saw the hand. But there was a body. In the next field. I could see the hand—'

'You mean a human body?'

'Yes. I think so.'

'Okay, Ms...?'

'Carter. Liz Carter.' The woman looked relieved to be asked a straightforward question.

'DC Sparrow here will take you back to your house. Did you say your husband was there?'

'My partner, yes. Rob. He's at home today.'

'Right. We'll take you back over there and I'll go and check what's down in the field.'

Donovan waited until Sparrow had led Liz Carter over the road and then pushed open the gate. The field was white with snow, disturbed only by the network of sledge tracks stretching down the hillside. She trudged cautiously down the slope, grateful she'd thought to pull on her heavy boots before leaving that morning.

A thick hawthorn hedge lined the bottom of the field. As she approached, Donovan crouched and peered into the undergrowth. The morning had darkened still further and it was difficult to make out what, if anything, might be lying under there.

There was something, though. Something white. Something that could easily be what Liz Carter had imagined.

Stepping cautiously, Donovan made her way along the hedgerow. She leaned over the gate and peered back along the far side of the hedge.

There was no doubt. She pulled out her mobile and quickly thumbed through the numbers to find Neil Ferbrache's number.

It took him a few moments to answer. 'Jesus Christ, Marie,' he said, before she could speak. 'You're worse than bloody Kenny Murrain. I've only just got started. Give me a chance before you start hassling—'

'It's not that. I've found something else. I hope you've got no plans for this afternoon, Neil. Because I think you're going to be here a while.'

CHAPTER NINE

As he left the building, Murrain glanced up at the sky. There was going to be more snow, he thought, and soon. Another heavy fall from the look of it.

Milton had given Murrain a knowing look when he'd said he was going for a walk. Murrain wasn't the sort of man who, in normal times, was given to leaving the office for a casual stroll. He certainly wasn't the sort of man who'd choose to go for a walk in the face of an impending snowfall.

Milton knew better than most that Murrain sometimes needed time to himself. Time to assimilate whatever half-formed thoughts and sensations were racing through his brain. Time to try to make sense of whatever his body or brain were telling him. Time, maybe, to give those impalpable feelings a freer rein.

'Bit of a headache,' he'd said to Milton. 'Fresh air might clear it.'

'If you say so.'

'I'll probably grab a sandwich on the way back. Want anything?'

Milton had shaken his head, his expression indicating he knew full well that this was nothing more than an excuse. 'I'll grab something from the canteen. Thanks, though.'

It wasn't exactly a headache, Murrain thought, as he waited for the lights on the main road to change. The A6 at least had been well-gritted and the traffic was moving smoothly, or as smoothly as it ever did in town. But even here some of the steeper roads remained inaccessible.

It was never just a headache. It was something else, something he could never accurately describe. A mental buzzing, a tremor. A loose connection, almost but not quite completing a circuit. An insistent bluebottle trapped somewhere in the back of his brain. He'd tried many times to talk about the sensation to Eloise, but had never found anything better than those unhelpful metaphors.

The other question was whether any of it meant anything anyway. There was no way he could answer that. Sometimes he'd been sure it had, that it had provided him with answers or insights he couldn't have derived any other way. At other times, he'd suspected the whole thing was little more than his own imagination. Shadows dancing behind his eyes, teasing him with meaning but revealing nothing.

He crossed the road, conscious of the slipperiness of the pavement beneath his shoes. The snow was still thick here, compacting rather than melting underfoot. There were few other pedestrians about. Clearly most people had had more sense. Although it was still only late morning, there was an eerie gloom to the light, as if he were observing the world through a dark filter.

Murrain was a tall, slightly ungainly man, who even at the best of times moved as if the floor might suddenly be whipped from under him. Today, hunched in his slightly shabby raincoat, he cut an awkward figure as he trudged cautiously down Wellington Road towards the town centre. His mind was already elsewhere, focused on the missing Kirsty Bennett.

This one was, at least in one sense, a little too close to home. Bennett's last agency job had been in the building adjacent to the police offices. On that final Friday, it was likely she'd walked down this same road, heading either into town or to the station for the train, depending on whether her colleagues' or her parents' understanding had been correct.

As he reached the turn-off for the station, Murrain looked around him with the air of a hunting dog sniffing the air. The faint but insistent buzzing in his head had not lessened, but he still had no idea what, if anything, it might be telling him. Possibly nothing more than that he was facing an incipient migraine.

He hesitated, then took the left turn towards the station, intending to follow the looped approach road that would bring him back to the main road further down the hill. The area had recently been redeveloped, with new office blocks opening up around the recently-landscaped station forecourt. The trains looked to be running normally despite the weather, and the snow around the station had already been trampled by countless feet.

Murrain was feeling nothing new here, though the original sensation hadn't diminished. His instincts were telling him that, whatever Kirsty Bennett might have led her parents to believe, she hadn't taken a train from here into Manchester and on to Leeds. But those instincts might well be worthless.

He continued past the station to the main road, turning left again down into town. He walked past rows of shops, the theatre and the Hat Museum, reaching the point where the road was elevated, the bus station on his left, the large shopping precinct on his right.

Then he suddenly felt something, an unexpected electrical jolt that stopped him in his tracks. There was an image, a half-glimpsed something, momentarily appearing behind his eyes. As so often, the image was too brief to discern, nothing more than a shadow.

Murrain looked at the surrounding landscape. It was as prosaic as it could be, characteristic of the unimaginative development of this side of town. A bleak bus station, an anonymous shopping centre, unnoticeable office blocks. The only remarkable addition to the view was the huge brick-built railway viaduct, an extraordinary product of Victorian engineering. But that only emphasised the ordinariness of the surrounding landscape.

He took a few more steps forward. There was no repeat of the sudden jolt, but he felt as if the continuing sensation in the back of his brain was growing stronger. As if there was something here he ought to be aware of.

Past the bus station, the land dropped away to reveal the dark strip of the River Mersey below the road. To his right, the Mersey disappeared under the shopping centre, literally built as an enormous bridge over the river. To his left, it stretched into the distance, its black tree-lined waters running incongruously between the office blocks and industrial buildings.

The sensation had grown stronger. There was something here. Something they ought to be investigating. But he had nothing that would justify the diverting of police resources.

Murrain stood staring out along the river, trying to allow his mind to grow blank. Sometimes that worked. Sometimes he could surrender to the feelings in his head, allow them to take over his rational mind. Sometimes, then, something emerged—a clearer sense of what was important, what he needed to understand.

There was a moment when he thought something was finally coming, when he could almost feel the meaning taking shape in his head. Then, agonisingly, he felt the buzzing of his mobile phone in his pocket, snapping him back into rationality.

He pulled out the phone and glanced at the screen. 'Joe?'

'Sorry to disturb you, boss—'

'No worries. What is it?'

'I've just had a call from Marie. She's out with Will Sparrow dealing with that body that was found this morning. Up in Merestone.'

'The walker or whatever he was?'

'That's the one.'

'What's the trouble? She suspect an unlawful killing?'

'Worse than that, maybe,' Milton said. 'We've another body.'

CHAPTER TEN

'Jesus,' Murrain said. 'How the hell are we going to get a full team up here if we need to?'

He'd somehow commandeered another four-by-four, and he and DC Roberta Wallace were heading up towards Merestone, Wallace at the wheel. Murrain had wondered whether to make this trip on his own, given the resource pressures on the team. Even with a second body, they had no evidence of foul play. But he was already sensing that this was something bigger. Joe Milton had been up to his ears trying to complete some urgent paperwork but had volunteered Wallace, a junior but well-regarded member of the team, to accompany Murrain.

Murrain always made an uneasy passenger, and today, as they negotiated the winding snow-covered road, he was having to close his eyes at every bend.

'Not sure it's going to be possible till the snow clears,' Wallace said.

'And that could take evidence with it. It's not helpful.'

Wallace's eyes were fixed on the road. As expected, the snow was falling again, even more thickly than earlier, heavy flakes filling the grey sky. Even with the wipers at maximum speed, visibility was severely restricted, their headlight beams penetrating only a few metres in front of them. 'I think we're almost there.'

'I bloody well hope so. No disrespect to your driving, Bert.'

'I kept us on the road, anyway. There were moments when I thought I wouldn't even manage that.'

'Thanks for sharing.' Murrain took a deep breath. 'There was me thinking you'd got it all under control.'

They turned another corner and the hamlet suddenly loomed in front of them, appearing through the snow as if a curtain had been pulled back. 'Probably picturesque in summer,' Wallace observed.

'Bloody isolated on a day like this.'

There was a marked police car and another plain four-by-four parked outside the churchyard. Wallace pulled in behind them. After a moment, the driver's door of the marked car opened and Marie Donovan climbed out, waving to them.

Murrain had swapped his battered raincoat for a more serviceable police waterproof. Pulling up the hood, he climbed out, Wallace following behind. They were hit by a blast of chill wind from off the valley, swirling the snowflakes into a blizzard. Snow was already drifting thickly against the walls and hedgerows to their left.

'Come and join us,' Donovan said. 'It's impossible to talk out here.'

When they were settled in the car, Sparrow hunched nervously in the front passenger seat, Donovan recounted what had happened since her and Sparrow's arrival.

'Robert Tilston?' Murrain interrupted. 'You mean *that* Robert Tilston?'

'The very same.'

'That takes me back,' Murrain said. 'He was an unpleasant bastard. Strange character, too. Hard to pin down. Not just your average old-school copper. I mean, not on the surface. He'd had a reputation as a moderniser at first. One of those who trots out all the jargon the politicians like and goes around reorganising everything for no good reason.' He allowed himself a smile. 'A bit like Eloise, I suppose.' Murrain's wife was a Chief Superintendent who, these days, was mainly tasked with leading organisational change across the force. To Murrain's slight amazement, she'd managed to do this while largely retaining most officers' respect and goodwill.

'That's not how I pictured him,' Donovan said. 'I always pictured him as the dinosaur's dinosaur.'

'He was that all right,' Murrain agreed. 'But he'd kept that under wraps for a long time. He'd always been hot on the old Christian values stuff, but the right side of what was acceptable. It was only when he got to Chief Officer level that the real evangelical stuff came out and he started with the hellfire and brimstone line. I don't know whether it had always been there and he'd just kept quiet about it. Or whether at some point he just flipped. Bit of both, probably. Obviously, by the end he'd completely lost it.'

Bert Wallace had been listening to the conversation with interest, but some bafflement. Now, her eyes widened. 'Oh, Christ, this is the guy who went to prison? Gay bashing? I remember reading about that.'

'Manslaughter and GBH to be accurate,' Murrain said. 'That was him.' He peered out of the window. 'This is where he lived? Seems suitably gothic.'

'Wait till you meet the three sisters,' Donovan said. 'It's a weird set-up.'

'And he came all the way back up here to die. But made no attempt to contact them?'

'That seems to be the size of it.'

'And now we have another body.'

Donovan nodded. 'Not much I can tell you about it. I didn't do much more than confirm he was dead. Didn't want to risk disturbing the scene, given Neil was already on-site. Body was covered in snow but it was white, probably male, probably youngish. Mid-twenties, maybe. Beyond that, you'll have to wait till Neil's done with it.'

'Don't envy Neil in this weather,' Murrain said. 'Suspect there's not much we'll be able to do today either. We'll need to wait till Neil's finished his business and we've got the bodies away, but I don't fancy getting stranded here all night. What's the position with the ambulance?'

'They've got a couple of all-terrain vehicles they reckon should be able to make it up here,' Donovan said. 'We're on their schedule. But there's a lot of demand.'

'We might as well try to make ourselves useful while we're stuck up here,' Murrain said. 'We can see if the sisters have any clue who our friend down there might be. I can do that. I wouldn't mind seeing the whites of their eyes.' They all knew this was one of Murrain's principles in any investigation. He liked to be face to face with those who seemed closest to the incident – to see their faces, read their eyes, hear their voices.

'We also need a statement from the woman who found the body,' Murrain went on. 'You think she'll be up to it?'

'She was shocked,' Donovan said. 'But I reckon she'll be okay once she's sat herself down and had a cup of tea. Her partner's apparently at home so she's not on her own with the kids. Shall I do that with Will? She'll probably respond better to a familiar face.'

'We'd better get on and do it, then.' Murrain gazed warily through the car window into the grey, swirling snow. 'That lot doesn't look like it's going to stop falling any time soon.'

CHAPTER ELEVEN

Neil Ferbrache wasn't a nervous or squeamish man. There was no room for that in his job. He supposed he must once have responded to his work in the same way any normal person would – with a mixture of revulsion, nausea and horror. At some point – he couldn't recall when or how – he'd adjusted and acclimatised to the work. It had become just another job, no different from turning up in an office or on a factory production line. In his darker moments, waking in the small hours, he wondered what that change might have done to him.

Mostly, he didn't even think about it. He turned up, did what he had to do, exchanged some friendly banter with his colleagues, packed up his case and left. That suited him fine. He never talked about his job outside work, even to his wife and family, and they were all content to leave it that way.

Even so, some parts of the job were shittier than others. Today wasn't one of the worst. That accolade was reserved for times like the night when he'd found himself, in the rain, in the mud, dealing with the aftermath of a road traffic collision that had left two young children dead and the third orphaned. But today wasn't great. He'd sensed almost as soon as he stepped into the far field what he was dealing with.

It was a dead body, all right, and from the covering of snow it had been lying there some hours at least.

It had taken Ferbrache some time to carry the protective awning down the hill. That had meant leaving Tilston's body unprotected, other than by a body bag, but there was little he could do about that until they got more resource up here. Ferbrache had already collected what little evidence he could. His main questions about Robert Tilston related to the cause of death. There was no obvious evidence of foul play, but Ferbrache had a suspicion the death had not been solely due to hypothermia or similar natural causes. One for the doc to advise on. Ferbrache was never one to speculate beyond the available evidence.

Once he was set up at the bottom of the hill, he worked systematically through his usual procedure, taking photographs, collecting samples, examining the body and surrounding area. Even in a case like this, it was a routine he could follow almost without thinking.

Eventually, he was able to turn the body over. For all his experience, he found himself taking a breath. As he'd cleared the snow around the body, he'd noted traces of blood on the surrounding earth, so he'd an idea of what to expect. But he was still taken aback. The body had been stabbed – no, that was an insufficient description. The body had been lacerated multiple times in vertical strokes down its back. It looked to have been a truly savage attack. Whatever weapon had been used, it had sliced through a substantial waterproof coat and the layers of clothing beneath, tearing deep into the flesh.

For all his experience, Ferbrache felt unnerved by the sight. For a moment, he wondered whether it might be the work of some animal rather than a human being, though he couldn't imagine what animal in these hills would be capable of such savagery. A closer examination of the wounds left little doubt that they were the result of some sharp instrument rather than claws or teeth.

He found himself involuntarily glancing over his shoulder. Death, he thought, had been relatively recent, probably some time in the early morning. Whoever had been responsible for this ferocious act had been standing in this spot only hours before.

Cocooned in the protective tent, Ferbrache suddenly felt unexpectedly vulnerable. Outside, the snow would still be falling and the day sunk in gloom. Someone could be out there, even standing immediately by the tent, and he would have no way of knowing.

He bent over the body, trying to maintain his concentration, forcing himself to follow the routines that had become second nature to him. Outside, the wind had risen as the snow continued to fall, the flapping canvas providing an eerie backdrop to his work.

Finally, conscious he had hurried the work more than usual, Ferbrache straightened up. He'd done everything he could for the moment. The only outstanding question was the victim's identity. He always made a point of leaving this to the end in cases like this, not wanting his judgement to be clouded by any assumptions about the character or background of the victim. He carefully turned the body over again, and began methodically to check the pockets.

Almost immediately, he pulled out an over-stuffed wallet. He took photographs of its interior and exterior, then, taking care to disturb nothing unnecessarily, he checked the contents. A small amount of cash, some receipts. A couple of bank cards. A driving licence. With his gloved hands, Ferbrache carefully slid out the licence card. There was no mistaking the likeness between the photograph and the blank white face of the corpse. Toby M Newland. An address in Merestone. A local, then. Though presumably a local who hadn't yet been reported missing.

It was difficult to imagine this death wasn't in some way linked to Robert Tilston's. The obvious conclusion, given his history, was that Tilston was the killer. But, although Ferbrache could only guess at the time of death, particularly given the low temperatures overnight, it was likely that Tilston had died before Newland. There had been no sign of blood on Tilston's body, and it was unlikely that the perpetrator of this killing could have avoided any trace.

Ferbrache finished packing up his equipment and dismantled the spotlights that he had directed at the body. It was still only early afternoon, but without the lights the tent was plunged almost into darkness. Ferbrache felt the same unease that had stirred within him earlier. He'd be glad to get away from this place.

There was little point in taking down the tent until the ambulance arrived. He might as well keep the corpse as undisturbed as possible by the weather. He ducked out of the tent, blinking at the heavy grey light. The snow had continued to fall while he'd been working, and was coming heavier than ever. Already the footprints he'd left earlier had been obscured. The snow was several inches deep on the flat field, drifting more densely against the hedges behind him.

If this continued, it was going to be hard to get any kind of vehicle up here. They'd have to give serious thought to getting the bodies down in one of the police vehicles. Assuming, he added to himself, that it was possible for the police cars to get out of this place.

He looked back. He could see only a few metres across the field, but something had caught his eye. A darker patch in the snow beyond the tent.

He had no doubt what he was seeing, even though it was disappearing even as he watched. A mess of footprints, a place where someone had stood, probably for several minutes, moving from foot to foot against the cold. Behind it, a line of individual prints stretched away to the far end of the field.

The footprints had to be very recent. Someone had been standing there while he'd been inside the tent carrying out his examination.

It meant nothing, of course. Some local attracted by the sight of the protective tent and the police warning notices. Ferbrache had taped off the scene, but could easily have missed one of the entrances to the fields, or maybe the warnings had simply been ignored. There was no reason to think anything sinister had occurred.

Even so, Ferbrache turned and strode back up the hillside at unusual speed, a chill in his bones that had nothing to do with the weather.

CHAPTER TWELVE

It was the sense of oppression that struck Murrain first. Part of it was simply physical. The dim lighting, the rich Victorian colourings that made the low-ceilinged rooms feel enclosed and claustrophobic. A damp stale scent to the air, as if nothing had stirred in here for many years.

That was part of it. But Murrain had known as soon as he entered the house that there was something more. He could almost hear the clamouring voices whispering somewhere behind his head. It was like that sometimes. A sensation he'd encountered most commonly in the mortuary. The sense that the dead, the lost ones, the others, were clustering around him. Trying to share what they knew. Trying to impart some truth he could never quite comprehend.

He didn't really believe that, even though he didn't know what he did believe. He couldn't bring himself to think the dead were literally out there wanting to commune with him. For all his experiences, he was too much of a rationalist for that. But it was something. An imprint in the air. A distant signal he was almost tapping into.

He'd rarely felt it in an ordinary domestic house. Not like this, anyway. Not with this strength and intensity. It had hit him as soon as he'd walked through the door, causing him to pause and catch his breath. Anne Tilston had looked back and regarded him curiously.

Before they'd approached the house, he'd spent some time trudging around the tiny hamlet, Wallace trailing in his wake. Murrain had said he wanted to get a feel for the place, check out Tilston's body, get a sense of the geography. But, with the snow still falling heavily around them, he knew he hadn't fooled Wallace. She knew enough about Murrain's reputation to recognise it was something else he was looking for. Some connection with this place. Something that would help him understand the presence of two dead bodies in this remote spot.

In the end, there had been very little. He'd felt something in the churchyard, some sensation. Some feeling that Tilston had chosen it as the site of his death for a reason. A reason, perhaps, even more significant than its proximity to the daughters he'd left behind. But Murrain couldn't begin to fathom what that reason might be.

He suspected this was going to be a difficult interview. As a junior officer, he hadn't known Robert Tilston except by reputation. He'd followed Tilston's arrest and trial, and he was conscious that the force had not treated Tilston's daughters well.

Senior officers had been in a blind panic about the reputational implications. They'd closed ranks and focused on limiting the damage. In retrospect, it might have been better – for the force as well as for the individuals involved – if that had included protecting the daughters from the attentions of the tabloid press. But that hadn't happened, and the young women had been subject to continued hounding and some lurid coverage, with information no doubt leaked by his less ethical colleagues.

Whatever the reasons, Anne Tilston had looked taken aback when she'd first opened the door to them. She'd seemed even more baffled when he'd shown her his ID.

'I thought you'd finished with us. And a Chief Inspector? My father's name must carry some weight even now then?'

'That's not the reason I'm here, Ms Tilston. Perhaps we can go inside and I can explain.'

She'd seemed reluctant even to let them through the door, but in the end she'd stood back and ushered them into the hallway. After a moment's hesitation, she led them through to the back of the house and into the kitchen, gesturing for them to sit at the table. 'It's probably better if we don't disturb my sisters unless we need to.'

'I'm afraid we may need to,' Murrain said. 'I'm not quite sure how to break this, Ms Tilston, but the fact is we've found another body.'

She looked up, startled. 'Another body? Whose?'

'We were hoping you might be able to help us with that. The scene-of-crime officer is down there at the moment, but we haven't yet been able to ascertain the identity.' It was odd, Murrain thought, how naturally he found himself slipping into this bland police-speak.

'Is this connected with my father?'

'We don't know. Again, we were hoping you might be able to shed some light on that. The deceased appears to be a white male, probably youngish, but that's all we know. Is it likely that your father would have been accompanied by anyone?'

She shook her head. 'You don't get it, do you? I told your colleague. We haven't seen our father since – well, since he went to prison. I know nothing about him and I care even less. I've no idea why he came here or whether or not he might have been accompanied.'

'I understand. You appreciate we have to check.' Murrain was about to say something more when he felt his mobile buzzing in his pocket. 'If you'll excuse me a moment, Ms Tilston.'

He rose and made his way back out into the hallway to take the call. It was Neil Ferbrache, who was typically to the point. 'We've an ID. One Toby Newland. Lives in the village. Looks like an unlawful killing, and a pretty nasty one. Stabbing, if that's not too polite a word for it.' Murrain could almost sense the hesitation down the line. 'To be honest, Kenny, it's left me a bit shaken.'

'Not like you. Must be a bad one.'

'It's partly that. And partly this place. And partly this weather, which isn't showing any signs of letting up. If it carries on, we're not going to get out easily, you know?'

The thought had already been troubling Murrain. 'I know. Do you want to get away?'

'I was planning to wait till the ambulance turned up. Though Christ knows when that will be. We can't just leave the bodies.'

'We could try to transport them down ourselves, if necessary.'

'What if we can't get down ourselves?'

'Then we have to find somewhere to store them till the weather clears. At least, decomposition shouldn't be an immediate problem in these temperatures. Where are you now?'

'In the van. With the engine on and the heater running full blast. It's bloody freezing out here.'

'We'll come and have a confab once we've finished in here. Decide how we handle things.'

'I'd suggest not taking too long if you want to get out of here tonight.'

'Message received.' Murrain ended the call and re-entered the kitchen. He could see that Wallace had been trying to engage Anne Tilston in small talk. Knowing Wallace, she'd probably managed to extract more information in the last few minutes than Murrain would have managed in an hour.

'Ms Tilston,' he said. 'Do you know a Toby Newland?'

'Newland? He lives a few houses along. Why?' But she had already read Murrain's expression and stopped. 'Oh my God—'

'We're not certain. Not until the body's been formally identified. Does Mr Newland have a partner or family at home, do you know?' For the moment, Murrain was sticking resolutely with the present tense.

'He lived alone. He only bought the place a few months back. He had various – friends, though. They could be a bit noisy sometimes...' She trailed off, as if conscious she was just filling the silence.

'Mr Newland had no connection with your father?' Murrain asked. He felt as if he was on the verge of sensing something here, but the feeling remained tantalisingly out of his mental grasp.

'Not that I'm aware of. Why would he?' She was clearly thinking. 'But, as I say, we knew nothing about our father. And we hardly knew Mr Newland, except as a neighbour to say hello to.'

The denial felt almost too pat to Murrain, too eager to dismiss the question. But that, Murrain conceded, might reflect nothing more than Anne Tilston's desire to maintain a distance from her father. 'And your sisters would say the same?'

She hesitated. 'I'm sure they would.'

Murrain was already climbing to his feet, recognising he could take the interview no further for the present. 'We'll need to take formal statements in due course, Ms Tilston.'

'We've nothing more to tell you.'

'We have to do all this by the book, as you'll understand. We'll leave you alone for the moment. We appreciate your time.'

There was something here, Murrain thought. Something in this house. Something in the incessant chatter of whispering voices trying to communicate. Something more than just the years of history, the decades of stress and anxiety and pain. Something he wasn't yet able to grasp. As they followed Anne Tilston to the front door, he found himself looking around at the worn carpets, the shabby peeling wallpaper, the gloomy old-fashioned lighting, wondering who or what it was that really lived here. Not just the three sisters, he thought. Something else. Something they knew or shared.

Something, he thought, to be feared.

CHAPTER THIRTEEN

'Oh, Christ! You bastards—!'

He was ducking and running but the flurry of snowballs was relentless. The first one had struck him squarely in the face, and he could feel his skin stinging from the blow. The next couple hit him on the back of the head, the melting snow dribbling down the back of his thin waterproof. Still running, he dragged up his hood, trying to protect himself from further blows, but could feel them pounding on to his shoulders and back. Behind him, there was mocking laughter.

It was always like this. The snow had just presented them with a new weapon. Usually it was little more than words, though they could sting enough. Sometimes it was physical blows. Never too hard, never really enough to injure him. But enough to make him aware the attacks were less playful than they pretended.

Afterwards, of course, once they'd taken him to the point where he was genuinely upset, occasionally even in tears, they'd claim they were just messing about. Can't you take a joke? Obviously he could. But he was smart enough to realise none of this was really done in fun.

He didn't even know why he hung around with them. Because he wanted to be part of a group, he supposed. Because he wanted a bunch of mates, even if they were mates who used him mainly as a whipping boy. It wasn't so bad in college, where he could always find places to get away from them if it became too much. But at weekends or on a day like this, when college was cancelled because of the weather, this was what it always turned into.

Another snowball struck him on the back of the head, and there were more jeers from behind. Someone shouting: 'Come on, Josh. Give us one back!'

He knew that was what they wanted. For him to have a go at fighting back, giving them an excuse to redouble their collective assault. Even so, as always, he felt obliged to go along with them. It was part of the game. It was the way it always went.

He grabbed a handful of the thick fallen snow, and, squashing it into a tight ball, turned and threw it back at them, not bothering to aim. Inevitably, the snowball fell short and there was more shouting. Three or four more balls flew in his direction, one striking him on the cheek. Jesus, he was sick of this.

They were at the far end of the bus station in the shadow of the flyover. He didn't even know why they'd decided to come down here. It was just a spot where they could cause some mayhem before an adult appeared to tell them to bugger off. It was a busy place generally, but today most of the buses weren't running.

They'd got him cornered down here, as the dark ravine of the River Mersey was behind him now. He had no alternative but to turn and make some pretence of fighting, even if they all knew how that would end. He half-heartedly made another snowball which he tossed back in their general direction. That one managed to catch one of them on the stomach, which provided a reason for them to launch another return barrage. He ducked his head and covered his face, allowing the snowballs to strike him, too fed up now even to make a show of resistance. He sensed they too were getting bored and would move on to something else before long.

'You okay there, Josh?'

That was always the first sign it was ending. The point where they started to show some concern. 'I'm fine.'

'You're looking a bit wet, mate.' This was from Daz, the ringleader of the group if anyone was. Once he took the lead, the others would follow.

'I'm fine.'

'You sure, mate? We were only playing around.'

'I know. It's fine.'

Daz was standing beside him, patting him on the shoulder as you might pat an obedient dog. Josh wanted just to hit him, but that wasn't part of the game. The rest of them were hanging back, a few metres away, waiting for a signal as to what they should do next.

'What's that?' Daz said.

Josh half-turned, assuming this was some new joke Daz was preparing. 'What?'

'Down there.' Daz was leaning over the fence, peering at the black waters of the Mersey. The rest of them were crowding behind, and Josh was happy to slip from between them. 'The red thing.'

'Dunno,' someone said. 'Someone's coat. One of them party balloon things. Could be anything.'

'Could be a body...' Daz adopted a half-hearted spooky voice.

'Fuck off, Daz. What would a body be doing down there?'

'I don't know, do I? Somebody pissed up who fell into the river. Somebody who topped themselves.' He paused for dramatic effect. 'A murder victim...'

'Bollocks. Hey, we could try throwing Josh in the river, though—'

Josh could tell they were losing interest now. They'd exhausted what little excitement the bus station had to offer, and were already thinking about where they could head next. That was always the way. They lacked the imagination to think of anything beyond mooching around town. Sometimes he wanted to suggest other things they might be doing, but no-one would listen to him.

He hung back, watching the others drifting towards the main road. Maybe he should let them go. He was feeling cold, anyway, in his thin waterproof. His shirt was damp from the snow that had run down the back of his neck.

He looked back at the object Daz had spotted. Something red, only just visible above the water despite its vivid colour. Probably a discarded item of clothing or packaging. But somehow it looked more solid than that. As if there really was something substantial there, the current washing around it.

He looked back. The others were heading back through the bus station, no-one caring that he wasn't following.

After a moment's hesitation, Josh reached into his pocket and pulled out his mobile. He'd end up looking stupid, no doubt, but he was used to that. Still peering towards the river, he began to dial.

'Still coming down out there?' DS Paul Wanstead was chewing morosely at a tuna and cucumber sandwich and flicking through a day-old copy of the *Daily Mirror*.

Joe Milton was at the window, a coffee in his hand, watching the street below. 'Harder than ever.'

'Bugger. Last thing we need is more of the stuff. How're the roads looking?'

'Main road's still clear, just about. Side-streets not so good, though.' Milton made his way back to his desk. 'What about our colleagues up in the hills? Anything from them?'

'Not since Kenny reported the second body. Wouldn't fancy being up there if the weather's as bad as it is here.'

'Likely to be worse. Doesn't take much to shut some of those Pennine roads. Hope they don't get stuck up there.'

Wanstead raised an eyebrow. 'You got something planned then?'

'You don't miss much, do you, Paul?'

'Just keep my eyes and ears open.' Wanstead was the longest serving officer on the team, the lynchpin that held the rest of the group together. Milton knew he prided himself on knowing – or at least reliably guessing – what was going on around him.

'It's not what you think, you know. We're just friends. That's all.'

'Aye,' Wanstead said. 'Friends. Does Kenny know?'

'That Marie and I are friends. I'm guessing so.'

'That's all right then.'

Milton shifted in his seat, looking uncomfortable. 'You trying to say something, Paul?'

'Me? No, nothing.' He gestured towards the window. 'But if you've got plans for tonight, you might need to put them on hold. Not looking good.'

'You reckon they'll be okay up there?'

'They're all grown-ups. Well, apart from young Will. And he nearly is. If they do get stuck up there, they'll find someone to take them in. Kenny can be quite persuasive.'

'I don't doubt it.' Milton had been on the receiving end of Murrain's influencing techniques on more than one occasion.

'Anyway, won't last, will it? Never does these days. Even if it carries on for the rest of today, it'll be slush tomorrow.'

'You're sounding very philosophical, Paul. Is that your motto for life?'

'Might as well be—' Wanstead stopped as his phone rang. 'Hang on.'

Milton went back to his administration as Wanstead made non-committal noises to whoever was calling him. 'Yes, obviously. We're a bit stretched ourselves at the moment, that's all. Just DI Milton and me at the moment. Okay, as soon as we can...' There was some more small talk before Milton concluded the call. 'You're not going to believe this.'

'The way things are going today, I'll believe almost anything. Go on.'

'We've only got another one. Another body. In town this time. Just up the road in fact.'

'Christ, just what we need.'

'How do you think the uniforms are feeling? Response teams are right up against it. Just had some choice words in my ear about that.'

'So what's this one?'

'Some young lad called it in, apparently. Didn't want to leave his name, but they dragged his details out eventually. Thought he might be wasting our time, but reckons he'd spotted something in the river by the bus station. Turns out he was right. Don't have any real details yet, but looks like it's a young woman.'

'Somebody managed to fall in the river? Suicide?'

'You tell me. They've called out the CSIs, but God knows how long it'll take them to get there. But somebody's got to go up there and manage the scene.'

'I knew that was coming. Don't suppose you fancy going out instead, Paul?'

'You know I'm more use here.'

Milton couldn't really bring himself to argue. Horses for courses, he supposed. Wanstead could work miracles with his knowledge of the internal systems – not to mention his uncanny expertise in knowing who to contact when the systems failed, as they frequently did. But it was a long time since he'd really worked out in the field. 'I get the picture. Can you keep Marty up to speed, just so our Chief Super doesn't think the whole team's gone AWOL?'

'He's been briefed on Kenny and the rest of them,' Wanstead said, predictably. 'I'll let him know.'

Milton pushed himself to his feet. 'And it's still bloody snowing out there. This is turning into a great day.'

CHAPTER FOURTEEN

Milton had searched the building in vain trying to find any available CID bodies who could accompany him. He'd been reluctant to attend on his own because he knew from experience that, even on a day like this, controlling a potential crime scene wasn't a one-person job. If the response teams were as stretched as Wanstead had suggested, they wouldn't be keen to spare resources any longer than needed. In the end, though, he'd had to resign himself to tackling it alone.

As the main arterial route into Manchester, the A6 had been well-gritted and, earlier at least, had been kept largely clear by the relatively heavy traffic. Now the traffic into town had lessened – people were increasingly staying indoors as the weather had closed in – and the surface was coated with snow, disturbed only by the wheel-tracks of the few passing vehicles. Milton drove carefully, keeping his speed low, as he covered the half mile up to the bus station.

The turning down into the bus station itself was even more perilous, the side-road thick with snow and steeply inclined towards the river. Milton was a skilled police driver but still felt the wheels slipping. He was relieved when he finally pulled into the station concourse and drew to a halt behind a marked car with its blue lights pulsing. Getting back up that hill might be more of a challenge, but he'd worry about that later.

Milton could see a couple of uniformed officers, a small knot of people milling around them. It was amazing how, even on the day like this when the bus station was almost deserted, this kind of incident could still attract a few rubber-neckers.

He made his way over, brandishing his warrant card at the uniforms and the people around them. 'Folks, can I ask that you clear the area, please? We have to get on with our work.'

'Yes, but what's—?' one of the onlookers began.

'Please leave the area, sir. There's nothing to see.'

As the small group reluctantly dispersed, Milton turned to the two uniforms. He knew one of them slightly by sight, the other not at all. 'DI Joe Milton.'

The first uniform stepped forward eagerly. 'Ben French,' he offered, then, gesturing at his colleague. 'Danny Yuill.'

'What's the story? All I know is there's a body in the river.'

'That's about it,' French said. 'Some kid spotted it.' He led Milton over to the fencing which separated the bus station from the drop to the river. 'Down there.'

The body was some metres below them and further along the river, only just visible from their vantage point. It was impossible to get much closer at this level, and Milton initially questioned whether what he was seeing was really human remains. Maybe everyone was getting over-excited about some optical illusion. 'You sure it is a body? All I can really see from here is a splash of red.'

French looked momentarily embarrassed. 'We had a pair of binoculars in the car. Danny's into this bird-watching stuff. You know, twitching. He makes a point of carrying them around, just in case he sees something unusual.'

Milton smiled. 'That right? Good job as it turned out.'

'When you look at it through the binoculars, you don't have much doubt. Let the DCI have a closer look, Danny.'

Once he had the binoculars, it took Milton only a moment to confirm the two officers were correct. It was a human body, most of it submerged below the surface of the water. It was unlikely to have entered the river at that point, Milton thought. There was no adjacent path from which it could have fallen or been dropped. Most likely it had been taken downstream by the current before being caught on the bank, perhaps on some branch or outcropping rock. It was now close to the river's edge, with only the red of a coat or jacket easily visible from above.

From its position in the water, there was little likelihood the individual could still be alive, though they needed to recover it from the water as soon as possible. Quite how they'd manage to do that was quite another matter.

As if reading his thoughts, French said: 'We asked for an ambulance. And the Fire Service. We thought they might have some ideas how to get down there. Reckoned they might be a while, though.'

'Everyone's stretched to the limit today, I know.' Milton looked around. 'We need to get a full team down here, but Christ knows when that'll be possible.'

In the end, it was another couple of hours before they'd begun to assemble even the bare bones of a team to control the scene. Eventually one of the CSIs, Rob Parry, had turned up and begun to set up, ready for the body being recovered. Between them, the police, fire and ambulance crews had managed to get the body on to a stretcher and hoisted back up to the bank. It had been clear immediately that the body had been dead and in the water for some time, possibly days.

There was little other information immediately available. The body was female and white, but there was no ID in the clothing. The face was battered and swollen. The clothing was unremarkable – a red waterproof jacket, a short fashionable-looking dress. Milton's recollection was that it matched what Kirsty Bennett had been wearing when she'd left her workplace on that final Friday evening. He wouldn't jump to any conclusions, but it seemed likely they'd found their missing woman.

'What do you think?' he asked Parry when the CSI had finished his initial examination.

'It's a nasty one. A very nasty one. A stabbing. Attacked from behind by the looks of it. Multiple wounds.' He paused, as if seeking the right words. 'Someone who carried on stabbing long after the victim was dead. Using a sharp instrument—probably a substantial knife.'

'Christ, I wasn't expecting that.'

'Me neither.' Parry didn't look obviously disturbed by what he'd been examining, but Milton knew the CSIs made a point of taking incidents like this in their stride. 'It was difficult to tell at first given the condition of the body. But when I turned it over—'

'You'd expect there to be a lot of blood? Where it happened, I mean.'

'The clothes at the back had been soaked in it, though again the water had had an effect. But, yes. Wherever she was killed, you'd expect a lot of blood.'

'How long do you reckon she's been in there?'

'A few days at least, I'd say.'

Milton looked back along the river. 'Wonder how far she might have travelled in that time?'

'No real way of knowing, is there? The water's not that deep generally, so the body might not have moved too far initially. Could have caught on the bottom. But with all this...' He gestured up at the heavily falling snow. 'Not to mention the rain we had before it, the river's been higher than usual over the past couple of days. Might have been enough to loosen it and bring it further downstream. I'm not really helping, am I?'

'Not so's you'd notice.' He knew Parry well enough to be sure he'd take the comment in the spirit it was intended. 'You're giving us all you can. It's just that there's not a lot to give. Not till we find out where she was killed, anyway.'

'That's about the long and short of it. You reckon this is your missing woman?'

'Clothes are a rough match, so looks like it. Surprised there's nothing on the body to identify her.'

'The only pockets are in the waterproof, and there's nothing in those. She probably had a handbag with her.'

'Good point. If so, it could have been stolen from her by whoever did this. Or it could have entered the river with her. Until we get an idea of where she went in, we're not likely to have much luck in finding it. I can't remember if any of her work colleagues mentioned a handbag, but if so we might be able to issue a description of it. You never know.'

'You never do. Don't know if there's much else I can do for you here, Joe. Best bet's probably to have the poor lass taken in and get the post mortem done as quickly as possible. Doc'll be able to tell you more about the time of death, the nature of the stabbing.'

'And that'll probably be four weeks next Thursday, the way things are going.'

'I heard we've had an excess of human remains today,' Parry said. 'Ferby's been up in the hills with your colleagues.'

'Nothing but trouble, you lot.' Milton peered gloomily up at the falling snow. 'Look at it.'

'Plenty more to come according to the forecast. Well into tonight. And as ever the whole country grinds to a halt. Except for the likes of us.'

'Even us, if it does carry on. Not sure how I'm even going to get back up the hill to the office. Might have to leave the car here and walk.'

'On that note,' Parry said, 'I may take the opportunity to make my escape while I still can. I'm never keen to leave my van unattended with all the equipment in the back.'

Milton helped him pack up, and watched while they finished clearing the scene. He was conscious they'd normally have spent much longer over an incident like this, but everyone was keen to move on. The body was loaded into the ambulance and taken off to the mortuary at Stepping Hill.

It was late afternoon now, growing dark, the snow still falling. After everyone else had departed, Milton stood looking down at the dark ribbon of the river.

This was going to be a big one, he thought. Kirsty Bennett's parents had already been doing their utmost to keep the story in the public eye. When this broke, the tabloids and the rest of the media would be all over it. No time to waste here. Time to get back to break the good news to Marty Winston and then to Kenny. What better way to end a perfect day.

He climbed back in the car and started the engine, waiting a moment for the wipers to clear the windscreen. As he pulled back out into the road, the snow was still falling, silent and relentless from the lowering sky.

CHAPTER FIFTEEN

'This must be the one,' Murrain said.

'I think so,' Bert Wallace agreed. 'Though the numbers don't make much sense.'

'The joys of village life.' Murrain stopped to appraise the building in front of them. 'Two tiny cottages knocked into one, I'm guessing.' He gestured to the small cluster of houses that comprised the remainder of the hamlet. 'Most of these look like conversions of one sort or another. No wonder the numbering doesn't work.'

The building before them was an attractive stone-built cottage that Murrain imagined pre-dated the Tilstons' Victorian house. This short row looked as if it had once been a terrace of farmworkers' cottages, each probably containing little more than a single room upstairs and down. Now, converted and gentrified, they'd be worth a few quid even up here, Murrain thought, with their views out over the valley and – when the weather was better than today – a relatively short commute into the city.

The cottage had been recently renovated, with new exterior paintwork and an impressive-looking oak front door. There were no lights showing and no other signs of life. He pushed open the gate and stepped into the small, snow-covered front garden.

The snow still showed no sign of abating. Murrain knew he'd have to make a decision soon about their next steps. If they didn't get away from here soon, they could easily end up stuck for the night. At the same time, he had to consider how best to protect the scene, how to deal with the two bodies, and what follow-up would be needed. The usual protocols would be difficult to apply until they could get more resource up here, and that wouldn't happen today.

He'd had a brief word with Neil Ferbrache after they'd finished with Anne Tilston. Ferbrache had been sitting in his van, waiting for the rest of them to return from their various tasks. He'd now extracted all the evidence he was likely to from the bodies themselves. There might be more to be gleaned from the surrounding area, but that wouldn't be easy until the snow cleared. As Murrain had pointed out earlier, the thawing of the snow might itself remove or compromise any evidence.

'If you've done everything you can for the moment, I'd get off, Neil,' Murrain had said. 'None of us wants to find ourselves stranded up here.'

Ferbrache had nodded morosely. He never liked to leave a job uncompleted, even if he knew there was little else he could do. 'Suppose you're right. It's not like there aren't plenty of other jobs waiting.'

But that was the problem, Murrain thought now. Of course there was always plenty of work waiting for them, but this was already a big one. They were all acutely conscious they couldn't do a complete job up here until the snow cleared, and that might be a day or more away. 'You've done everything you can here, Neil.'

'What about the bodies?'

'I'm still hoping the ambulance will get up here. If not, we'll have to try to get them down ourselves.'

'They're all neatly bagged up.' Ferbrache's tone carried an air of professional pride. 'Only question is, can I trust you lot to bring the tent back safely?'

'You know us, Neil.'

'Aye, Kenny. That's the trouble. You're right, though. I'd better go and make myself useful back in the civilised world.'

He'd left Ferbrache manoeuvring his van in the narrow lane, and rejoined Bert Wallace to track down Toby Newland's cottage. Now he stood gazing up at it wondering what they might find inside. He had felt no particular sensation as they approached the building, nothing more than the low-level mental static that had been present since they'd arrived in the village.

Murrain pressed the bell, hearing it sound somewhere in the depths of the house. He already had the sense the house was unoccupied. He pressed the bell again, holding it down for longer. 'Let's have a look round the back.'

The cottage was at the end of the terrace, and a narrow passageway led to the rear of the house. The snow in the passageway, like that in the front garden, was undisturbed. Any earlier footprints would have been long re-covered.

The passage emerged into a small garden, bounded by a stone wall on two sides and a wooden fence between it and the adjoining property. Murrain tramped across the snow to the rear door and tried the handle. To his surprise, the door was unlocked. He glanced back at Wallace and stepped cautiously inside.

The sensation hit him almost as soon as he stepped inside. It was like a blow to the head that made him physically flinch. He couldn't have said whether it was painful – the feeling was too rapid and fleeting and there were no physical after-effects. But the intensity was greater than anything else he had experienced.

The kitchen seemed undisturbed. A mug and a breakfast bowl were unwashed in the sink but otherwise the room was tidy. There was nothing to suggest anything out of the ordinary had occurred. But Murrain could still feel the steady mental pulse that suggested something wasn't right.

'Do you want me to come inside with you?' Wallace asked from the doorway.

'You'd better stay there for the moment. If we've got a crime scene, we don't want to disturb it any more than we need to. I'll give the place a quick once over and we can decide what to do.'

'Give me a shout if you need me.'

Murrain made his way further into the house. The kitchen opened into a narrow hallway, with rooms leading off both sides, the front door ahead of him. The left hand room was a sitting room, containing a sofa, a couple of armchairs, a large flat-screen television, and a couple of well-filled bookshelves. Like the kitchen, it was tidy and undisturbed. There was a paperback crime novel on the sofa and a stack of DVDs by the television. Those were the only signs the room had been occupied.

The room on the right was clearly used as a dining room. It was largely filled by a pine dining table and the surrounding half-dozen chairs, and had the air of a room used only on special occasions. The whole house had an oddly unoccupied feel, Murrain felt, as if Newland had spent little time here.

Satisfied there was nothing of interest on the ground floor, Murrain made his way upstairs. The layout of the upper floor mirrored the rooms below. There was a bathroom ahead of him which sat over the top of the kitchen, and bedrooms leading off both sides of the landing.

The bathroom was as tidy as everywhere else. There were a few toiletries on the window-sill, and a pile of neatly rolled towels set on a stand by the bath, but no other personal possessions.

The bedroom on the right had the air of a guest bedroom. The bed was neatly made and looked as if it hadn't been recently used. There were a few anonymous pictures on the walls, and a short row of books on a shelf in front of the window. The books looked as if they'd been placed there in a half-hearted attempt to make the room feel homely, rather than because they reflected the taste of the owner.

The steady mental pulse had been growing stronger in the back of Murrain's head. It was a more familiar sensation now, the buzzing of a loose connection. There were images too, he thought, or the ghosts of images. Shadows behind his eyes that never coalesced into anything he could recognise.

He stepped back out on to the landing. The door to the second bedroom was closed. As he approached it, his senses were struck by something else. It took him a moment to disassociate the new sensation from those already crowding his brain. To realise it was physical, rather than mental or psychological. Something much more straightforward. Something he recognised only too well.

He reached into his pocket for one of the pairs of thin plastic gloves he always carried. He slipped one of the gloves on to his right hand and, taking care to touch as little of the surface as possible, pressed down the door handle.

He thought he'd already prepared himself for what he would find inside. But he was wrong.

The blood was everywhere. The double bed and the covering duvet were soaked a deep red. There were splatters of blood across the pale wallpaper, and a thick pool on the floor, already congealing.

In the centre of the bed, half-covered by the matted duvet, there was a body. A young man, naked, his torso a mess of lacerations.

The stench of blood was overwhelming. Murrain stood holding his breath, taking in as much of the scene as he could. It was difficult to believe that whoever had committed this act had not themselves been covered in blood, but it was difficult to detect any signs of a trail leading from the body. There was no obvious sign of a murder weapon.

He stepped backwards out of the room. The pulsing sensation in his head had reduced now, although there were still unintelligible images skittering across his vision. Back on the landing, he took a second to look around, seeking signs of blood, any traces the killer might have left. There were marks on the dark carpet but he couldn't be certain of their origin. That would be a question for the CSIs and Forensics in due course.

He made his way downstairs and back out to the kitchen. It was only as he stepped back outside into the winter air that the full significance of his discovery really struck him.

Three bodies. Two of them savagely murdered. The killings very recent. The killer, potentially, still out there.

Wallace was outside the back door, stamping her feet against the cold. The snow was still falling. She had clearly read his expression before he could speak. 'You found something?'

Murrain took a breath, enjoying the crisp air in his lungs, trying to forget the stench of blood. 'We've another one.'

'Christ, really?'

'The same as Newland, as far as I could judge. Male. Youngish. Probably no more than early-twenties. In bed. Stabbed.'

'The same way as Newland?'

'Pretty much. But from the front not the rear. Hell of a mess in the bedroom. Rest of the house apparently undisturbed.'

Wallace looked around. 'No sign of any disturbance out here. Though the snow would have covered anything from earlier. What the hell's going on here?'

'Christ knows. This one started strange and just gets weirder. And this snow's starting to get to me. It feels like the world's closing in on us.'

'I know what you mean. It's so bloody quiet. It doesn't feel natural, not to a Manchester girl like me.'

Murrain smiled. 'We'd better get on, before we start spooking each other out. Get this place properly sealed off. Head back to the others and decide what to do next.'

'What are the options?' Wallace said. "This whole place gives me the creeps.'

That was the question, Murrain thought. Their options were rapidly diminishing. The first two bodies were firmly bagged up and could, in principle, have been taken down in their vehicles, assuming there was still no sign of the promised ambulance. The new body was a different matter. They had to leave the scene undisturbed until the CSIs had had a chance to do their work. That in turn meant ensuring it was properly protected. Ideally, that meant keeping a direct eye on the place, although in the circumstances the chances of any intruder contaminating the site were remote.

Except.

Except that the killings were recent, and they had no idea of the identity or location of the perpetrator. His first, obvious thought had been that Robert Tilston had killed Newland. He had been a man with a history of violence, and the coincidence of his death and the two killings suggested a connection. It was possible, but Tilston had looked a relatively frail figure, at least in death. Would he have had the strength or stamina to have committed these two savage murders before quietly lying down to face his own death?

If not, the implications were even more bizarre – that some third-party was responsible for the two killings. If so, given the weather, it was unlikely that third-party had had an opportunity to move far from the vicinity. A brutal killer could be somewhere close by.

He knew he'd been silent for too long, and Wallace was guessing at least part of what he was thinking. 'Lets get back to the others. Get our heads together, see what we know. Then decide what to do.'

CHAPTER SIXTEEN

Chief Superintendent Marty Winston was a decent enough bloke, Milton thought. Not perfect – officers at that level always had their particular foibles – but better than most. He was generally supportive, prepared to listen, and willing to take responsibility when he needed to. All that, in Milton's view, gave him a head start over most of the senior officers he'd encountered.

At the moment, though, Winston was looking as if he'd rather be anywhere else. He was pacing up and down his small office as if about to make a break for freedom. 'You're sure about this?' he asked, for what was probably the fourth time since Milton had entered the room.

'Like I say, not entirely. We don't have a firm ID on the body yet. There were no identifying items on the body or the clothing – we think there was probably a missing handbag – but the clothing matches what we understand Bennett was wearing when she went missing. I thought you'd want the heads-up as soon as possible.'

Winston stopped pacing and slumped back down behind his desk, as if all the energy had suddenly drained from him. 'Of course. You were quite right.' He closed his eyes, with the air of seeking some external inspiration. 'Where's Kenny? Have you told him?'

'Not yet. He's still out at that incident up in Merestone.'

'Bloody Robert Tilston turning up like a bad penny. And now there's some second body?'

'Apparently. A stabbing. I don't know much else.'

'Why does everything happen at once? As if we haven't enough on our plate on a day like today. I imagine half the staff will have buggered off early.'

'They were told to. Anyone whose presence wasn't essential. Last thing we want is for our own staff to start getting stuck and adding to the chaos.'

'I know. I'm just venting.' Winston allowed Milton a brief smile. 'One of the problems of high office. You mostly have to keep your frustrations bottled up. It's usually Kenny gets the blunt end of it. Today, you've drawn the short straw. Sorry.'

'No worries. I'll just find some DC to take it out on. Isn't that why we have these ranks?' At least when Winston expressed frustration, it was generally just against the world at large. Many of his colleagues preferred to direct their ire at those who worked for them.

'So what about your body?'

'They've taken it to Stepping Hill. Once they've got it tidied up we'll need to get the parents in for a formal ID. Confirm it really is her.'

'Poor buggers. They must have been desperately hoping for a positive outcome.'

'I don't know what they really think. They're aware she hadn't used any of her bank cards since she went missing. That must have sounded a few alarm bells even though we hadn't spelled it out. But people cling on to whatever they can.'

'We all do. Okay, so we get a firm ID. But this thing's got bigger implications. Whether or not it's Kirsty Bennett on that slab, we've a killer at large. And from what you've said a pretty brutal one.'

'Very brutal. I've seen a few knife victims, but never anything like that. Crazed stuff.'

'And we don't know whether the killer is someone known to Bennett, assuming that's who the victim is, or whether this is just some random act. Jesus, this is a nightmare. We can't sit on the story. Until we've got some idea of the killer's motives, we've at least got to urge the public to be vigilant. If there's some psycho out there—'

'Normally, I'd say that was unlikely. These things usually turn out to lie closer to home. But this didn't look like your usual domestic.'

'I'd better take this one up the line. And get Comms involved. Decide how we're going to play it. Don't want to start a full-scale panic. Only consolation is that the media will be full of "snowmageddon" stories for the next day or two.'

'Yeah.' Milton peered past Winston through the office window. In the gap between the adjoining buildings the sky was still dark and snow-filled. 'That's some consolation.'

'Any word on the ambulance?' Murrain asked.

'I've just chased it up. We're "on the list".' Marie Donovan paused. 'But it's a long list.'

'And I'm guessing that dead bodies don't take priority over live ones.'

They had reconvened back in the larger of the two four-by-fours. Sparrow and Wallace were in the rear, with Murrain and Donovan taking the two front seats. Outside, the snow was continuing to fall. Ferbrache had managed to make his escape, though he and his colleagues would be needed back up here as soon as the weather allowed.

Donovan and Sparrow had taken a statement from Liz Carter, but her account of finding the body had added little. She and her husband had seen or heard nothing unusual over the previous night. She'd been shaken by finding the body, and, for the moment, Donovan had provided her with no further information about the nature of the death and had made no reference to Robert Tilston's body. There was no point in stirring up the couples' anxieties, although Donovan had recommended they should stay inside and not answer the door to anyone else until the police had ascertained exactly what they were dealing with. Now it looked as if that might be worse than Donovan had imagined.

Murrain had already phoned in to see what resources were available to put checks on the surrounding roads in case their killer had already escaped the vicinity. The answer, as he'd expected, was that all operational units were already stretched to the limit. He'd managed to extract a promise from the control room that they'd divert whatever they could, but he had little confidence it would actually happen.

He'd left messages for Marty Winston and Joe Milton, both of whom were apparently at some Comms meeting. Murrain had been surprised by that – it seemed an odd priority on a day like this – but, since he tended to leave that kind of administration to Milton, he assumed it was some routine meeting he'd forgotten or never been told about.

The control room had also broken the unwelcome news that most of the smaller roads in the vicinity were now impassible. The key trunk roads had largely been kept open, with the familiar exceptions of the Snake and Woodhead Passes over the Pennines, but even some of those were becoming difficult to navigate. There was no chance of getting any additional resource to them for the remainder of the day. And, it was implied, the chances of Murrain and his team getting away from there were receding by the minute. His question to Donovan about the ambulance had been largely academic. Even if by some miracle they reached the top of the priority list, it wouldn't be worth trying to get a vehicle up here just to pick up the dead.

'So what do we do then?' Wallace said from the rear seat, echoing the question that had been dominating Murrain's thoughts for the previous few minutes. The truth was he didn't have a ready answer.

'I'm not sure we've much choice,' he said, finally. 'I reckon we're stuck up here till this lot clears.'

There was a silence in the car, though he suspected he was only confirming what they'd each already concluded. He just hoped that Ferbrache had made it down in time, and wasn't now stuck in some snow-drift halfway down the hill.

Then there was the question of their killer. If there was even the possibility that the killer was still in the area, Murrain and his team owed a duty of care to the inhabitants of the hamlet. Whatever the killer's motivations, they were clearly dealing with a highly dangerous and potentially unstable individual. Until Murrain knew differently, he had to consider everyone here at risk.

'We can't just sit in the car,' Wallace pointed out. 'Not if we're going to be here till this lot clears.'

'Time to commandeer some space, then,' Murrain said. 'Create ourselves an informal incident room. I suggest we start with the Tilstons. They looked as if they had a few unused rooms in that place.' He realised he felt more relaxed now their immediate fates had been decided. 'Besides, after all the grief he gave the force, I'd say Robert Tilston owes us one.'

CHAPTER SEVENTEEN

The first few hundred metres hadn't been too bad. The snow had settled thickly on the road surface, obliterating the tracks left only hours before. But initially the downhill slope was relatively gentle, and Ferbrache had been able to maintain control of the vehicle, keeping his speed low and steering as gently as he could.

The terrain became more challenging as he rounded the first bend. Almost immediately, the road fell away, dipping more steeply towards the valley. As he straightened the van, Ferbrache could feel the wheels slipping. He steered cautiously into the skid and regained control, but was already gaining speed. He touched the brake carefully, trying to avoid a further skid. He was approaching the next bend, the road becoming even steeper. He slowed almost to a halt, and then tensely guided the van into the curve.

Despite his efforts, he felt the rear wheels losing grip. He pressed the brake again, trying to bring the vehicle to a stop, but knew he'd lost control. The van continued to slide, the brake pedal already to the floor.

'Bugger—' To the left, the hillside fell more steeply away into the woodland. Previously, Ferbrache had seen the snow as little more than an inconvenience. He was a reasonably skilled driver, and his major concern had been that the road might simply be impassable and he'd find himself stuck here. Now for the first time he registered that, if the van were to leave the road, he could be in real physical danger.

He touched the steering wheel again, trying to ease the van away from the edge without worsening the skid. The rear wheels were sliding unnervingly close to the drop. Unsure how best to respond, Ferbrache pressed the accelerator, hoping to gain enough traction to drag the van from the precipice. For an agonising moment, he thought he had failed, but suddenly the wheels caught and the van moved forward. The acceleration almost caused him to lose control again but he brought the vehicle to a halt sideways across the narrow road. He dragged on the handbrake, his body pulsing with adrenaline.

There was no question. He wasn't going to get down this road until the snow cleared. As far as he could recall, the next stretch of road was even steeper and more winding. The risk was too great.

Sighing, he climbed out of the van and surveyed the scene. He was reluctant to leave the van obstructing the road, but nervous about even trying to manoeuvre it off the carriageway. In practice, it was unlikely anyone would get up here before he was able to move it.

The snow still showed no sign of abating, and was already filling the tyre tracks he had left on his descent. He could see little alternative but to tramp his way back up to the village and break the bad news to Murrain and his colleagues.

The surrounding woodland was eerily silent, even the crunch of his own footsteps deadened by the thick carpet of snow. He was only a few hundred metres from the edge of the village, but the buildings were not yet visible over the summit of the hill. He glanced back, uneasy at his own isolation. It was only mid-afternoon, but the gloom was already thickening.

He quickened his pace, more anxious than he wanted to admit. This place spooked him. Even on a bright summer's day, it would be steeped in its own isolation. A spot where bad emotions would fester.

Jesus, he thought, I'm turning into Kenny bloody Murrain. Ferbrache prided himself on his rationality, his ability to focus on the facts and the evidence. It was what made him good at his job. It was what made him the person he was.

He finally reached the summit of the hill, the dark cluster of houses ahead of him. The police vehicles were parked as before, but there was no sign of Murrain or his colleagues. As he drew level with the two police vehicles, he saw a jumble of footprints leading from one of the vehicles towards the Tilstons' house. If that was where they were, Ferbrache couldn't see he had much alternative but to join them.

He never heard any sound. During his walk back up the road, he'd been trying to reassure himself that, in the snowbound silence, at least it was impossible for anyone to approach him unheard. In that last moment, he realised he'd been wrong. That the silence really was all encompassing.

That was his final, almost irrelevant thought, before he felt the sharp agonising pain on the back his head.

CHAPTER EIGHTEEN

'Is there really no alternative?'

Murrain glanced behind him at the grey sky swirling with falling snow. 'I can't insist, Ms Tilston. I'm simply asking for a favour, given the conditions out there. It looks as if we're stuck here until the weather clears. It's too cold for us to risk staying outdoors—'

'Is there really nowhere else you could go?'

Murrain's honest answer, just at that moment, would be that he'd rather go anywhere than into this oppressive, shadow-filled house. Even standing here on the doorstep, he could feel it, stronger than earlier. A chorus of ghosts, a cacophony of inaudible whispering. A sense of threat, or perhaps merely a sense of warning. 'I wouldn't want to impose on Mr and Mrs Carter. Not with their children in the house. There's no sign of life in the other houses as far as we can see.' Perhaps not the ideal choice of words, he reflected, given what was lying in Toby Newland's house. But they'd carried out a circuit of the village, partly to warn any other residents to remain indoors and to answer to no-one but the police team, and partly in the hope of finding some more conducive accommodation.

'A couple of them are holiday lets,' she conceded, her tone suggesting she was assessing the truth of what he'd just said. 'I don't know about the others.'

'We'll make ourselves as unobtrusive as possible. We just need a room where we can base ourselves until this clears up.' He leaned back, the snow catching in his tightly-curled hair, and gazed up at the facade of the house, as if to remind her how large it was.

She seemed to take the hint. 'All right. It's just that my sisters are a little – well, prone to nerves. I don't like them to be disturbed more than necessary.'

Murrain felt a sudden additional tremor in the back of his brain. Her words felt significant, though this wasn't the moment to delve further. 'We're very grateful, Ms Tilston.

We'll be as discreet as we can. And we'll be on our way as soon as the weather allows.' Which, he added silently to himself, might well not be until the morning, but they'd deal with that problem when it arose. He imagined the possibility would not have escaped Anne Tilston.

'There's a room at the back you can use,' she said. 'It used to be – we called it the study. It was the room our father used.'

Murrain presumed that, given the circumstances, the room would not have been much entered since Robert Tilston's departure. 'That sounds fine. I'll tell the others.'

That was one problem solved, at least temporarily. They'd spent the previous thirty minutes bringing Tilston's and Newland's bodies up to store in the rear of one of the four-by-fours. Although Ferbrache had bagged the two corpses up neatly, carrying them through the snow had been challenging. As they'd hoisted Newland's body up the hillside, Will Sparrow had managed to slip at least twice, though on both occasions the main injury had been to his dignity.

The bodies would be safe enough until the morning, and in this weather there was little risk of any further significant decomposition. There was nothing they could do about the third body until the CSIs had had an opportunity to examine the scene. They had no means of securing the rear door of Newland's property, so Murrain had been able to do little more than festoon it with police tape.

When Murrain returned accompanied by the rest of the team, Anne Tilston was standing at the door waiting. Her manner had lightened in the interim – Murrain assumed she had now resigned herself to their presence – and she greeted them pleasantly enough. 'I'll take you through to the study. I've dug out a spare kettle and some coffee and milk. You must need warming up.' The tone was welcoming, but Murrain suspected her real motive was to minimise their need to leave the designated room. Fair enough, he thought. He'd probably feel the same in her position.

The study was as bleak and shabby as the rest of the house. A mahogany desk, presumably once used by Robert Tilston, stood against the far wall. There were a couple of bookshelves containing a selection of out-of-date books on policing, a couple of legal text books, a handful of crime fiction paperbacks, and various other unidentifiable volumes. In the centre of the room there was a large table, also mahogany, with matching chairs. Two leather sofas were set against the nearer walls. Murrain wondered whether the room had ever been used for dining. It was difficult to envisage anyone enjoying a pleasurable meal in here. Even the kettle and mugs which Anne Tilston had set out at one end of the table looked incongruous.

This dark Victorian style must once have been fashionable, but now the room had a forbidding air. The unease which Murrain had felt since re-entering the house was stronger here, as if the presence of the late Robert Tilston was still haunting the place.

'Will this be sufficient for you?' Anne Tilston said, with a frostiness in her tone that suggested she had at least partly read Murrain's thoughts.

'This is fine,' Murrain said. 'We just need somewhere to base ourselves until we can get out of your hair. But there is one other thing. Until we're sure exactly what we're dealing with, we'd advise you to stay inside. If you think there's any sign of anyone outside the house, please let us know at once.'

'You think whoever did this is still out there?'

'It's possible.'

'I usually take Dougie for a walk in the evening. My dog,' she added, unnecessarily.

'I'd advise you to stay inside this evening, Miss Tilston. Please. Until we know what the situation is. In the meantime, we'll try not to disturb you any more than we need to.

She nodded, not obviously reassured. 'We'd appreciate that. Please help yourself to the coffee.'

'Not exactly "make yourselves at home",' Marie Donovan commented, once Anne Tilston had left the room.

Murrain shrugged. 'We're imposing on her. She's good reasons to dislike the police. I don't suppose we can expect anything more.'

Bert Wallace was at the window staring out at the still-falling snow. It was almost dark now. 'What happens if we're stuck here for the night?'

'I'd say that was pretty likely, wouldn't you?' Donovan said. 'I assume that thought had occurred to our host, too. Probably another reason she wasn't too welcoming.'

'We'll just have to make the best of it.' Murrain glanced round the room. 'Though if we're stuck in here, I don't think any of us will be getting much sleep.'

Wallace turned her back to the window. 'The other thing we're still rather dancing round is that there could well be a multiple killer out there. A very violent multiple killer.'

'That possibility hadn't exactly escaped me,' Murrain said. 'But I don't know what more we can do for now. If he's made it down into town, we can only hope our lot pick him up before he can do any more harm.' The main concern, as they all knew, was if the killer had become stranded somewhere between here and the edge of the town and had been looking for shelter. There was no way of warning everyone in this rural location. Even if they made an announcement on the local news – which was one of the options Murrain wanted to discuss with Marty Winston – it wouldn't be broadcast till later.

'You said "he"?' Donovan said. 'Are we sure about that?'

'They were pretty brutal attacks,' Murrain said. 'And would have required a fair degree of physical strength. But, no, I'm not sure.' An image flickered momentarily behind his eyes. Something glimpsed, and then gone.

'You okay, Kenny?' Donovan said.

'I—' He shook his head. 'Yes, I'm fine. Well, as fine as I can be in this place.'

'Maybe we should make a break for freedom,' Will Sparrow said. 'Ferby must have got out all right.'

'I assume so,' Murrain said. 'If he'd got stuck somewhere, he'd have been in touch.'

Bert Wallace looked sceptical. 'You never know with Ferby, though, do you? Likes to be Mr Self Sufficient. I can imagine him leaving his van in some snow drift and struggling on down the hillside to civilisation.'

Murrain sighed. 'I suppose I'd better check. He might be able to give us some idea what it's like down there.' He pulled out his mobile and flicked through his address book to find Ferbrache's number.

After a moment, he frowned. 'Ringing but going to voicemail. That's not like Ferby. Usually the only time he doesn't answer is when he's engrossed in a crime scene.'

'Probably can't get a signal,' Donovan said. 'I imagine it's hit and miss up here.'

Murrain nodded, still staring at his phone as if it might provide the answer. 'I guess so. I'll try him again in a while.' The glimpsed image had gone, but he could still sense something, something he couldn't quite discern, overlain on the persistent sense of discomfort he had felt since entering the house.

He looked up at Will Sparrow, who was already pacing impatiently up and down the room. 'I know how you feel, Will. I'll be only too glad to get out of this place. But I don't think we can risk heading down until the weather improves. That road will be lethal.'

In this job, you just wanted to be getting on with things. Even Murrain, for all his mental distractions, was essentially a pragmatist. He wanted to make something happen. He juggled his phone in his hand for a moment, then thumbed Joe Milton's number again.

The phone rang briefly, Murrain expecting it to transfer to voicemail. Then, unexpectedly, Milton answered.
'Boss?'
'How was the Comms meeting?'
'Long story. Just got back and picked up your message. Sounds like we have a hell of a situation between us.'
'That right?' Murrain glanced up at the others, who were busying themselves making coffees. Sparrow was at the window, staring out as if willing the snow to disperse.
'We may have found Kirsty Bennett. Or at least her remains.'
'Shit.' Murrain had already partly resigned himself to this outcome, but it was still painful to have it confirmed. 'What's the story?'
He listened in silence as Milton recounted the finding of the body. After a long pause, he said: 'Describe the state of the body again.'
'Lacerated, I think would be the best phrase. Savage stuff. Repeated slashings. Not quite like anything I've ever seen.'
Murrain was silent for a moment longer. 'No, me neither. Not until today.'
'You—' Milton stopped. 'You're kidding.'
'The other news is that we now have two bodies here. Both in the same condition.'
'Christ. You think this is more than coincidence?'
'Like you say, I've never seen a body in that state before. One hell of a coincidence.'
'I'm not getting this,' Milton said. 'What about Tilston? You think he—'
'Doesn't seem like it. Ferby couldn't be certain, but Tilston was most likely dead before the first killing occurred. From what I saw of his body, I don't think he'd have had the strength to do this anyway, though who knows?'
'So where does Tilston's death fit in? Another coincidence?'

'Doesn't seem likely, does it? But I'm all out of bright ideas at the moment. On top of that, it looks like we're stuck here for the duration. How are you planning to handle the Bennett case?'

'Was just talking to Marty about that. We need to have a proper discussion once you get back. Plan was to designate you as SIO, but for me and Paul to get on with setting up everything in the meantime. We haven't confirmed the body's identity for certain yet. The clothes and the appearance broadly match, though.'

'Anyone spoken to the parents yet?'

'That was going to be my next task. They're out in Bramhall somewhere. I'd rather speak to them face-to-face. I'll try and round up someone to come with me and head out there. Not that we've many spare hands.'

'What are the roads like down there?'

'Pretty awful. The A6 is just about passable, but even the other A roads aren't great.'

'Good luck with that.' Both of them understood that Murrain wasn't primarily talking about the roads.

'It's got to be done. Then we'll have to get them in to do the formal identification. God, there are times when I really hate this job.'

'Do me a favour, Joe. Don't jack it in till I'm able to get down off this bloody hill, will you?'

'I'm promising nothing, the way today's going.'

Murrain allowed himself a laugh. 'Tell me about it. I'd better give Marty a call and put him in the picture.'

The subsequent call to Marty Winston went much along the same lines, though punctuated by Winston's periodic expletives. 'So how long do you reckon you'll be stuck up there?'

'God knows. It's not looking good at the moment. We might be here overnight.'

'How are the Tilston sisters going to take that?'

'I'm planning to cross that particular bridge when we come to it. But I'm guessing Anne Tilston's got a pretty good idea what's coming.'

There was silence at the other end of the line. Murrain sensed that Winston's grasshopper mind was flicking around what he'd been hearing. 'You reckon there really is a link between your killings and Kirsty Bennett?'

'MO sounds very similar, doesn't it? We can't discount it, let's put it that way.'

'And you think your killer might still be up there?'

'Again, we can't discount the possibility. Depends whether he got away before the snow closed in. Assuming he wanted to get away.' Murrain paused, a momentary blurring skittering behind his eyes.

'You've warned everyone up there?'

'As best I can. Seems to be just this household and the Carters around. They've been told to stay in, check their locks and not answer the door to anyone.'

'You think that's enough?'

'I hope so. I don't want to cause a complete panic. Not unless I really need to.'

'I'll have another chat with Comms. We're going to have to put some sort of bulletin out if there's a possibility he's made it down. If this is linked to the Bennett case, we can't take any chances.'

They finished the call, and Murrain stood for a moment with the phone in his hands. Winston had a point. Murrain didn't know whether he'd done enough. The other option would be to bring the Carters in here. But he didn't want to scare the children more than necessary, and he was conscious of what Anne Tilston had said about her sisters' nervousness. On the other hand, they potentially had a killer outside, and they had no knowledge of what might have motivated his actions.

'How's it looking?' Marie Donovan asked.

'Not good. From what Joe said about the roads, I think we may well be here for a while.'

Bert Wallace had risen to join Will Sparrow at the window. Outside, the snow was falling as relentlessly as ever. 'Christ,' she said. 'Stuck in Wuthering bloody

Heights. Now all we need is for Cathy's ghost to come tapping at the window.'

CHAPTER NINETEEN

Ferbrache didn't know at first if he'd actually lost consciousness. He felt as if he'd been lying in the snow forever, though he knew it could be only a matter of minutes. He was face down, his face jammed into the compacted drift. As his mind returned to something approaching coherence, he registered that whoever had struck the blow might still be standing there, looming over him, waiting to complete the task.

For a long moment, he remained motionless, holding his breath. Finally he twisted his head slowly and looked behind him. In the pale glow of the short string of streetlights, the road was deserted, pristine white in the falling snow. There was a small scuffle of footprints around his own feet, but it was impossible to tell which were his own and which might belong to another. He could see no prints leading towards or away from his prone body. It was as if his assailant had appeared from nowhere and disappeared in the same way.

He must have been unconscious, then. Long enough for the falling snow to have at least partially covered any prints. His body felt bruised and there was a dull ache in the back of his head. There was a real possibility, though, that he was lucky to be alive.

He climbed slowly to his feet, his senses alert for any movement in the darkness. Then he jumped as, somewhere close at hand, there was the sharp sound of a dog barking.

It occurred to him now that he'd heard the same sound earlier, half-registered, in almost the same moment he'd felt the blow to the head. The urgent yapping of a dog. Perhaps that was what had distracted his assailant.

Ferbrache couldn't immediately work out where the barking was coming from. Somewhere around the Tilstons' house, he thought, though he couldn't be sure if the dog was outside or barking loudly from within. He stepped cautiously into the garden, expecting that, at any moment, the dog would come tearing around the side of the house, barking furiously to repel the intruder.

But nothing happened. After a moment, the barking quietened and, as Ferbrache took another step forward, the front door of the house opened, throwing a triangle of light on to the snow-covered path. 'Who's there?'

Ferbrache blinked at the bulky figure silhouetted in the doorway. 'Kenny?'

'Ferby?' A pause. 'You okay?'

'Not exactly.' Ferbrache moved until he was standing in the light from the doorway.

'Bloody hell, man,' Murrain said. 'With all due respect, you look terrible. Let's get you inside. What happened?' He stepped out into the snow and took Ferbrache's arm, supporting him as they entered the house.

A middle-aged, anxious looking woman was hovering behind Murrain. One of the Tilston sisters, Ferbrache assumed. Her expression was far from welcoming.

Murrain turned to her. 'Don't worry, Ms Tilston. Neil here is our Crime Scene officer. We thought he'd managed to make it out of here earlier, but it looks as if he ran into the same difficulties we did. I'll take care of him. I'm sorry if it's caused you any unnecessary alarm.'

'It was Dougie,' she said. 'He only barks if there's someone outside. I thought—'

'Yes, of course. Dougie could be quite a reassurance tonight. If he shows any other signs of being disturbed, let us know straightaway.' Murrain was leading Ferbrache towards the rear of the house.

Ferbrache said nothing until Murrain had ushered him into the study. 'Just grab a seat, Neil. Will, can you rustle up a drink for him? I think the cold's got to you, Ferby.'

It took Ferbrache a moment to find his voice. 'Not just the cold. Some bugger hit me on the back of the head.'

Murrain turned. The rest of the group had fallen silent. 'Where was this?'

'Outside in the road. I got stranded down the hill and decided the safest thing would be to head back up here. Then—'

'Christ. When was this?'

'I'm not sure, exactly. I think I was out cold for a bit. But probably only for a few seconds. I could hear that bloody dog barking just before it happened.'

'Maybe that's why you escaped with just a blow to the head,' Murrain said. 'We heard the dog going frantic in the kitchen. Apparently he only does that if there's someone unfamiliar outside the house.'

'And there were two of us,' Ferbrache said.

Murrain looked round at the rest of the team. 'I think this changes things. It means we know the killer is still here. And it means that, whatever the motives for the two previous killings, he's prepared to attack randomly. Marie, can you contact the Carters again. I don't fancy the idea of them being unprotected if we do have some sort of lunatic on our hands. It might be easiest to get them over here so we can keep an eye on everyone together.'

'You really think there's that much of a risk?' Marie Donovan said, though her tone suggested she didn't disagree.

'There's no way of knowing, is there? But, given what's happened, I don't think we can take a chance. It's probably better to keep us all together rather than splitting up.' Murrain turned back to Ferbrache. 'I don't suppose you caught any glimpse of your assailant?'

'Nothing at all.' He blinked and looked up at Murrain. 'Christ, Kenny, I'd have sworn there was no-one behind me. It was as silent as the bloody grave. Then—'

'It's this bloody snow. Makes everything unreal. Let's have a look at the damage. Not the first time I've said this to you, Ferby, but you need to get your head examined. Once we get out of here. If you were unconscious…'

'I know. Concussion. Certainly feels painful enough.' He waited while Murrain examined his scalp. 'How's it looking?'

'No blood,' Murrain said. 'You're going to have a bit of a bump there, though. Doesn't look too serious but you can never be sure, even with a head as thick as yours.'

'Ha bloody ha.'

Across the room, Marie Donovan was ending her call to the Carters. 'Not sure I pitched that right. Wanted them to take it seriously without alarming them. Well, one out of two's not bad. Hope I've not freaked them out too much. I've said we'll escort them over here.'

Murrain nodded. 'I'd better square this with the Tilstons. They're not going to be happy.' He stopped, suddenly looking weary. 'Jesus, what a job. We've just gone round in circles since we got here. We've not even spoken to the other two sisters yet. And every time we turn around another bloody body appears.'

CHAPTER TWENTY

The clock in the corner of Joe Milton's computer screen told him it was still only 4.30pm, but it felt much later. Darkness had long since fallen, and the main road outside was quieter than he'd ever seen it. The building felt deserted, with all but the most indispensable staff leaving early in the hope of making it home before the weather finally closed in. Even Paul Wanstead, normally the last one to leave, had decided to throw in the towel. 'If I get stuck here all night, I'll never hear the bloody last of it,' he'd grumbled as he pulled on his coat. 'Helena already reckons I'll find any excuse not to go home.'

Which left Milton as pretty much the last man standing. There didn't seem much point in heading back to an empty house, just so he could open another couple of beers and half-watch yet another box-set on Netflix.

Not that there was much to do here. He'd spent the last hour doing anything he could to prepare for what appeared to be at least two murder enquiries. He'd made some progress in identifying candidates for the investigation teams, finding accommodation and resources, and generally getting the basics in place. But as the afternoon dragged on he was hitting the law of diminishing returns.

There was something oddly dreamlike about the atmosphere in the building. Normally, with major incidents kicking off, there'd be a buzz of activity, constant comings and goings as they pulled the teams together. Now there was near silence, the room darkened by the gloom of the heavy skies outside. It seemed wrong, and Milton felt oddly discomfited.

But it wasn't just that. He'd been trying to keep the thought at bay all afternoon, busying himself with phone calls and administration. The truth was he was worried. Worried about what might be going on up in Merestone. Worried about the prospect of a highly dangerous and apparently random killer on the loose. Above all, worried about Marie Donovan.

He knew Donovan was more than capable of looking after herself. She'd proved that on more than one occasion. And Murrain wouldn't allow any of the team to take unnecessary risks.

It wasn't even as if he and Marie Donovan were an item. They'd been out together a few times. Not exactly dates. A few drinks after work, which more recently had stretched into dinner. Maybe they were close to taking the next step into something more serious. But at the end of those evenings neither seemed quite able to initiate it.

He wasn't quite sure why, at least in his own case. He was definitely a free man now. Gill had made that quite clear during that brief, very uncomfortable visit to Paris. He'd come away from that trip still unsure whether Gill was seeing anyone else, but with no doubt that their own relationship was well and truly over.

He didn't want to leap into a relationship with Marie simply on the rebound. And Marie Donovan had plenty of reasons to be wary of becoming too closely involved with anyone. He couldn't really blame her for keeping him at arms' length. They'd ended up circling round each other like nervous teenagers, not committing to anything beyond a pleasant friendship. He wondered whether there was, or ever would be, much more to it than that.

None of that stopped him worrying. And, however much he might tell himself otherwise, his anxiety about Marie Donovan was of a different quality to the understandable concerns he might have about Bert Wallace, Will Sparrow or even Kenny Murrain. They were close work colleagues and, in some cases, friends. Marie Donovan already felt like something more.

He hesitated for another moment and then dialled Murrain's number. The call was answered almost immediately. 'Joe?'

'Just thought I'd better touch base again and see how things were going.'

'Not great, since you ask. I was just about to call you and Marty. We've had another development.'

Milton felt the cold clutch of fear in his stomach. 'Development?'

'Ferby was attacked.'

'Is he OK?'

'Seems to be. We'll need to get him checked out properly once we get out of here.'

'You reckon it was our killer?'

'Unless we've got a whole convention of violent lunatics congregating in Merestone, I'd say so.'

'Christ.'

'Quite. It means he's still here somewhere. Which I suppose at least means that he's not anywhere else. Small mercies.'

Milton was staring out of the window. The snow was still falling, and even the main road below looked deserted. 'You're all together?'

'We are,' Murrain said, with a faint emphasis on the first word. 'There seems to be just one other family in the village at present, so I want to get them safely in here with us. I may being over-cautious, but—' He paused. 'Look, Joe, whoever this is, they're a dangerous bastard. We need to get this stopped. We need a full-scale manhunt up here as soon as it's feasible. Helicopters, heat-seekers, the lot. That was why I was calling Marty. And I want to find out what the chances are of getting a bloody snowplough up that road here as soon as we can.'

Milton had rarely heard Murrain sounding quite so rattled, and he wasn't even sure Murrain recognised it. Murrain wasn't the type to be unduly disturbed by the normal rigours of police work – even the prospect of facing a violent killer. More likely, Murrain sensed something else. Milton knew better than to delve into the matter before Murrain was ready to tell him. It did little to alleviate his own anxiety, though.

'I'm happy to support Marty in drumming up whatever resource we can at this end,' Milton said. 'I wouldn't be too optimistic, though, even with a killer on the loose. Even the chopper's grounded by the weather. There are strong winds as well as lousy visibility. Everyone else is stretched well beyond capacity.'

Milton heard a sigh from the other end of the line. 'Yes, I know. Every snow plough in the district will be keeping the key routes open. I just feel so powerless stuck up here. I want to get things moving.'

'How's the team?'

'Going stir crazy, just like me,' Murrain said. There was an extended silence, and for a moment it sounded as if Murrain might offer more. Finally, he simply said: 'Okay, let's both lobby Marty and see what we can get out of him. But I suspect the answer will be not much until the morning.'

'I'll keep you posted, boss,' Milton said. But Murrain had already ended the call, distracted by whatever demons were prodding at his brain. Milton had worked with the old man for a good few years now, and knew him better than most. Better than anyone except the long-suffering Eloise, probably. But he'd never quite fathomed what was lurking in the depths of Murrain's mind. There were times, and this could be one of them, when he thought it was probably better not to know.

CHAPTER TWENTY-ONE

'Christ, Kenny,' Marty Winston said. 'You're sure he's still hanging around up there?'

'I can't see who else could have attacked Ferby,' Murrain said. It always took a while for Winston to absorb unwelcome information. 'At least it means he's not at loose in a more populated area.'

'That's something,' Winston agreed. 'Though we've put a warning out on all the local media now. Potentially dangerous. Not to be approached.'

'You've still got Kirsty Bennett's killer. We don't know for sure the killings are linked.'

'You always know how to brighten my day, Kenny. Look, as soon as I can get some resources up to you, I will. We're really up against it down here. We've even had parts of the M60 shut. Virtually all the B-roads to the east of the city are shut. None of the Pennine routes are open. Chances of getting anyone up to clear the road to Merestone—'

'I get the message, Marty. I wasn't really expecting anything else. I just wanted to let you know how things stood up here.'

'I'm not planning on going home tonight. Even assuming there was a chance of getting there.' Winston lived somewhere the other side of Wilmslow. 'There aren't that many of us still left in the office, and anyone who's gone home isn't going to be able to get back before the morning. I'll keep monitoring things and we'll get some back-up to you as soon as it's humanly feasible.'

'I know, Marty. We'll be okay till the morning. We'll huddle together for warmth. But whoever's out there is bloody dangerous. We can't afford for them to get away from here.'

'Don't take any unnecessary risks, Kenny. Not without back-up.'

'Believe me, Marty, I'm not planning to.'

The question, Murrain thought, after he'd ended the call, was what counted as unnecessary. His main priority was to keep everybody safe. His own team. The Tilston sisters. And the Carters. He looked up at Will Sparrow, who was still staring out of the uncurtained window. 'No sign of letting up, Will?'

'Heavier than ever, I reckon. I can't remember the last time it was like this.'

'Time to brave the cold and fetch the Carters. Let's go and warn Anne Tilston what's coming.' He looked around at the other members of the team. They were like caged animals, he thought. Even Ferbrache, still recovering from the blow to his head, was shifting uncomfortably in his seat as if he'd rather be anywhere else. Marie Donovan was pacing at the far end of the room, and Bert Wallace was messing with the coffee mugs, supposedly on the pretext of making another drink but obviously just looking for something to occupy her time.

The unease Murrain had felt since entering the house had grown even stronger. It wasn't only what might be lurking outside that worried him. It was what he felt might be lurking within.

He'd called Eloise and spoken to her briefly before calling Marty Winston. She'd been heading home but was expecting to be on call, trying to hold together the thin resource they had available to deal with whatever the night might throw at them. 'There aren't many calls coming in at the moment. Everyone's hunkered down for the evening, and there's no-one out on the streets. But we just need one thing. Any accident, incident, and we'd be well and truly up against it.'

She was worried about him, he could tell, but neither of them was able to acknowledge it. That went with the job. Eloise could always tell what he was thinking. She could read the unease in his voice. She'd be concerned, not just by his circumstances, but because there was something he wasn't articulating. 'Just keep me posted. Let me know if anything happens.'

'Nothing's going to happen. Our killer will have hidden away somewhere. All we're going to get is more and more of this bloody snow.'

'Even so.' She'd left it at that, ending the call before he could offer any response. They knew each other too well.

The only solution was to stifle his unease by taking some action. He gestured to Sparrow to follow him back out into the narrow hallway. The light was even dimmer out here than in the study, and it took his eyes a moment to adjust before he registered Anne Tilston standing further along the corridor. She looked as if she'd been waiting for them to emerge. 'I was coming to see if you needed anything.'

'We're fine for the moment,' Murrain said. 'But we were coming to see you. We've another request to make.'

She stood in the centre of the hallway, as if to block their way. 'Request?'

'Yes, I'm sorry. You saw my colleague in there. I think that whoever attacked him was our killer. There's—'

'I'd assumed so. Who else would have attacked him?'

'We can't afford to take any risks. I want to fetch Mr and Mrs Carter and their children back here. Just so that we're all in one place and we can keep an eye on everyone.'

Her face registered no surprise. 'You think they're in danger?'

'I honestly don't know. I don't know who the killer is or what their motives might be. But I can't afford to take any chances. Do you think you can manage to accommodate them? For the night? We'll need beds for the children, but I don't imagine the rest of us will get much sleep.'

'We've a spare room down here, with a couple of twin beds. I don't know about the parents—'

'I'm sure we'll all manage. I'm very grateful for you putting up with all this.'

'Did we have any choice?' The question sounded straightforward, with no undertone of bitterness.

'In theory you did, I suppose. But I'm not sure what we'd have done if you'd said no. I really ought to express my gratitude to your sisters too.'

'That won't be necessary. Really.'

Something in her voice made him hesitate before responding. 'We will have to speak to your sisters before we're finished, you know? I appreciate the need for sensitivity. But we need to do this properly. I've been remiss in not interviewing them already.'

'My sisters won't be able to tell you anything of value.'

'Nevertheless—'

She held up her hand. 'I think I'd better show you something. To avoid any misunderstanding.' She glanced at Will Sparrow who had been watching this exchange with apparent uninterest. Murrain knew the young man had been taking in every word. 'If your colleague wouldn't mind waiting here for a moment?'

Sparrow obediently stood back as Anne Tilston led Murrain along the corridor to what he presumed was the main living room. She ushered Murrain inside. He followed her, opening his mouth to greet the two sisters, and then stopped.

The two women were sitting facing him. One – the older of the two, he thought, though it was difficult to be sure – was in a sophisticated-looking electric wheelchair. Her head was tipped back, eyes fixed on the ceiling. It was impossible to know whether she had registered his presence.

The second sister was in a more conventional motorised wheelchair. She was facing Murrain, but her eyes were blank and unresponsive, as if focused on some point far behind him.

Murrain turned back to Anne Tilston. 'I'm sorry. I didn't realise—'

'There's no reason you should have done. It received a little coverage in the media at the time. Mainly of course because of who our father was.'

Murrain had no recollection of reading any news relating to the Tilston family, at least until the small flurry of stories that had accompanied Robert Tilston's release from prison. 'I don't recall it, I'm afraid.'

'A car accident. On the road down from Merestone, in fact. The weather was – well, not like today but icy. Charlotte was driving.' She gestured towards the woman in the larger of the two wheelchairs. 'Emily was in the passenger seat. I was in the rear. We were just going shopping. Charlotte lost control. I don't know why or how. It's a blank to me now. I remember us setting off. I remember the first part of the journey, down to where the road begins to curve. After that, nothing until I woke up in hospital. They'd initially thought Charlotte was dead. I suspect it might have been better for her if she had been.'

'I'm sorry.' Murrain was conscious of how far short his words fell from what really needed to be said. 'Is she—?'

'Quadraplegic. Brain damaged. A little short of being a vegetable.' There was no sentiment in the tone. 'She shows some responsiveness, but it's impossible to know how much she really understands or appreciates.'

'And your other sister?'

'Emily? She was much less badly injured. Physically, anyway. But again, very severe brain damage. She's more responsive than Charlotte.' Anne Tilston took a couple of steps forward. 'Emily?'

Emily Tilston blinked, her eyes suddenly focusing. Her mouth moved, but no words emerged. Her eyes flickered rapidly from Anne to Murrain and back again, and Murrain detected something in her expression that might have been curiosity or enquiry. Just as suddenly, the glimmer of apparent comprehension died and Emily Tilston's eyes reverted to their previous unfocused state.

'That's how it is. Sometimes she even says a few words. Nothing complicated, but enough to show she's aware of what's happening.'

'Do you take care of them by yourself?'

'As best I can. We were offered support by social services, but I prefer to take care of them myself, as long as it's possible.'

'We've just added to your burden. Is there anything we can do?'

'It's very kind of you. But, no. I think I'd rather just handle it by myself. In the circumstances.'

Murrain didn't feel able to enquire quite what circumstances she had in mind. 'Please let us know. I'm very conscious we're imposing on you.'

'There was nothing else you could do. You won't get out of here tonight. You couldn't just stay in your cars.' It was as if, having made clear her initial reservations, she was determined to make the arrangement work.

'I'll see if the Carters can bring some food over with them. And I'll make sure you're reimbursed for any expense.' Murrain wasn't entirely sure how he would manage this, short of digging into his own pocket.

'I can dig something out. We've cheese and bread. There'll be stuff in the freezer, I'm sure. If you really think this is necessary.'

'All we know is that we're dealing with someone who's violent and dangerous. That's why I'd prefer us all to be in one place.'

'Safely in numbers?'

'Something like that.' He allowed her a faint smile. 'And me covering my back, of course.'

'Of course. I'd expect no less.' It wasn't entirely clear if she was joking. 'Anyway, as you can see, you're unlikely to obtain much information from interviewing my sisters.'

'We'll try not to disturb you any more than we have to. And my offer holds. If there's anything we can do—'

'Thank you.'

Murrain wanted to say something more, but could think of nothing worth saying. With a final glance at the two seated sisters, he stepped back out into the hallway, closing the door behind him.

'What was all that about?' Will Sparrow was standing by the front door, looking impatient at the delay.

'I'll tell you when we get outside.' There was something nagging at Murrain's head. A feeling he'd had when Anne Tilston had been describing the car crash. As so often in moments like that, an image had crept into his mind. An image he could barely discern and couldn't begin to interpret. Three figures, and somewhere a fourth. That was all he had, all he'd been able to hold on to. Even that was already melting away. He walked past Sparrow and opened the front door, feeling the tug of the rising wind as he did so.

If anything, the weather had worsened still further. The snow was still falling and the wind was growing stronger, icy off the valley, piling drifts against the house walls.

'Jesus.' Sparrow pulled his coat more tightly around him. 'Bloody brass monkey weather.'

Murrain closed the door behind them, feeling an unexpected sense of isolation as the lock clicked into place. 'This would have been heaven when I was a kid.' Sparrow's voice was raised to carry over the wind. 'Now I just want it to stop.'

'You and me both,' Murrain said. 'Come on, then.'

Their walk to the Carters' house was short but slow, as they trudged through the thickening snow drifts, the wind forcing them back with every step. It was not yet evening, but the darkness was already complete, the small cluster of streetlights adding little to the visibility. There was a moment, at the midpoint of their trek between the two houses, when Murrain almost became convinced they had lost their way and were stepping unknowingly out into the desolate open countryside. A moment later, the bulk of the Carters' cottage loomed out of the dark.

Murrain could understand now how Ferby had been attacked with no recollection of his assailant's approach. The snow and wind swamped any other sound and reduced visibility almost to nothing. Murrain had to keep glancing at Sparrow to remind himself he wasn't alone. Sparrow himself had fallen unusually silent. Murrain could see that the younger man was peering backwards every couple of minutes, his eyes darting around for any sign of a threat.

The snow had drifted even more thickly outside the Carter's house, piled high against the wall and front door. Murrain pressed the bell and heard movement within. 'Chief Inspector Murrain,' he called through the letterbox.

There was a moment's silence before the door opened on a chain. An eye appraised them and then Murrain heard Rob Carter's voice. 'It's okay. It really is them.' He laughed, but there was little humour in his tone. The chain was released and the door opened, Rob Carter ushering them quickly inside. He had shut the door even before Murrain had had the chance to remove the snow from his boots.

'I'm sorry about that. But you know—'

'You're doing exactly the right thing, Mr Carter. I don't want you or your family to be taking any chances.'

'It all just seems so ridiculous.'

'We have two killings. And an attack on one of our colleagues.'

'It's just that you don't expect to have to face this kind of thing. Not at home.'

'Not anywhere.' Murrain followed Carter through the living room, Sparrow trailing behind them. 'Are we all ready?'

'As we'll ever be,' Carter said. Liz Carter was sitting on the sofa with the two young boys beside her. They were already wearing their coats, and there was a suitcase and a large full-looking carrier bag propped against the sofa. 'I've just scraped together whatever suitable foods I could find,' she said. 'There are a couple of loaves, and some cheese and cold meats and stuff like that. We had quite a bit left over from Christmas still—' She stopped, as if conscious she was gabbling. 'I just thought—'

'I was going to suggest that you did just that, Mrs Carter.' Murrain gave her a smile. 'I just wish my colleagues and I were in a position to contribute. But we'll be happy to help consume it.' His smile was unwavering. He could see Liz Carter was genuinely scared. Her husband was bustling about in the background, also clearly at a loss but doing his best to suggest he was in control of events.

It was several more minutes before they were ready to leave. The two Carter boys had both been entrusted with a small bag to carry, probably simply to help distract them from what was going on.

The walk back was uneventful, but more tense than he'd expected. Sparrow led the way, with the Carters clustered behind him, the two boys stumbling along between their parents. Murrain followed in the rear, trying to make his frequent glances over his shoulder as discreet as possible. He didn't seriously expect the killer would launch an attack on them as a group, but he had no real idea what this person might be capable of.

Anne Tilston had been watching from the front window and emerged at the door to greet them. Whatever her true feelings, she was clearly making an effort to make the Carter family feel welcome. She led them into the house, encouraging them to remove their coats and shoes inside the entrance, and took them through to the kitchen. 'I thought this was probably the best place to start with. It's the warmest room in the house with the Aga going. We can sort you some drinks and get you back to room temperature.'

Murrain smiled his thanks to her, and gestured to indicate that he and Sparrow would join their colleagues back in the study. He'd already checked with Anne Tilston, as they'd been making their way back down the hall, that all the external doors were locked and as secure as they could be made. He'd have a further check round himself once everyone was settled.

He was reassured by what he'd seen so far. The front and rear doors were both solid, with lockable bolts on the inside. The ground floor windows he'd seen were all secured with good quality locks. He imagined that, even discounting their history, three women living alone in this remote location would have been careful to ensure the house was secure.

Back in the gloomy study, Donovan, Wallace and Ferbrache were sitting round the large oak table. It looked as if they'd been interrupted in the middle of a particularly unproductive seance, Murrain thought. Joining hands and trying to contact the living.

'Carters okay?' Donovan asked.

'Seem to be,' Murrain said. 'Trying to persuade the kids that it's a big adventure. They seem to have accepted it's the right thing to do. Nobody's panicking, which is the main thing.'

'So what do we do?' Donovan said. 'Just sit and wait?'

'I'm not sure there's much else we can do. Marty's pulling out whatever stops he can, but not much is likely to happen tonight.'

'You never did tell me what Anne Tilston said to you, boss,' Sparrow said.

'The two sisters. Charlotte and Emily. They're both very severely disabled.' Murrain lowered himself on to one of the chairs around the large table. 'Injuries resulting from a RTC. Both suffered substantial brain damage.'

Donovan frowned. 'Oh, God, I think I remember that, now you mention it. It got some coverage at the time because of the Robert Tilston connection. But I can't remember anything about how things turned out.'

'How things turned out,' Murrain said, 'is that both sisters ended up with very substantial physical and cognitive disabilities. Must be a hell of a burden for Anne Tilston.' He looked up at Donovan. 'I'm sorry, Marie. You'd know all about that.'

'Too much.' Her late husband had been similarly disabled as a result of a highly progressive form of multiple sclerosis. 'The poor woman. Then all this comes and adds to her troubles.'

Murrain sat back as she spoke, feeling a sharp pain in his forehead. It felt almost as if his vision had focused on something very close, some image too near to discern clearly. He blinked and, almost immediately, the sensation had passed, impossible to recapture. 'I asked if we could give her any help, but she refused.'

'It's a personal thing, isn't it? I used to resent the care workers coming in, even though I knew full well I couldn't manage without them. As for strangers offering to help—'

'Just makes me feel even worse that all this has been foisted on her.'

'It might do her good,' Bert Wallace offered. 'It can't be easy being stuck out somewhere like this.'

'Nothing to stop her moving,' Sparrow said, bluntly. 'Get a pretty penny for a place like this. Move to somewhere that's been properly adapted for disabled people.'

'But it's their house,' Wallace said. 'She's lived here since she was a child. She may not want to move.'

Sparrow looked sceptical. 'Not exactly got the happiest of memories, presumably. I wouldn't want to stay here.'

Murrain gestured for them to keep their voices down. 'That's not our business. Our business is to keep everyone safe until we can get this all sorted tomorrow. Nothing else.' He pushed himself to his feet. 'Speaking of which, I think we'd better earn our keep. I'd like us to do a bit of a patrol round. Check all the security inside. And, if we feel brave enough—' He looked round at the team. 'Maybe do another little recce outside. Be interesting to see if there's any sign of anyone lurking around the house. At least in this weather, they can't avoid leaving footprints.'

Ferbrache looked up for the first time since Murrain had returned. 'I wouldn't be too sure of that if I were you, Kenny old son. The bastard who hit me seemed to come out of nowhere and buggered off in pretty much the same way.'

Murrain regarded him for a second then laughed. 'That's your great gift, Ferby. No matter how bad everyone's feeling, you always know just how to make them feel that little bit worse.'

CHAPTER TWENTY-TWO

Joe Milton had made little progress since his telephone conversation with Murrain. He spent half an hour in Marty Winston's office discussing what action they could take that night, before eventually concluding there was almost nothing they could realistically do. The weather was showing no signs of improving, though the Met Office had advised the snow was likely to cease some time in the small hours of the morning. Milton had no real idea what Winston's domestic circumstances might be, but it appeared that both men were resigned to staying in the office for the duration. Not that the following day was likely to be any easier.

For the moment, he returned to his office and sat playing in a desultory fashion with his computer. He didn't fool himself he was doing anything worthwhile. It was simply displacement activity, filling the time until he was in a position to do something more productive. He'd been flicking again through the interview notes relating to Kirsty Bennett, with the frail hope he might spot something useful he'd missed on previous readings. It was possible, he told himself, that the confirmation of her death might shed some new light on the various statements.

There was one statement in particular that had caught his attention when he'd first read it. He recalled one of Bennett's former office colleagues had mentioned that Bennett might be 'seeing' an older man. It took Milton a few moments to scan through the statements to find the one he was looking for. An interview with a Mrs Rena McKenzie, one of the permanent clerical officers who'd worked alongside Bennett.

The statement was characteristically uninformative. McKenzie thought she'd heard Kirsty Bennett say something about an older man, but when pressed she'd been unable to recall the context of the supposed mention or any further details. 'It was just something she said in passing. I was probably only half-listening.' Or more likely, Milton thought, it's something you've unconsciously concocted because you're trying to give us some useful information.

That was the most common problem with witnesses. Not that they were dishonest or unforthcoming. But that they wanted to be helpful. They were put on the spot by some uniformed officer and felt obliged to come up with something. In most cases, they genuinely believed what they were telling you. But years of interviewing witnesses had taught Milton that people could persuade themselves of anything. Sometimes there was a kernel of truth in the memory they'd constructed. Often there seemed to be nothing at all.

As far as he could see, no other witness had made a similar suggestion. Most of Bennett's former colleagues had no knowledge of her personal life. Others reported that she'd talked about 'friends' but had given no indication she was in any kind of relationship.

Even so, the comment had nagged at Joe Milton's brain. Sitting here reading it again, he realised it had dragged up a memory from somewhere else. Another case he'd been looking at over the last few days.

The case files Murrain had been examining were all still held in the secure cabinet by his desk, with the keys in the combination-locked box by Paul Wanstead's desk. It took Milton another few minutes to recall the combination – they tended to leave that kind of thing to Wanstead – and a little longer to dig out the most relevant files. There was a mass of material, and previously Milton had only skimmed through most of it, alighting every now and then on something potentially interesting or relevant.

The sheer volume of documents looked daunting. He had no precise memory of where he'd come across the reference, although he knew which files Murrain had drawn to his attention as most relevant. On the other hand, it wasn't as if he had much else to occupy his time.

In the event, it took him less time to find the first reference than he'd expected. He wasn't even sure if this had been the one he'd recalled. He had a half-memory of reading through this particular set of interview notes, but little else of their content had lodged in his brain.

The file in question related to the disappearance of one Martin Venning, a twenty-year old who'd been living in a shared flat in Levenshulme. Venning had been estranged from his family, quite possibly – or so Milton had read between the lines – because he was gay. It was hard for Milton to believe that any parent would really care these days, but there were plenty of unreconstructed types out there.

Whatever the background, Venning had moved out of the parental house in Birmingham at the age of sixteen following a bust-up with his parents. Both parents had been interviewed as part of the enquiry, but the notes shed little real light either on the reasons for Venning's departure or what might have happened to him since. His housemates in Manchester had apparently got on with him well enough, but he hadn't mixed socially with the others and they'd known little about his life outside the house, except that he'd worked for one of the big retailers in the city centre and seemed to have had his own circle of friends. But they'd been unable to provide much information about these friends, and the case notes suggested the investigating officers had had little success in tracking any of them down.

Like Kirsty Bennett, Venning had left his workplace one Friday night, supposedly heading off to meet a bunch of friends in the Northern Quarter. The police had tracked down CCTV coverage of him walking through the city centre early that evening, but there were no later sightings. He'd never returned to the house and hadn't turned up for work the following Monday.

In the absence of close friends or family, it had taken a while for anyone to become concerned about Venning's disappearance. The Human Resources department at his workplace had tried to contact him at home, but it wasn't unusual for employees to depart their minimum wage jobs without notice. His fellow housemates barely noticed his absence for a few days, and then assumed he'd gone off somewhere without bothering to tell anyone.

It took another week or so for anyone to wonder why Venning might have disappeared without taking any of his possessions, and another few days beyond that before the landlord was persuaded to consult the police. Reading a case like this, Milton wondered how many people simply fell off the grid each year without anyone even noticing. Even the police hadn't taken the case particularly seriously.

As the days had stretched into weeks, they'd interviewed Venning's housemates, work colleagues and immediate family with little success. Venning's bank account had been left untouched, apart from some ongoing direct debits, so there was cause for concern. Or there would have been if anyone had been sufficiently interested in Venning's fate.

The comment that caught Milton's eye was in an interview with one of Venning's housemates, in response to a question about Venning's friends or acquaintances. The housemate had responded: 'He kept all that close to his chest really. Not that we ever talked about it much. He gave the impression he hung around with another crowd, up in the city centre, but he was pretty cagey about it all. It was all a bit "you wouldn't know them because they go to a different school". You know?'

Milton knew or could imagine. A good dollop of bullshit to cover for an unacknowledged loneliness, probably. But other housemates had reported that Venning was often out in the evenings, so he'd presumably gone somewhere. When pressed the first housemate had added: 'I got the impression he might have been seeing someone. Someone in particular, I mean. Maybe an older man—'

There it was. Probably something and nothing. The reference had emerged only when the interviewee had been pushed to come up with something further. Even then the interviewee had offered nothing of substance. He didn't know how or why he'd formed the impression Venning had been seeing someone. He couldn't remember whether Venning had actually told him or had mentioned seeing an 'older man'.

Still, the reference was there. Milton skipped through the rest of the interviews but there was no further confirmation, although one of Venning's work colleagues had also said, again with no supporting evidence, that he'd formed the impression Venning was in a relationship. No mention of an 'older man'.

Milton pulled another stack of the files towards him. He was a decent speed reader, and it took him only about fifteen minutes to skim through each of the files. He couldn't swear he hadn't missed anything of significance, but he'd spotted no similar references among the interview notes. He was struck mainly by how similar these cases were. Young people disappearing between leaving work and arriving anywhere else. Individuals without close family connections or at least living away from their parental home. Individuals who hadn't been forthcoming with others about their personal lives and relationships. Individuals who, with the likely exception of Kirsty Bennett, had never been seen again.

He took out more files and started the process again. The first gave him nothing except another variant on that same characteristic narrative. Halfway through the second, he came across another reference to an 'older man'.

The missing person in this case was a student at one of the universities, a young woman called Tanya Davis. The story was similar to the others. Davis had been something of a loner, with various acquaintances from her lecture and tutorial groups but no close friends. She'd gone missing one Friday afternoon or evening. The last confirmed sighting of her had been at a tutorial earlier in the day, although one of her neighbours in the hall of residence thought he'd heard music from her room in the early evening. It seemed she'd left the hall sometime after that and failed to reappear.

It wasn't unknown for students to have weekends away without notification, and, as with Martin Venning, no-one had registered her absence until the following week. It was only when she had failed to turn up for a scheduled tutorial on the Monday morning that anyone became concerned. Her parents had been contacted, but they'd had no word from her since a phone-call earlier the previous week. That wasn't unusual, as she'd normally called them only once a week or so, mainly just to reassure them she was all right.

Beyond that, the story was similar to Venning's. The police were unable to track down any CCTV sightings of her in the vicinity of the university after the Friday evening. Her bank account and debit cards remained unused. Her mobile was turned off and never located.

The police had interviewed friends and family, but made scant progress. Her family had known little about her life at university, other than that she'd seemed 'happy enough'. Her acquaintances at university seemed to know nothing about her private life, and assumed she'd spent most of her time working. One of her fellow tutorial students, however, had commented: 'I thought she had friends outside university. In fact, I think she said she was seeing someone, an older man. She was cagey about it, so I assumed he was married or something.' On this occasion, the comment had been offered unprompted, but again the interviewee had been unable to substantiate it beyond: 'I don't know. It was just something she said once.' There were no clues as to the identity of the older man and, though the investigating officers had raised the question with other friends and family members, no-one else had formed a similar impression.

By now, Kenny Murrain would be experiencing some kind of buzzing in the back of his brain which would at least give him a steer as to whether any of this was worth pursuing. All Milton was feeling was a burgeoning ache in his frontal lobes that was more to do with tiredness and lack of coffee than anything else.

He was wondering whether to embark on a further set of files when his mobile buzzed on the desk. He glanced at the screen before taking the call. 'Marie?'

'Hi Joe. How's everything?'

'Everything's—' He stopped. 'I'm stuck in the office with the snow gradually mounting up outside. But I'm guessing that things might still be better than they are with you. Am I wrong?'

'It sounds like we're more or less even. Although in fairness we do have a violent killer stalking the building, so I think we win.'

'I've got Marty Winston,' he countered. 'But you probably do. Seriously, how is everything?'

'I'm going a bit stir crazy in here. That's one reason I called. No offence to the rest of the team, but I wanted to hear from someone who wasn't stuck in these four walls.'

He decided to accept that as at least approaching a compliment. 'Any developments?'

'Not really. You know about Ferby. We've got the Carter family here now. Everyone's treating it as the great British adventure. Dunkirk spirit, all that.'

'Except you?'

'Except any of the team, to be honest. We're none of us happy with that bastard prowling round out there while there's nothing we can do about it. I've been lobbying Kenny to let us go look for the bugger, but he won't hear of it.'

Milton wasn't sure whether she was joking. 'Don't do anything stupid, will you?'

'The story of my life is doing things that are stupid. Why should I change now?'

'You—' She really was joking, he decided. 'It's cold outside, though.'

'There is that,' she acknowledged. 'But, no, I'm not planning to head out there on my own. We've been having a debate about what to do. Like I say, we're none of us happy to be cooped up here. Kenny wants to err on the side of caution, probably rightly, until we can be sure of getting some back-up out here. He wants to check the exterior of the house, but we'll do it in pairs and stick close to the building.'

'The thought even of that made Milton feel uncomfortable. 'Take care. Marty's pulling out all the stops to get some resource sorted.'

'But I bet nothing'll be forthcoming now till the morning. If then. You'd think a violent killer would have some sort of priority, wouldn't you?'

'You'd think. But I guess it shows how far up the creek we are. And very short of paddles.'

She laughed, and it occurred to him, not for the first time, how much he enjoyed the sound of her voice. Not just her voice, but the way she thought about things. How her sense of humour dovetailed with his. He wanted to say something more before they ended the call but couldn't think what it might be.

'I'm sure we'll survive,' she said. 'Though that kind of cliche doesn't feel entirely appropriate in the circumstances. Speaking of which, I'd better go. Kenny's starting to round us up to go out on patrol.'

'Have fun. And take care.'

He dropped his phone back on to the desk and sat back in his chair, gazing out of the window at the night sky. The snow continued to fall, as heavily as ever, and the darkness had an orange glow from the streetlights of the town and Manchester beyond. He shivered unexpectedly, suddenly feeling very cold. Maybe the office heating had gone off, though it seemed early for that.

He dragged another file towards him, and wearily opened it up, preparing to plough through another mass of verbiage. It was like all detective work, he thought. Almost always a wild goose chase.

Except, of course, for the times when it wasn't.

CHAPTER TWENTY-THREE

It wasn't until they stepped outside that Murrain realised how much he'd been inwardly praying for a change in the weather. He'd never enjoyed snow even as a child. He'd always found it oppressive, slightly threatening. The heavy looming skies, soaking woollen gloves, frozen feet inside his Wellington boots, ice dripping down his neck from a snowball thrown by a schoolmate. Those were his memories. There must have been times when he'd had fun, building snowmen or sledging, but he couldn't summon any of those recollections now.

He'd had better experiences with his own son, on those increasingly rare occasions when snow had fallen in these parts. He'd made a point of playing with Joe in a way his own rather distant father never had. He'd bought a cheap plastic sledge and taken him over to Lyme Park to race down the gentler slopes, alongside dozens of other screaming children. They'd even had a shot at building a snowman once when the snow had hung around for a day or two. There hadn't been enough to make a full-sized figure and the whole thing had ended up lop-sided and misshapen. But they'd had a good laugh about the 'snow goblin' squatting on the lawn until the thaw had left nothing but a lump of greying ice on the sodden grass.

Years ago now, and even those few memories were soured by what had come after. Joe would almost have been old enough to take his own children playing in the snow.

'Not showing any signs of letting up,' Marie Donovan said from behind him as they clustered under the porch. The snow was thick and pristine, the earlier footprints long re-covered. The wind had increased and they could hear the rhythmic creaking of the trees that lined the hillside.

'Not obviously,' Murrain agreed. 'I can't remember the last time it snowed like this. It's usually something and nothing, even up in these parts.' He took a first step out into the open air, pulling his waterproof tightly around him. A blast of the wind caught him squarely in the face, unexpectedly strong. 'Let's get this over with, people. We don't want to spend any longer out in this than we need to. Marie, why don't you go with Will round the front of the house, and Bert and I can check round the back? We can all meet up at the rear door. Should only take five minutes, then we can get back into the warm.'

Most likely, they were wasting their time. But all of them were itching to be doing something. Given only the mildest encouragement, they'd be out there scouring the countryside for the killer. Most police officers weren't given to undue reflection. They wanted to be making progress, getting results, taking action. Murrain was more prone to inner contemplation than most, but he shared the growing frustration.

His own unease had been growing. There was something in the house itself that made him feel uncomfortable. The feeling was intangible as always, tantalisingly outside his conscious mind. When Anne Tilston had revealed her sisters' condition, he'd thought that might be it. Sometimes he could sense disability or illness even when it was not immediately apparent.

But he felt sure now that wasn't it, or not all of it. Too much about the house felt wrong. Its history, the mysteriously lingering presence of Robert Tilston, the shared past. It was as if there was a ghost haunting the place, something much more potent than Tilston's lifeless body stiffening in the rear of their police vehicle. Now, as the afternoon had worn on and the light had faded, that ghost felt closer than ever.

They split up in the way Murrain had suggested, and he and Bert Wallace tramped round to the rear of the house. 'What are we looking for, exactly?' Wallace said.

'Probably nothing. I want to check all the windows on the ground floor from the outside.' He'd made an internal circuit of the ground floor with Anne Tilston before they'd come out. She had hovered behind him protectively, as if he wasn't fully to be trusted.

Internally, the security had seemed pretty good. There were decent-looking mortice locks as well as lockable bolts on front and rear doors, and solid locks on the ground floor windows. A solitary able-bodied woman living with two severely disabled sisters in this remote spot would have legitimate concerns about security, even without the Tilstons' history.

There were only a couple of ground floor windows on this side of the house. Presumably, the place had been built to take maximum advantage of the views of the valley offered from the front.

'Looks secure enough,' Wallace offered.

'I just wanted to make sure there were no vulnerabilities that weren't evident from inside. And to check if there were any signs of life out here. If our killer's still hanging about close by, I'd like to know.'

Most of the garden was at the far end, between the house and the churchyard where Tilston's body had been found. At this side, there was only a relatively narrow strip of land, bounded by a large *Leylandii* hedge with woodland beyond. This part of the garden lay in the shelter of the house, protected from the winds off the valley. The snow had drifted less thickly here. Apart from their own scuffled footprints, there was no sign anyone had passed through here in the recent past.

They proceeded along the garden and checked the second window. It looked as solid as the first. The room beyond, the bedroom used by the two disabled sisters, was in darkness. The two sisters would be the greatest point of vulnerability if the killer were to enter the house. Anne Tilston normally slept upstairs, but the plan tonight was that everyone would remain downstairs, with a couple of camp-beds set up for the Carters in what had been a spare ground floor bedroom.

Wallace had obviously been reading his thoughts. 'You think the killer might try to break in here?'

'I can't really see it. I don't know why anyone would want to take the risk. But why would anyone want to break into Newland's house and do what they did? We can't really make any assumptions.'

'The house looks solid enough. But my guess is that, if someone wanted to get in, they probably could.'

'That's what concerns me. The security's decent, but it's just domestic stuff. Enough to deter most opportunistic house-breakers. But, with this one, who knows?' Murrain could feel it again, that familiar buzzing in the back of his head. He peered into the darkness, half-expecting something to give substance to his feelings.

They continued on their way, tramping through the snow. Every now and then, Murrain paused and flashed his torch beam around the narrow garden. As they rounded the corner of the house into the broader rear garden, they saw Donovan and Sparrow approaching from the far side of the house.

'Anything?' Murrain called.

Donovan shook her head. 'Nothing. Everywhere looks secure enough. No footprints.'

They gathered by the rear door. Murrain handed Wallace the torch and fumbled for the keys that Anne Tilston had lent to him, his fingers numb from the cold. Behind him, he heard Wallace talking quietly to Will Sparrow, obviously responding to some comment he'd missed. 'There, look. Where I'm pointing the torch.'

The two younger officers were peering into the dark, flashing the torchlight across the snow-covered ground. Murrain looked quizzically at Marie Donovan who shrugged.

'What is it?'

'I'm probably being stupid,' Wallace said, exchanging a glance with Sparrow. 'Will thinks I am, anyway. But I reckon there are footprints over there. They're almost covered in snow but they must be relatively recent, the way this lot's been coming down.'

At the same moment, Murrain sensed something. He blinked, startled, at what seemed like a visual image. A figure in the darkness, standing motionless, staring back at them. Then it was gone, and there was only the blank white ground and the endlessly falling snow.

Wallace was right, though. There was a trail of footprints out there, stopping perhaps ten metres away from where they stood. They were barely visible, already obscured by the further snowfall.

He took the torch back from Wallace and walked over to where the footprints ended. There were two adjacent lines, he saw now, one blurring the other. The trail of someone who had approached the house, then stopped and returned.

The footprints must have been made within the past half hour or so. That would have been some time after the attack on Neil Ferbrache.

'What do you want to do?' Marie Donovan said from behind him.

He paused for only a moment. 'Let's check it out.'

He sent Will Sparrow back to the car to dig out a couple of batons, conscious of how badly prepared they were. He had noted Sparrow's momentary hesitation, even though the car was fully visible from where the rest of the team was standing. They were all spooked. It was partly the atmosphere, the deadening effect of the falling snow, the steady roar of the wind, the strangely pale darkness. But it was also the sense that they were dealing with something, someone, who didn't seem entirely human. The sheer savagery and randomness of the attacks. The lack of any evidence of the killer's presence, other than the footprints before them now, fading even as they watched.

'Okay?' he said to the others. With the flashlight in one hand and the baton in the other, he led the group across the garden, following the vanishing trail of footprints. It was already hard to discern the tracks, but he could see they led away from the house in the direction of the thick hedge that divided the Tilston's land from the churchyard.

Just before the hedge, the footprints veered to the left back into the corner of the garden. He shone the torch across the ground. As far as he could judge, the prints led to the rear of the garden and then returned, but it was difficult to be sure.

In the corner of the garden, at the furthest point from the house, there was a small wooden shed. It was well concealed behind a row of overgrown bushes, and he'd not registered it earlier.

There was a fastening on the door designed to take a padlock, but no sign of any lock. The door was slightly ajar. Murrain gestured for the others to stay close behind him, then pulled open the door, shining the full beam of the torch inside.

The shed was empty. He ran the light slowly around the walls, the light catching on an array of garden tools in various states of repair. There were few other contents – a couple of old tins of paint, a small tower of plant-pots, a half empty bag of compost.

Behind all those, a small pile of blankets and an old, stained pillow.

'Someone's been in here quite recently. Everything else has a layer of dust. The tools haven't been used since at least last summer. But these have been moved.'

'You think someone's been sleeping in here?' Donovan said.

'Looks like it, doesn't it?' Murrain moved the torch beam into the space behind the mound of blankets. There was a large plastic water bottle, half full. The water looked clean, as if the bottle had been refilled relatively recently. 'Or at least sheltering in here.' He straightened and took another look around the small shed. 'Not my idea of home. But better than being out in the cold, I suppose.'

He'd been expecting to feel something as he'd entered, but as so often his instincts had deserted him just when he might have expected some insight. He thought there was something there, some flickering connection, but nothing that he could capture.

'You think they'll come back here?' Donovan said.

'Maybe. But if they were planning to come back, you'd have thought they'd have left some possessions. Apart from the water, there's nothing.'

'Maybe that's why they came back,' Bert Wallace offered. 'To pick up their stuff before heading off.'

'But heading off where?' Murrain said. 'Seems odd to abandon a decent shelter in weather like this, unless you've a better prospect to go to.' He'd initially found the sight of the blankets reassuring, as if he'd needed persuasion that they really were dealing with another human. Now, though, he was just chilled by the thought that the killer might have been sheltered here for days, like an animal waiting for its prey.

Back outside, Murrain led the team along the edge of the garden, trying to follow the trail of prints away from the shed. It was already becoming difficult, the prints reduced to little more than slight indentations in the smooth snow. The front of the garden, adjacent to the road, was bounded by a low wooden fence, and it appeared that whoever had left the prints had scrambled over the top. On the far side of the fence, the wind was driving the snow into deep drifts. Any footprints on the verge or road beyond would have been long obscured by the blizzard. Once again, it was as if the killer had only briefly materialised as a physical presence, then vanished again into the snow-filled night.

'You okay, Kenny?' he heard Donovan say.

'I'm fine. Well, at least—' He laughed. 'You know.'

'I know. This is a nightmare, isn't it?'

'I wish it was. Then we'd have a chance of waking up. It feels as if we're trapped in limbo. Nowhere to go. Nothing to do but wait, without even knowing what we're waiting for.'

'We'd better get back inside. They'll think something's happened to us.'

He nodded. 'That's the trouble, isn't it? Nothing's happening. But it feels, every minute, as if something might. And we don't know what that something could be.'

CHAPTER TWENTY-FOUR

Joe Milton had lost track of how many files he'd worked through. All unresolved missing persons cases from recent years. All young people who had unexpectedly disappeared, sometimes missed, more often not or not much. Some were no doubt individuals who, for whatever reason, had chosen to step off the grid. But that was increasingly hard to do, and all the cases provided substantive reasons for concern – bank accounts and cards unused, mobiles dead, no physical sightings beyond a given point. In roughly half the cases so far, Milton had come across at least a passing reference to an 'older man'.

He was opening another file when the office door opened and Marty Winston's face peered into the room. 'Still here, then?'

'I reckon we're both here for the night. Still coming down out there.'

'At least I've been able to relieve some other poor bugger of his stint on the duty rota,' Winston said. 'Coffee?'

'Why not? Anything to keep me awake.'

Winston gestured towards the stack of files on Milton's desk. 'Light reading?'

'I'd got as far as I could with setting up the MIR for the Bennett case. Thought I'd go back to these. Kenny was looking through them earlier. Similar missing persons cases from the last few years.'

'Kenny hoping his spider sense would start tingling, eh?'

Milton followed Winston into the small kitchen area on the opposite side of the corridor. Most other officers had some idea of Murrain's distinctive approach, and Winston was no fool. Even so, he'd never previously heard the Superintendent refer to the topic.

'Something like that,' Milton said, finally. 'You know how it is with Kenny.'

Winston was filling the kettle. 'I know something about it. You want to tell me more?'

'I think that's up to Kenny.' Milton had the sense he was being drawn into a conversation he'd rather have avoided. 'It's his business, I mean.'

Winston leant back against the worktop. 'It's mine if it affects the way he approaches investigations.'

'He's a very professional officer.' Milton was conscious he was already sounding more defensive than he'd intended or wanted. 'Does it all by the book. You know that.'

'I know that. I'm not trying to put you in a difficult position, Joe. If I'd any issues with Kenny – which I haven't – I'd take it up with him face to face. I'd just like to know more about this – how would you describe it? This gift of his?'

'I don't know how Kenny would describe it. Look, I'm not trying to be difficult either, but you ought to talk to him face-to-face if you really want to know about it. Kenny knows everybody talks behind his back, but it's not a subject he's comfortable with.'

'That's why I raised it with you. I've tried to talk to Kenny about it, but he does his best to avoid answering.'

So maybe you should take the hint, Milton thought. 'I think it's all something and nothing. He gets – well, feelings about things. He'd be the first to say they're far from reliable, but a few times they seem to have given him a steer when we had nothing else to go on.'

'Doesn't sound much more than the old copper's intuition.'

'Maybe it isn't. Kenny makes no great claims for it. If anything, he hates its unreliability.' Milton knew he was saying more than he'd intended, but perhaps it was the best way of shutting the conversation down.

'He thinks it's taken him in the wrong direction sometimes?' It sounded a leading question.

'From what Kenny says, it's not that what he's feeling is wrong, it's more that he doesn't always know how to interpret it. It doesn't always mean what it seems to mean.'

'That sounds convenient. I mean, it's the kind of thing a fortune teller might say. You know, the death card doesn't always mean death, sometimes it just means that a change is coming...'

Milton felt his mood shifting to irritation. He hadn't initiated this conversation, after all. 'Well, like I say, you'd have to ask Kenny.'

Winston finished spooning coffee into the mugs and poured on boiling water. 'Sorry, that was crass. I'm not asking you to be disloyal. I'm just genuinely interested. I know Kenny gets results. I'll back off. Tell me about those files you're going through.' He followed Milton back through into the office, and sat down opposite Milton's desk. 'Anything interesting?'

'Probably a waste of time. It was just that now we know – assuming the body's identified as hers – that Bennett was killed, I thought it might be worth revisiting these.'

'Kenny was already doing that?'

Milton could feel his defensive hackles rising again, but made an effort not to rise to any bait being offered. 'We didn't – don't – have any real leads on the Bennett case, though that might change now we know her fate. Kenny was looking for patterns. Anything that might give us a clue where to start. You know how it is.'

'I know exactly how it is. A lot of this job feels like you're wasting your time chasing shadows, but that's usually how you start to make progress. Ballsaching stuff, though.' He gestured again towards the stack of files.

'Tell me about it. But that's where Kenny was coming from. And, yes, maybe just hoping for a touch of the old intuition. I thought it might be worth another look now we've a different perspective.'

'Not to mention these two corpses up in Merestone or whatever the place is called. If they really do demonstrate the same MO.'

'I guess it's too early to say that.' Milton was aware of Winston's occasional eagerness to jump to the wrong conclusion. 'If they are connected, we've got something different again.'

'So did you find anything?'

'Not really. Just—'

'Just?'

'In several of the files I've come across references to the missing person having a relationship with an 'older man'.' Speaking the words out loud made the supposed finding feel even flimsier.

'An older man? Anything more than that.'

'No, that's just it. It's only ever a passing comment. Never any detail given. Usually just mentioned by one interviewee in each case. Not corroborated or even echoed by any other witnesses.'

'You said usually just mentioned by one interviewee. Any exceptions to that?'

'Just one, so far.' Milton flicked through the files and then handed one to Winston. 'Young woman called Amy Barnes. Slightly different from most of the others in that she seems to have been more gregarious. Most appear to have been very private, reclusive individuals, which is part of our difficulty.'

'So what was the story with Amy Barnes?'

'Early twenties. Had moved over to Manchester from North Wales. Pretty much the usual – looking for a decent job, bit of excitement, move to the big city out of the small town. Mother widowed, but a largish extended family back home. Got a job working in a call centre and was doing okay. Recently been promoted to team leader. Well liked and respected by the people she worked with.'

'And?'

'Same story. She went missing. She left work one Friday night – that seems to be another recurring pattern here – saying she was going to meet someone, but she'd arranged to meet up with her usual gang later in the evening. She never turned up.'

Winston was flicking through the file, stopping apparently at random to read excerpts from the notes. 'A bit more forthcoming than some of the others. She was definitely seeing someone.'

'Looks like it. Or at least that was the impression she gave. But still cagey on the details. At least three of her work colleagues reckon she'd implied she was in a relationship, but wasn't keen to discuss it.'

'Married man?'

'Maybe. But there's no other detail. Even with this one, it looks as if no-one could really remember anything specific she'd said. Just an impression.'

'What about her mobile phone records? If she really was seeing some guy, she must have phoned him.' He paused, thinking. 'Or, more likely, he'd generally have phoned her, I guess. Not exactly my area of expertise, to be honest.' He laughed awkwardly.

'Me neither,' Milton said, wondering as he spoke if that was entirely true. He'd never been unfaithful to Gill. If anything, it was quite likely that she'd been unfaithful to him, technically at least. Even so, his burgeoning relationship with Marie Donovan, limited as it still was, had left him with an odd sense of guilt. 'There's a report on that in the file. They got access to her mobile records. From memory, there were two or three numbers they couldn't account for among the usual stuff to family, work colleagues and the like. They were pay-as-you-go numbers bought with cash. No account, no address, no traceable user.'

'Burners?'

'Probably just cheap pre-paid mobiles bought from a supermarket. Not necessarily suspicious, but does smack of someone who wanted to remain incognito.'

'Which could just be someone who wants to make sure his wife didn't find out. Separate phone, not kept at home. No chance of her accidentally stumbling across an incriminating text.' Given it wasn't Winston's area of expertise, Milton thought, he sounded surprisingly knowledgeable.

'Leaves us no further forward, anyway. Except Amy Barnes was calling someone, or more than one person, we weren't able to identify.'

'I assume there was no suggestion she was involved in anything dodgy?'

'No hint of it. Just your typical young single woman. Less of a loner than most of the others, but still with parts of her life she kept private for whatever reason. But no suggestion of anything untoward.'

Winston sipped at his coffee. 'How many of these cases have we got?'

'A dozen over five years that roughly seem to fit the pattern. That's as far back as we've gone, and that's just central and south Manchester. We haven't followed it up in the north of the city yet.'

'It was Kenny's decision to look back at these files?'

'Sort of. Like I say, we were just looking for some background. Any relevant patterns. Kenny picked up on the recurrent pattern - loners, private individuals, typically going missing in the evening after leaving work. The lack of any kind of indication of what might have happened to them.'

'Now we have a body. And evidence of foul play.'

'Which may or may not link to the killings up in Merestone,' Milton added.

'Christ, Joe. Do we really want to go where this seems to be leading us? The idea that we might have had a multiple killer operating for years, and we haven't even bloody noticed?'

'It's possible. I mean, it's an old coppers' thing, isn't it? How many killings just go under the radar? The ones that seem like accidents or natural deaths or someone just falls off the grid and isn't even missed. How many patients did Shipman kill before anyone noticed there was even anything amiss?'

'The trouble is, no one wants it to be true. Not the relatives. Not the friends. Not even us. They want reassurance and we want an easy life. You see it with every missing person case. They want to believe that the individual's just going to walk back into the house one day. They carry on believing that long after you know it's not going to happen.'

He looked gloomier than Milton could recall seeing him. 'And, meanwhile,' Winston went on, 'Kenny and the team are stuck up in Merestone with a killer prowling round outside, and we're stuck down here, sitting on our arses, waiting for the bloody snow to clear.' He took a large mouthful of coffee and shook his head, with the air of a dog shaking off water. 'Christ, this isn't like me. Let's get down to something, Joe. Anything. Even if it's just more ploughing through those bloody files.'

CHAPTER TWENTY-FIVE

Anne Tilston had gathered the Carters in the kitchen. Liz Carter was sitting with the boys at the kitchen table, playing a card game to keep them amused. Tilston was standing at the Aga, stirring a large pot. 'I dug some soup out of the freezer. There's plenty for all of us, with the bread and cheese.'

Murrain nodded. 'We're very grateful, Ms Tilston.' He had no appetite himself, but he recognised that none of the team had eaten since the early morning, apart from Sparrow who always seemed to carry an emergency chocolate bar in his pocket.

'Did you find anything outside?' Anne Tilston asked.

Murrain glanced at the two children, and decided this was probably not the moment to reveal what they'd discovered in the shed. 'Nothing very significant. We can talk about it later.'

Tilston still had her back to him, stooped over the Aga, but he saw from Liz Carter's expression that she'd understood the implication behind his response. 'Where's your husband, Mrs Carter?'

'He went to sort out the bedding for the children. Anne's been very good at organising them somewhere to sleep.'

'I found a couple of old camp beds,' Anne Tilston said. 'Haven't used them for years. They seem sound enough.'

'The boys can sleep on those. Rob brought a couple of camping mattresses with us. We'll be fine for tonight.' Her cheeriness sounded feigned, Murrain thought. Something she was maintaining for the children.

'What about you and your team?' Anne Tilston said. 'Do you want me to try to sort out something for you?'

'I really don't want to put you to any trouble. I don't imagine we're going to get too much sleep anyway. We'll probably just take turns on the sofas in the study, if that's okay.' He turned to the others standing behind him. 'We'll cope, won't we?'

Will Sparrow looked as if he might be about to offer a contrary opinion, but Bert Wallace said, 'We're fine. I'd rather keep my wits about me in any case.' Her tone suggested this might be a battle that Sparrow had already lost.

'I'll just go and double check on your husband,' Murrain said to Liz Carter. The situation was already beginning to get to him. There was no reason to be concerned about Rob Carter's safety. But Murrain had felt that familiar stirring in the back of his brain when Liz Carter had been speaking.

He stepped back out into the hall. Anne Tilston had allocated the Carters a room halfway along the corridor, opposite the study. It was, she'd told Murrain, the room she normally slept in herself if either of her sisters was having a bad night. The two sisters themselves shared the room next door. Murrain couldn't imagine what challenges must be involved in getting the two women prepared for bed each evening.

The door to the room was standing slightly ajar. Murrain pushed it open. The room looked as if it was normally sparsely furnished – just a single bed, a wardrobe which had seen better days, and a small chest of drawers. Two folding camp beds had been set up next to the single bed, and a camping mattress was spread on the floor beside those. The beds had been made up, but there was no sign of Rob Carter.

Murrain turned back into the hallway. He pushed open the door of the study and peered inside. Neil Ferbrache was alone, fiddling with his mobile phone.

'All okay?' Ferbrache said. 'I'm just trying to check the weather forecast and the traffic but the signal's pretty crap up here.'

'You haven't seen Rob Carter, have you?'

'I said hello to him in the kitchen earlier. I've been in here since then. Don't tell me you've lost him?' The tone was jocular, but the two men knew each other too well.

'I hope not. He was making up the beds for the kids in the room over the way. But he's not there now. He's not gone back to the kitchen.'

'I heard someone moving about out there. But nothing since then.' Ferbrache followed Murrain back out into the hallway. Murrain could feel his unease growing, but he couldn't tell whether it was just anxiety or that more significant inner voice.

He took another few steps towards the front door, conscious now of a breeze. 'The bloody front door's open.'

For a moment, he wondered if they'd somehow failed to close it behind them when they'd left the house. But he knew that wasn't the case. Anne Tilston had closed it firmly, and he'd heard the sound of the key turning in the mortice lock. At the time, it had felt disturbingly absolute. They'd re-entered the house, as agreed, through the rear door, directly into the kitchen.

He hurried down the hall, Ferbrache behind him. The front door was half open, flurries of snow drifting in.

Rob Carter was standing in the doorway, a lit cigarette cocooned in his hand. He started and turned guiltily at the intrusion. 'Oh, thank Christ. I thought you were Liz.'

Murrain mentally counted down from ten, one moment away from giving Carter the mother of all bollockings. 'That's the thing you're mostly worried about, is it, Mr Carter? Your wife catching you smoking?'

Rob Carter blinked and looked around, as if it had only just occurred to him where he was standing. 'I mean, she knows that I still do. But I try not to at home because of the kids—' He stopped, finally reading Murrain's expression. 'I just thought—'

'What did you think, Mr Carter? We've brought you across from your own home because there's a potential risk to yours and your family's safety. My colleague here was attacked just a few metres from where you're standing. What did you think exactly?'

'I didn't really think, I suppose. I thought I'd just be out here for a second...'

'Mr Carter, this isn't a game. I've no idea whether we're really in danger tonight, but there's a sufficient risk for us to take every precaution. I'm not scaremongering. I'm just trying to be prudent. I'd ask for your full co-operation in that. If you really can't manage without another cigarette, let us know and we'll make sure someone accompanies you. What I don't want is anyone going AWOL tonight. Is that clear?'

'I'm sorry.' Carter tossed his cigarette butt into the snow, and followed Murrain and Ferbrache back into the house. 'You won't tell Liz, will you?'

'About the smoking?'

Carter gave a weak grin. 'No, about what a prat I am.'

Murrain was beginning to form an impression of Carter, and he suspected Liz Carter already knew very well what sort of man her husband was. 'No, Mr Carter. She won't hear that from me.' He turned and focused on ensuring that the door was securely locked and bolted.

Once Carter had retreated down the hallway, he turned to Ferbrache. 'Hard work this, sometimes, isn't it?'

'Pillock. He'd probably benefit from someone hitting him on the back of the head. Still, no harm done this time, I suppose.'

'No. But he might have been bloody lucky.'

'How do you mean?'

'You didn't notice out there?'

'I was too busy focusing on chummy's cheesy grin. What was it?'

'Just outside the gate. More footprints.'

'Made since you returned from your patrol?'

'I'm pretty certain there was nothing out there when we went past. None of us went out the gate. Anyway, our prints will have been covered by now.'

'So our killer's still out there? Still near the house.'

'We knew that already. There were prints at the rear, and there's an old shed out back that looks as if it's been recently occupied.'

'You think we should go out there?'

As before, Murrain found himself hesitating. He knew how ill-equipped they were to tackle whatever they might find. 'I really don't know. It feels as if whoever this is, they know the terrain out there much better than we do. In the dark, in weather like this, they'll be impossible to find. At least as long as they're lurking round here they're not a danger to anyone else.'

'If they stay lurking round here.'

'There are no other residences close by. And nobody in their right mind would try to walk far in these conditions.'

Ferbrache nodded slowly, as if absorbing what Murrain had been saying. 'I think you're right, Kenny. But maybe we need to bear in mind that, whoever we're dealing with here, they're a long way from being in their right mind.'

CHAPTER TWENTY-SIX

By the time Murrain and Ferbrache returned to the kitchen, the Carters, along with the rest of Murrain's team, were sitting around the table, hungrily devouring bowls of soup. Anne Tilston ladled out another two portions, and the two men gratefully accepted them and joined their colleagues. Murrain still felt no real appetite, but the warmth of the soup would be welcome after their excursion outdoors.

He lowered himself into a seat next to Bert Wallace, exchanging a glance with Rob Carter who was now seated on the opposite side of the table.

'Great soup.' Wallace gestured towards her bowl. 'God, I was starving. I hadn't realised.'

'It's been a long day.'

'And not over yet. Boss, can I have a word in a minute?' Wallace had lowered her voice to something just above a whisper.

'Whenever you like. Some problem? I mean, apart from all the obvious ones.'

'Better not in here. Back next door when we've finished eating.' Her eyes, Murrain realised, were fixed on Anne Tilston, who had seated herself at the far end of the table.

They finished their soup and, muttering excuses, Murrain followed Wallace back into the study, leaving the rest of the team helping themselves to the cheese and cold meats Anne Tilston had set out in the middle of the table.

'What is it?' Murrain said.

'Just a small thing. The Robert Tilston case.'

'What about it?'

'I was thinking about Tilston's death. How weird it was. Why he should have made his way back up here to die. Then not even make contact with his daughters.'

It felt to Murrain as if Wallace's words had triggered something in his mind, one of those almost imperceptible shiftings of the neurons that sometimes opened up new insights for him. With everything else that had followed, he'd almost come to disregard Tilston's death. Whatever its motivation and background, it seemed almost insignificant compared with the violent deaths afterwards. Except, of course, there remained the question of whether the death was simply a coincidence, or whether it was somehow linked to everything that had followed. As Wallace said, the circumstances of Tilston's death seemed inexplicable in themselves. 'And?'

She hesitated, as if unsure how to approach this. 'Do you know anything about the family? I mean, were you aware of the background when Tilston was convicted?'

'Not really.' Murrain was unsure where this was leading. 'Though there was a lot of internal gossip in the force. But I was just a lowly sergeant – I'd recently been promoted, if I remember correctly. I'd come across Tilston a few times, but had no real contact with him. I was never interested in delving into the detail. Why?'

'It's just that earlier, while we were sitting around, I did a bit of digging around on the internet on my phone.' She looked vaguely embarrassed, as if she'd been caught out wasting time. 'Signal up here's a bit iffy, but I found a few things. Archive stuff from the nationals, mainly.'

'Anything interesting?'

'I don't know whether any of this means anything. There was a fair bit of stuff about the three sisters, especially in the tabloids. They were all fairly young then, so you can imagine the coverage it got.'

Murrain could remember some of it. Innuendo-laden nonsense about the three young women. Questions about whether Tilston had abused his own daughters. They were never more than questions, but once Tilston was convicted he became fair game for any kind of semi-accusation. It was all too possible, of course, and the fact that no charges of that kind had been brought against Tilston didn't necessarily mean much. The whole affair had been embarrassing enough for the force as it was. Murrain could easily imagine strings might have been pulled to contain the reputational damage.

'What caught my eye,' Wallace went on, 'was that one of the accounts – not one of the tabloids, but in the Telegraph, I think – also mentioned a brother.'

'I don't remember any reference to a brother.'

'A younger brother. Who'd died as a child.'

'Branwell?' Murrain said.

Wallace looked baffled. 'Not quite. Bradley, I think. Why?'

'Just the Bronte connection. They must have chickened out of going the whole way.'

Wallace was still looking puzzled, but had clearly decided to ignore another of her boss's eccentricities. 'It looks as if he died when he was only a few months old. Some sort of accident, though the article didn't give any details. But there was a suggestion that Tilston tried to use the death as a mitigation for his actions in court. Never recovered from the grief, that kind of thing. But it had been years before so he probably got short shrift. I found a few reports of the trial but couldn't see any mention of it.'

'This was presumably before the mother left?'

'It looks as if she walked out on the family just a few years before Tilston was charged. Seems to have retained her privacy fairly effectively as far as I can see. No real mention of her at the trial.'

'I wonder where she is now,' Murrain mused. 'She's somebody we need to track down, once we get started. But what about the son? It's interesting, but I'm not sure where it gets us.'

'It probably doesn't get us anywhere. It's just that the story also said the son was buried in the churchyard next to the Tilstons' house. It was one of those details they'd included to make the whole thing sound even more dark and morbid.'

'It's a thought,' Murrain said. 'Maybe he came back to say goodbye to his late son rather than his living daughters. I don't suppose any of us thought to look at the occupant of the grave where he was found?'

'We can check in the morning. From what I remember, the grave was one of the more recent-looking ones.'

'It's a possible explanation, though, Bert. Good work.' Murrain always felt slightly awkward dishing out praise, especially when the recipient was a female officer universally known as Bert. He'd never felt comfortable with the nickname.

'Doesn't get us very far, though, does it? Tilston's death's the least of our concerns.'

'I don't know,' Murrain said. 'The whole thing's so bizarre. Interesting that Anne Tilston didn't mention the brother's grave.'

'Maybe didn't occur to her. She'd have been pretty young when he died.'

'She must know he's buried out there, though. I just get the feeling that there's something we're not being told.'

'It was interesting looking back through the story,' Wallace said. 'There wasn't a huge amount on-line after all these years. Most of it was just news reports on the trial. The Telegraph feature was the longest. More of a background piece about the family.'

'Anything about the mother?' Murrain dropped his head, avoiding Wallace's eyes, trying to grasp the momentary sensation that had skittered across his mind.

'Not much. She wasn't featured in the piece. Reading between the lines, it looked as if they weren't able to track her down. There were a few snide suggestions she'd gone to ground. Avoiding the media.'

'You couldn't blame her for that. If they'd found her, they'd have been camped out on her doorstep.' Murrain was still trying to focus on the elusive thought or feeling, but it was gone.

'From the article, it looked as if they pretty much laid siege to the daughters until they got some quotes from them. But there wasn't much about the mother. Just said that she and Tilston had split up a few years earlier. As far as I can tell, she walked out and left Tilston with the children.'

'That's a bit odd in itself, isn't it? Leaving him with the children, I mean.'

'It's not unheard of, is it?' Wallace said. 'We don't know the circumstances. The article implied it might have been because she knew what Tilston was up to. But the way it was phrased suggested they didn't have any evidence to support that.'

'If she did know, it'd be even stranger to leave the daughters behind, surely?'

'You'd have thought so, wouldn't you? But there could be any number of reasons why she walked out.'

Murrain stepped back over to the window. The curtain had been left open, and he could see that the snow was still falling. He was feeling the same unease, the same sense of oppression he'd felt when he'd first entered the house. 'Everything about this feels wrong,' he said, conscious Wallace was watching him curiously. 'Tilston coming back here to die. Random, apparently unconnected killings.' He paused. 'Even those two poor sisters.'

'Three poor sisters, I'd say,' Wallace added. 'Can't be much of a life being stuck here as the carer for the other two. This place feels about as desolate as it gets even if the weather wasn't like this. I wonder why they've not sold up and moved somewhere more – well, more civilised, I suppose.'

'People stay put for all kinds of reasons.' Murrain remembered he and Eloise had talked endlessly about moving house after their son had died, but it had never happened. Neither of them had acknowledged it, but he suspected it was because they hadn't wanted to sever themselves from the boy who'd grown up there.

There was a knock at the door and Marie Donovan peered into the room. 'Is this a private meeting or can anyone join in?'

'I've just been filling Kenny in on a bit of digging I was doing on the internet,' Wallace said.

'Apparently there was a Tilston brother. Died as a child. More interestingly, he's buried next door.'

Donovan came into the room, followed by Sparrow and Ferbrache. 'Liz Carter's trying to get the boys settled for bed. Thought we'd better leave them to it. They seem a bit over-excited by the prospect of meeting real police officers.'

'The real excitement was meeting a CSI, if you ask me,' Ferbrache said.

'Nothing more thrilling, Ferby,' Donovan said. 'So what's this about a brother?'

'Nothing much, really,' Wallace said. 'Like I say, younger brother. Died in an accident as a child. Buried in the churchyard. I thought that maybe explained why Robert Tilston had gone back there.'

'That's interesting,' Donovan said. 'When I was first talking to Anne Tilston about who was living here, she made some half-joking comment about there not being a Branwell. Something about the way she said it felt a bit odd, but I couldn't put my finger on it.'

'She may have thought it was none of our business,' Murrain commented. 'But it might have cast a little light on why her father had chosen to return to the churchyard, rather than coming to the house.'

'I don't get the impression her father's actions or motives are high on her list of things to care about,' Donovan said. 'One other thing, though, since we're talking about Anne Tilston.' She'd dropped her voice, though the door into the room was firmly closed. 'I was chatting to Liz Carter while Anne was sorting out something for her sisters. She reckoned there was some bad blood between Anne and Toby Newland.'

'What sort of bad blood? Murrain asked.

'Maybe not the best choice of words in the circumstances. Liz clearly felt a bit awkward raising it. She said it wasn't much more than gossip. It was mainly just an impression she'd got from conversations she'd had with Newland. Apparently, she hadn't had much contact with him or with Anne Tilston for that matter. Newland worked in Manchester and had a flat in the Northern

164

Quarter. This was mainly a place he came to for weekends, so she hadn't run into him very often. She was surprised he'd been up here today. Must have been caught out by the snow.'

'Doubly unlucky, if so,' Murrain said.

'Too right. Anyway, Liz thought the animosity between Anne Tilston and Newland stemmed from homophobia as much as anything else. Apparently, Newland had a habit of bringing young men up here for the weekend.'

'Young men plural?' Murrain asked. 'Not the same one?'

'That was what Tilston reckoned. I don't think Liz Carter had any interest one way or another. She said she'd occasionally seen Newland arrive with someone, but had no real idea who. Newland apparently thought Tilston disapproved.'

'I wonder what form her disapproval took? Presumably obvious enough that Newland was aware of it.'

'I've no idea. Don't think Liz did either. She didn't want to make too much of it.'

Ferbrache had settled himself back on to the sofa, nursing a mug of coffee. 'If you're suggesting Anne Tilston might have been behind what happened to Toby Newland, then forget it. She's a slight figure. She wouldn't have had the height or the strength to have done that.'

'Stranger things have happened,' Murrain said. 'But you know what you're talking about, Ferby.'

'Aye, I do. Not about many things, admittedly. But this is my specialist subject, poor bugger that I am. I'm not saying it's completely impossible, if the circumstances were right and the assault weapon was sharp enough. But what was done to Newland would have needed some real welly. I reckon whoever did it would have had to be a similar height to Newland, at least. He was a good six foot.'

'Okay, so we can probably rule that out,' Murrain said. 'But we should interview Anne Tilston properly. If there was something between her and Newland we need to find out what. She might at least be able to give us some insights into Newland's lifestyle. Maybe that's where the answer lies, and Tilston's death is just a red herring. That should probably be our priority tomorrow assuming we can ever get out of this place. Finding out more about Mr Newland and his background.'

'Not to mention identifying the other victim.' Donovan said. 'I'd been assuming that it was Newland's partner so we'd be able to identify him easily enough. But it sounds as if that might not be the case.'

Ferbrache was looking startled. 'Other victim? What other victim?'

'Oh, Christ, Ferby,' Murrain said. 'I'd forgotten you didn't know. We thought you'd already made your escape by the time we found him, so we weren't about to summon you back up.'

'Well, thanks for that,' Ferbrache said. 'So what's the story?'

'Upstairs in Newland's house. In the bedroom. In bed, in fact. Apparently the same, or a very similar, MO. Savage stab wounds, slashing. But attacked from the front rather than behind.'

'In bed?' Ferbrache repeated.

'Could have been attacked in his sleep, I suppose. Which would explain how someone could get close enough to do it.'

'Especially if he'd been under the influence of something,' Ferbrache agreed. 'That'll be something to check. You've sealed off the scene.'

'As best we could. And the rest of the house. Just hoping that in these temperatures, the scene won't decay too much overnight.'

'Best we can do,' Ferbrache agreed. 'Can't say I fancy heading out there again before morning.' He rubbed the bruised spot on his head. 'I've had more than enough dealings with our friend for one day. But this isn't your average domestic, is it? I mean, not that we thought it was, given what happened to Newland. But it's not some one-off.'

'Then there's the question of whether it's linked to Kirsty Bennett.' Murrain realised Ferbrache hadn't been acquainted with that piece of this unfathomable jigsaw either. 'They've found a body, Ferby. In the Mersey. Sounds similar to what we've got up here.'

'Jesus,' Ferbrache said. 'You really think—?'

'I don't think anything, Ferby old chum. Not yet. But it's got to be a line of enquiry, assuming that the MO is as similar as it sounds.' He shook his head, as if trying to dislodge whatever was continuing to echo in his brain. 'What worries me is that Bennett wasn't the only missing young person on our books. There were others with similar stories.'

He walked over to the uncurtained window. If this weather continued, it would be no easier to access this place in the morning. The resources of the emergency services would be stretched even thinner. It felt as if they were under siege, with the cavalry indefinitely delayed.

Ferbrache and Donovan were slumped on the threadbare sofa. Wallace and Sparrow were seated at the table, Wallace playing idly with her mobile phone.

'Bert,' Murrain said. 'Are you still getting a decent wifi signal?'

'Not bad. Fades occasionally but mostly 4G. Not a lot of battery life left, though.'

Sparrow leaned forward, looking as if he'd just woken up. 'What sort is it? Think my charger will fit it.'

'Good,' Murrain said. 'Since we're stuck here, let's at least try to do something. At least some more digging on the internet, Bert. Anything more you can find about the Tilstons. Robert Tilston. The sisters. The car accident. The mysterious brother. And the mother.'

'I don't know—'

'There probably won't be much after all this time. But it feels to me like there's something not right with this picture, and I'd welcome anything that sheds any light on what that something might be.'

Wallace was looking sceptical. 'If you think it's worth it.'

'It's not like there's much else we can get on with,' Murrain said. 'But I'm open to ideas.'

'Joe's still stuck in the office, as far as I know,' Donovan said. 'Sounded as if he was looking for things to occupy himself. We could ask him to do some on-line digging into the Tilstons. There must be some stuff about the accident, at least. Maybe about the brother's death, depending on the circumstances. Worth a shot, anyway.'

'Anything's worth a shot at the moment,' Murrain said. 'Once she's finished dealing with her sisters, I'll see if I can get a word with Anne Tilston again. I don't think this is quite the time for a formal interview – we can do that in the morning. But I might just see if I can tease out anything about this brother.'

They were all doing little more than clutching at straws, he thought. But at least it would create the illusion of activity. He felt he needed something, anything, to calm the endless static that continued to trouble his brain.

CHAPTER TWENTY-SEVEN

Marty Winston had eventually returned to his own office, leaving Joe Milton to continue checking through the remaining files. Milton had found a couple more references to an 'older man', both as inconclusive and unhelpful as the previous mentions. But he was becoming convinced there really was a pattern here. Something worth pursuing, once they finally managed to get the inquiry properly kicked off.

He was still wondering whether he should try to make the journey out to Kirsty Bennett's parents. But the control room had advised that even the A6 was now becoming close to impassible. The gritters and snowploughs were out where possible, but they could do little more than alleviate the worst of the impact. They were keeping the motorways largely open, though stretches of the M62 and M61 across the Pennines were closed, but the major trunk roads were gradually succumbing to the endlessly falling snow. The number of serious call-outs had reduced, simply because most people were now staying put wherever they were. The last major incident had been a gridlock on the M60 caused by a jack-knifed lorry, but they'd cleared that an hour or so back. The control room were taking numerous calls about stranded vehicles, but there was little they could do other than advise drivers to seek shelter.

The general guidance to the public was not to make unnecessary journeys. The visit to Bennett's parents was necessary enough, but there'd be little benefit in making it tonight.

As he opened yet another case file, his mobile buzzed on the desk. Marie. As before, his first thought was to feel absurdly pleased – and, yes, slightly relieved – at the prospect of hearing her voice.

'Marie? Everything okay?'

'Yes, fine. Or as fine as it can be in the circumstances.'

'How was your expedition outside?'

He listened while she recounted what they'd found in the Tilstons' garden.

'Shit. You reckon that place is secure?'

'As secure as a domestic house can be. And I can't see why whoever it is out there would have any interest in trying to get in.'

'I'm sure you're right.' He wanted to offer reassurance but his words sounded hollow even to his own ears 'Probably just desperate to get away. Anyway, what can I do for you?'

'It's a bit of an odd request, and I don't know how much you'll be able to do. But you've got access to some of the on-line files—'

'Go on.'

'It's about the Tilstons. Kenny's got this bee in his bonnet.'

'Is this one of Kenny's usual bees?'

'You know how it is with Kenny. How cagey he is about that stuff. But it might be. There's something troubling him, certainly. It might just be he's going stir crazy like the rest of us.'

'I take it he's not with you at the moment?'

'No,' she said, 'and I don't mean to be disrespectful. It's just that – well, like I say, you know how it is with Kenny.'

'Only too well. I also know that, when he gets one of these bees stuck in his bonnet, it's usually worth paying attention. So what about the Tilstons?'

'A couple of things. Not about Robert Tilston, oddly enough, though there's obviously plenty odd there. But more about the sisters. And the brother.'

'Brother? I thought just the three sisters lived up there.'

'It is. The latter-day Brontes. But it turns out there was also a brother. Died as a young child. Some kind of accident.'

'Branwell?'

'We've been through all that. No, Bradley. Bert found some brief details of the story on-line, but nothing about the nature of the accident.'

'Why does it matter?'

'He's apparently buried in the churchyard next door. Where Robert Tilston's body was found.'

'What does Anne Tilston have to say about all this?'

'That's the thing. She didn't mention it.'

'There's no particular reason why she should, though, is there? I mean, if the brother died years ago.'

'Only that it might be a reason why Tilston headed to the churchyard rather than coming to the house.'

'She might not want to acknowledge that possibility, however much bad blood there was between them.'

'Of course. There's probably nothing in this. But, like I say, Kenny—'

'I get that. It's never a good idea to ignore Kenny on something like this. He doesn't do things lightly, especially where his – feelings are concerned. Most likely, he couldn't even explain to you himself why this might be important, but something will be driving him in that direction. You said a couple of things?'

'The other's about the other two sisters. Emily and Charlotte. Turns out they're both very severely disabled. Car accident. Severe brain damage and physical injuries. I've not seen them, but from what Kenny says they're both in a pretty bad way.'

'Tragedy certainly knew how to hit that family, didn't it?'

'Seems so. Which is interesting in itself. That may be one of the things influencing Kenny's thinking. If bad things keep happening, maybe there's a reason.'

'Something more than bad karma?'

'I don't know what I mean. But we seem to have rather a lot of accidents here. Maybe just coincidence. Maybe bad luck. But maybe—'

'Not all necessarily accidents?'

There was a hesitation, as if he'd made something more explicit than she'd intended. 'It sounds far-fetched when you put it like that. But again—'

'Kenny. Yes, I know. We've come across stranger things. When you see patterns emerging, it's probably better not to ignore them.' He thought about the pattern he'd begun to see in the case files. 'So what do you want me to do?'

'Only if you've time—'

It was Milton's turn to laugh. 'Time's about the only thing I'm not short of. Food, yes. Even milk, I think. I might have to go and raid one of the other teams' fridges, if I'm stuck here much longer. But time – no, I've more than enough of that.'

'I think all Kenny's looking for is whatever information we can find on the Tilstons. Obviously, there's plenty of stuff on Robert, but at the moment he's more interested in the others. The sisters and this mysterious brother. We're looking at public domain stuff on line, but Kenny wondered whether there would be anything more you could track down internally.'

'I can try. But I won't be able to get access to most of the files. Pretty much everyone's buggered off here. I can try the PNC, but I presume none of these will be nominals so the chances of finding anything useful are pretty low. I assume neither the brother's death or the accidents would have been classed as major incidents?'

'I doubt it. The car crash sounds as if it was just that. Careless driving at most, but the driver was Emily, so I doubt anyone would have taken that further in the circumstances. The brother we don't know about – there was only a passing mention in the piece Bert found – but if there'd been anything significant there, the story would have got wider coverage after what happened with Tilston. Seemed to be just a footnote. Sounds like a wild goose chase, doesn't it?'

'Does a bit. But, like I say, it's not like I'm rushed off my feet here. Suppose the other thing I could do is give Paul a ring.'

'Paul Wanstead?'

'Who else? He's the closest thing we've got to a one-man corporate memory round here. As well as being the prince of HOLMES 2. If there's a fact about the force that Paul doesn't know, it's not worth knowing. Or so he's always telling me.'

'Worth a try. If he doesn't mind being disturbed?'

'This is Paul Wanstead we're talking about. Probably the only person in the world who's envious of me being stuck in the office.'

'I'll leave it with you. I'm not hopeful we'll find anything useful, but you never know. Kenny's going to have another word with Anne Tilston, but I think he wants as much background as possible before he wades in.'

'Does he think she might be lying? Why would she?'

'That's the question, isn't it? But, well—'

'I know. Kenny. Okay, leave it with me. And Marie—?'

'Yes?'

'Just take care, won't you?'

There was a moment's silence, then she said, 'Yes, of course, Joe. We all will. Speak later.'

He sat there after she'd ended the call trying to interpret her tone in those last words. It had felt dismissive, but he was conscious of his own sensitivities. Maybe she hadn't wanted to admit — or let him know — that she was feeling as anxious as he was. Or maybe she just didn't want his concern.

Either way, there was no point in obsessing about it. For the moment he had something to get on with. He thumbed through his phonebook and pressed Paul Wanstead's mobile number.

CHAPTER TWENTY-EIGHT

For the moment, the kitchen was deserted. Murrain assumed the Carters were getting the children off to bed, and Anne Tilston was doing what needed to be done with her sisters. He couldn't begin to envisage what that might entail every night.

Waiting for Anne Tilston to reappear, he dialled Eloise's number. He knew her too well to imagine she'd have been worrying unduly about him, but they had an unspoken understanding, as serving police officers, that they should at least check in with one another periodically.

Her opening words on answering the phone were: 'Don't tell me you're going to spoil my evening and get back after all?' That was, as their conversations went, characteristic.

'No chance, you'll be delighted to hear. Take it you're sitting with your feet up knocking back a glass of wine.'

'Feet up, yes. Wine, sadly, no. Doing my bit on the duty rota tonight. Thought I might as well offer since you wouldn't be around to provide the usual night of passion.'

Eloise was a Superintendent. These days, she'd largely moved on from operational duties into management and project roles. The major risk she faced now, she always told Murrain, was death through sheer frustration as she took on yet another supposedly undeliverable change management assignment.

She was good at it, though. She was well-organised, personable, good at cultivating the higher ranks, and a natural leader. All qualities which, apart from arguably the last, Murrain himself felt he singularly lacked. Which is why she was a Super, on course to be promoted to Chief Super, while he'd probably exceeded his potential by making DCI. Not that any of that remotely worried Murrain. He was doing what he was good at and enjoyed, and so, despite her repeated complaints, was she.

'Reckon you'll get called in?'

'Called in, no. From what they're telling me, the level of incidents has calmed down now, mainly because nobody can move an inch. So should be okay unless there's something unexpected. But no doubt someone will be wanting the benefits of my razor-sharp judgement.'

'At least you're not snowed in out in the back of beyond.'

'There is that. How are things?'

He filled her in on developments since they'd last spoken. She was already aware the killer might still be in the proximity, but they hadn't spoken since they'd completed the patrol of the garden. 'Christ, we need to get a team in the area bloody quickly, don't we?'

'They'll be welcomed with open arms, as soon as anyone can be bothered to put themselves out to come and help us.'

'The whole thing's so bloody frustrating. The TV news is full of the usual "why does the country always grind to a halt with a few flakes of snow" stuff. Even our warning of a potential killer on the loose got short shrift compared to some reporter standing on a snow covered bridge telling us that parts of the M62 are shut. Never seems to occur to them that we haven't had snow on this scale since — well, you're older than me. Maybe you can remember when?'

'I'm three weeks older than you, El, as you well know. Or you probably don't since you never remember my birthday. But I take your point. Speaking of the dim and distant, what do you remember about the Robert Tilston case?'

'Not a lot. Bit before we met, wasn't it? I was just a PC. Seem to recall everyone was totally shocked and not remotely surprised, if you see what I mean.'

'That was my recollection. Don't think there was much love lost for Tilston in the force. Authoritarian bully. All that bloody hammer of God stuff. It was shocking — well, obviously because he was a senior police officer, but also because he'd always set himself as this pillar of moral rectitude. But most of us just saw what he did as an extreme extension of the behaviour they'd always witnessed on duty.'

'I'm not aware he actually beat up many junior officers.'

'Not physically. Verbally and psychologically he did. At least, that was the word on the corridor. The worst kind of bully.'

'I was fortunate in not having many dealings with him. Saw him at one or two formal things, but that was all really, Remember we all followed the trial closely, though. Real rubbernecking stuff.'

'Hard not to,' Murrain said. 'It was extraordinary. You remember anything about the daughters? From the trial, I mean.'

'Not a great deal. Press were pretty salacious about it, from what I remember. Three teenage daughters. Always good for the front page of the tabloids.'

'That was my recollection. Fairly nasty stuff. Pretending to care about their well-being but really just peddling the usual titillation. You recall much about the mother?'

'Not really. She didn't seem to be in the picture at all. But I suppose she had every incentive to keep as far away from it all as she could.'

'Media would have tried to track her down, though, surely?'

'I suppose. But the story had enough in it anyway, so maybe they didn't try too hard.'

'Did you know the daughters had been involved in a serious car crash? Elder two now very severely disabled. That one had passed me by entirely.'

'That was just a few years back, wasn't it? Remember reading something about it. But it wasn't a big story. Tilston was very old news by then, so the connection wouldn't have meant much to a lot of people. I hadn't realised that was the outcome, though. Think at the time it just said they'd suffered potentially life-changing injuries. They're still up there?'

'Still living in the house here. Anne Tilston's their sole carer.'

'That must be hellish. Why stay in a place like that?'

'People always have their reasons, don't they?'

'Maybe she feels guilty? You know, survivor's guilt. Feels she owes it to them to keep things going as they were. Or as close to that as possible. That's how it affects some people.'

'Maybe.' Murrain was thinking, as he knew Eloise must be, of their own feelings after Joe's death. 'She could hardly be blamed for the car accident, though.'

'No, but she might blame herself for not being with them. Can't recall the details, but I have a feeling she was supposed to be going with them and then decided not to for some reason.'

'That can't be right. She told me she was in the car, but somehow escaped without serious harm.'

There was a moment's silence at the other end of the line. 'Maybe I'm misremembering,' Eloise said, finally. 'Or maybe the media got it wrong at the time. They usually do.'

'Not necessarily by accident, either, in my experience. If it helps to make the story a bit sexier.' Murrain looked up, hearing the sound of footsteps in the hallway. 'Look, El, I'd better go. Just wanted to let you know I was okay.'

'Don't go milking it. You might be stuck in the back of beyond, but at least you're not on the duty rota tonight.'

'Fair point. Do you want me to give you another call later?'

'Not unless you've a reason to. I'm planning to get an early night. I can tolerate being disturbed if it's official business. But not if it's just you banging on about ancient history.'

This, Murrain reflected, was Eloise's unique way of telling him she loved him and that she was delighted and relieved he'd called. At the same time, he knew better than actually to disturb her once she'd gone to sleep. 'Won't call unless it's an emergency, then.'

'If this killer breaks in brandishing a machete, you've my permission to disturb my beauty sleep. Short of that...' There was a moment's pause, as if even she realised she might have taken this too far. 'Take care, Kenny, won't you?' she said, finally, as she ended the call.

CHAPTER TWENTY-NINE

'Paul? It's Joe.' The phone had rung for so long that Milton had almost given up expecting it to be answered. He'd persevered only because he knew Wanstead almost never went anywhere beyond his twin poles of work and home.

'Joe?' Wanstead made it sound as if he was trying to distinguish Milton from one of the many thousands of other Joes he knew. 'I was upstairs.'

'Sorry to disturb you if you're busy—'

'Busy? Christ, no. She's watching one of the soaps, so thought it best to make myself scarce. You know what women are like.'

Milton couldn't begin to imagine what Wanstead's wife might be like while watching a TV soap, or why that might necessitate Wanstead absenting himself upstairs. Wanstead's domestic arrangements remained largely mysterious to the rest of the team. 'Just wanted to pick your brains briefly, if that's okay?'

'You want me to come in?' Wanstead sounded hopeful. 'I could give it a go—'

'Have you seen the weather out there, Paul? You were lucky to get home in the first place.'

'Lucky.' Wanstead's tone suggested he barely knew the meaning of the word. 'I guess so. Anyway, what can I do for you?'

'Marie just called from Merestone.'

'Are the poor buggers still stuck up there?'

'Looks like they're up there for the night. They're all huddling together for warmth in Robert Tilston's old place.'

'Rather them than me. I wouldn't want to spend any time where Tilston's been.'

'Kenny's after some more information on the three daughters.'

'This one of Kenny's hunches?'

179

'She wasn't sure. But, well—'

'It's Kenny. Aye, I know. I've worked with him long enough. So how can I help?'

'Thought you might be a more reliable source than any files I'm likely to be able to access tonight.'

'Mr Memory, eh? Well, I remember Tilston well enough. And his trial. I was one of the many applauding from the sidelines. I was only a young officer, but I'd already had a couple of run-ins with him.'

'Doesn't sound like you, Paul.'

'Doesn't it? You mean I'm not a cantankerous, stubborn old bastard?'

'Well—'

'I was just the same then, as it happens. I like things to be done properly. By the book. And for all that he liked to clamber on his high horse, you couldn't always say the same about Robert Tilston.'

'That right?'

'I happened to be in the wrong place when he was trying to bend the rules. Bullying a young finance clerk into signing off some dodgy expenses he was trying to push through the system. He'd known that if he went through the proper channels, the FD would have told him where to get off, Deputy Chief or not. So he tried to slip it through with some junior. Said junior told him he couldn't, and Tilston came down doing his voice of God routine. I was there trying to sort out some expenses query of my own, and I told him he was out of order.'

'Good career move.'

'Aye, well. That's probably why I'm still stuck as a Sergeant and you were a bloody Inspector before you'd left university.'

'So what happened?' Milton ignored the now familiar jibe.

'Let's say he didn't take it well. At least it deflected the fire away from the poor bloody clerk.' He paused. 'And she was grateful enough to say yes when I subsequently asked her out. And that, to cut a long story short, is why she's now sitting in the next room glued to Eastenders.'

'Ah.' This was probably the most that Wanstead had ever revealed to Milton about his personal life. 'And what about Tilston?'

'My card was marked. It's surprising how petty senior officers can be when they put what they laughingly call their minds to it. Found myself shoved from pillar to post. One crappy non-job after another. So I wasn't exactly distraught when justice finally caught up with our friend Tilston. If you ever want an example of karma in practice, I reckon that would be it. Don't think there were many people shedding tears.'

'What about the daughters? You know much about them?'

'I followed the trial pretty closely. Wanted to make sure the bastard wasn't going to find some way to wriggle out of it. Wouldn't have put it past the slippery old sod. The papers were interested in the daughters because it gave the whole thing a human interest angle. Not to mention an excuse to put pictures of three teenage girls on their front pages.'

'How old were they?'

'Late teens. Actually, the eldest was probably older than that. Early twenties, even. That's why they were just left to live up in that place after Tilston was sent down. Two of them were already adults, and the third was probably seventeen or something. So they could fend for themselves.'

'What about the mother? What happened to her?'

'That was one of the funny things. There was a fair bit in the trial about how Tilston had brought up the three daughters by himself. You know, all the stresses and strains of being a single father, and how that had contributed to his behaviour. All bollocks, of course.'

'Was it?'

'Well, you know. It wouldn't have been easy for him at times, I'm sure. Especially doing a job like his. But he wasn't short of a bob or two. Had pretty much full time help. He tried to use it all as mitigation, but the impression you got was that he hadn't actually seen much of the daughters while they were growing up. Just left them in the hands of a childminder.'

'Still might not have been easy for him or them.'

'For them, maybe not. For him – well, I'm not inclined to cut him much slack. But maybe I'm not the most impartial judge. But from what I recall the actual judge at the trial wasn't too impressed by that line of argument, either.'

'So what was the funny thing?'

'Just that the mother just didn't really feature. As far as I can remember the story, she'd walked out on him some years earlier. It wasn't clear why. Or why she'd left and made no attempt to gain custody of the daughters. From what I recall, they weren't even divorced. She'd supposedly moved down to the west country somewhere, but then just gone off grid.'

'Sounds a bit odd. Was there any attempt to track her down?'

'For the trial? Not that I recall. She wouldn't have been a material witness. I suppose, if they'd thought it worth it, she might have been called as a character witness. By the prosecution, presumably, given she'd walked out on him. I don't know whether any attempt was made to track her down, though. We had a bit of an inside track in the force, but there were pretty tight Chinese walls, as you can imagine.'

'What about after Tilston was convicted?'

'I don't know. Maybe social services would have made an attempt to track her down. But, like I say, two of the daughters were adults and the third not far off. My guess is they just let it lie.'

'Surprising that someone can just disappear like that. Press don't seem to have tracked her down either.'

'I imagine once it all blew up she'd have had good reason to keep her head down. And we don't know she wasn't in contact with Tilston. I don't even know that she wasn't spoken to as part of the enquiry. You'd have to check that in the files. I just know she never appeared at the trial.'

'Do you know anything about a son?'

'A son? Tilston's son, you mean? There were just the three daughters, as far as I recall.' There was a moment's silence, as if Wanstead was thinking. 'No, you're right. There was something at the trial. It was during all the mitigation stuff. You know, all the pressures that had finally got to Tilston and driven him off the rails. Not just the wife walking out. But also the loss of a son. Very young. There was a suggestion that both Tilston and the wife had been grief stricken, and that was one of the reasons the marriage had failed. Tilston had never recovered from the trauma. Blah, blah, blah. Again, don't think anyone was persuaded.'

'Do you remember how the son died?'

'An accident. This was before my time in the force, so I can only remember what came up at the trial. Something at home. A fall – down the stairs, maybe, or outside. I don't know. A head injury is what springs to mind.'

'Any suggestion Tilston might have been culpable?'

'I don't recall anyone making that suggestion. My feeling is that Tilston hadn't been around, and that if anyone had been to blame it would have been the wife. But I don't remember any suggestion of foul play or negligence. Though you know how it is. Maybe we applied slightly different standards in the case of a respectable middle-class wife of a senior police officer than we would to a harassed single-mum on a council estate.'

'You're getting cynical in your old age, Paul.'

'I've always been a cynical bastard. Anyway, why are you interested in the son? Or why is Kenny?'

'According to this article they stumbled across, the son's buried in the churchyard by the house.'

'So that might be a reason why Tilston made his way back there? Makes some sort of sense, I suppose.'

'It might.'

'Not sure I'm being much help here, though,' Wanstead said. 'All I can give you is gossip and the fruits of my fading memory.'

'Better than nothing. Sorry if I'm keeping you away from Eastenders.'

'Sod off. Anything else?'

'Just one more thing. You recall anything about the elder sisters being involved in a car crash.'

'That was just a few years ago, wasn't it? After Tilston's release. Nasty business. I'd forgotten about it till Tilston made his reappearance this morning. One of those hillside roads around Merestone. Icy day. Eldest sister lost control of the car, and they plummeted – well, I don't know how far, but a good few hundred metres down the steep hillside, making contact with a selection of trees on the way down. From what I remember, they were lucky to get out alive.'

'Not so lucky, maybe. The two elder sisters are apparently both severely disabled. Physically and – what's the word? – cognitively, from what Kenny said.'

'Makes sense. They were in intensive care initially, and they thought it was likely that neither would pull through. I know they were in hospital for a long time after that, but I never heard what the outcome was. Poor buggers.'

'Was there an investigation at the time? I don't remember anything about it.'

'There was. Fatal RTC. The vehicle examiners examined the car to ascertain if there was any cause other than the ice. Other than that, though, there were no witnesses and the two women were in no state to be interviewed. The car was too wrecked to yield much useful, even if there'd been something to find.' Wanstead hesitated for a moment. 'Actually, I do recall having a look at the file afterwards. I know I shouldn't really have done. Didn't have any good reason, other than curiosity.'

'Because of your history with Tilston?'

'Something like that.' Wanstead was sounding embarrassed which, Milton thought, was something of a first in itself. Whatever else he might be, Wanstead was a stickler for the rules or least for his own, sometimes distinctive, interpretation of the rules. 'I found some justification for accessing the file. It was interesting. The investigation was initially pursued pretty seriously because the circumstances of the crash were potentially suspicious.'

'Suspicious?'

'Well, questionable, let's say. It was a straight stretch of road compared with most of them up there. The police got there fairly quickly — another driver spotted the crashed vehicle only ten or fifteen minutes after it happened — and there was no sign of any serious black ice there. It was a mystery as to why the vehicle had left the road at that point. There were questions about whether the elder sister had driven the car off the road on purpose—'

'As in a suicide attempt?'

'Suicide and potential murder or manslaughter, given that the middle sister was in the car with her.'

'Just the middle sister? What about Anne Tilston?'

'She wasn't in the car. That was the angle the press picked up on, along with the Robert Tilston connection. She was supposed to be travelling with them but had changed her mind at the last moment. You know, miracle escape stuff. They looked at the suicide angle, and also whether there was something wrong with the car itself. It had been fairly recently serviced, so there might have been some sort of negligence.'

'And?'

'Zilch. The examiners did their stuff, but the damage to the cars was so bad that they could really only draw tentative conclusions. They couldn't identify any evidence of negligence or foul play. They interviewed the third sister, but she'd seen no signs that either of her sisters might be contemplating self-harm. In the end they put the whole thing to bed and the Coroner recorded a verdict of accidental death. Which is most likely what it was. On a road like that, you've only got to lose concentration for a moment. Anyway, there you have it. I think you've pretty much plucked my brains clean of any titbits of information about the Family Tilston. Hope it was worth the effort.'

'Always grateful for your input, Paul. You know that. Seriously, you've given me more than I expected. Not sure where Kenny's hoping to get with this, though.'

'He's probably as bored as I am. Clutching at straws. Mind you, Kenny's straws are often worth clutching, if you'll pardon the expression.'

'We'll see.' Milton paused, thinking. 'One more thing, actually. What about Tilston himself? I mean, I know about the trial. But he's been out for a good few years now, and I'd heard he'd turned over a new leaf. You any idea what he's been up to?'

There was silence for an unexpectedly long time before Wanstead responded. 'I've kept a bit of an eye on him, if that's what you're getting at.'

'No, I didn't—' Milton realised he'd hit a nerve.. It was a side of Wanstead he hadn't seen before. They thought of Wanstead as Mr Reliable, the lynchpin who held the whole team together. He was the guy you could depend on to get the MIR up and running, to make sure all the technology was in place, to check and double-check that all the documentation was how it should be. But there was a doggedness there, a stubbornness, that suggested Wanstead wasn't someone you'd want as an enemy. If you crossed him, Milton suspected, he wouldn't be quick to forget.

'I've not done anything untoward,' Wanstead went on. 'But I've never trusted the bastard. He was a slimy, duplicitous toerag who hated himself and the world. He went out to hurt innocent people for no reason at all. I've never bought all this stuff about him turning over a new leaf in prison. He was smart enough to know how to play the game. How to say and do the right things. Show the appropriate levels of remorse. He wouldn't have had an easy time inside, and he'd have got out as soon as he could manage it. That's my view.' There was an unprecedented passion in Wanstead's voice, and Milton wondered whether there might be something more in it than simply some work-based victimisation from years before.

'He's not committed any crimes since leaving prison, though, has he?'

'Not that we know of. He continued with the religious stuff. Toned down the fire and brimstone crap, obviously. He was working for the last few years with some Christian charity doing stuff with the homeless, addicts, that kind of thing.'

'Sounds admirable enough. Atoning for his crimes.'

'Aye, it sounds like that, doesn't it?'

'You think there was more to it?'

'It was Robert bloody Tilston. I know there was more to it.'

'But there've been no accusations, have there? No complaints?' Milton was beginning to wonder how sound Wanstead's judgement was on this.

'Not that I'm aware of. I'm not even necessarily suggesting Tilston abused his position. Maybe the charity stuff was just a smokescreen. Maybe there was something else. I don't know. But he was a malicious, exploitative, evil bastard. People like that don't change.'

'But you've no evidence he's done anything wrong?'

Milton heard Wanstead take a breath, as if he'd realised he was pushing this too far. 'No, you're right. As far as his record's concerned, he's been clean as a whistle since he left prison. I just don't believe it.'

'Whatever he might or might not have done, he won't be doing it any more.'

'That's something,' Wanstead conceded. 'I just hope the bugger's rotting in hell.'

'I'll let you get back to the telly, Paul. I've obviously wound you up too much.'

'It doesn't take a lot where Robert Tilston's concerned. He won't be missed.'

Milton ended the call, feeling more uneasy than when he'd started. He'd never seen Wanstead react that way before. While Wanstead might not be one to set the woods on fire, his judgement and thinking were generally pretty solid. If Robert Tilston had made him lose his usual perspective, there must be some good reason for that.

Something more, Milton thought, than just a grudge over fiddled expenses.

CHAPTER THIRTY

'Is there anything I can do to help?'

Anne Tilston looked down and up the length of Murrain's body with a sceptical expression, as if he'd perhaps just offered to swim the Atlantic or slay a dragon on her behalf. 'I don't think so. But thank you for offering.' She was carrying a tray laden with half-eaten foodstuffs — cups of water, two plates of some kind of mashed vegetable concoction. A bowl of yoghurt. Clearly what passed for her sisters' supper. Murrain could imagine how difficult it must be to persuade the two women to eat.

'You've taken on a lot tonight. I just wondered—'

'I can cope by myself, thank you. We're used to this kind of situation. We get cut off up here quite frequently. Not just in the winter. We've had trees down on that road. Had to wait till the Council could get up here to clear it.' She sounded as if she was talking simply to distract him from any further offers of assistance.

'I can imagine,' Murrain said. 'Have you considered moving somewhere more accessible?' As he asked the question, he was conscious it sounded more accusatory than he'd intended. 'I mean you could presumably get a decent price for this place?' Oh, for goodness sake, Kenny, he thought, stop digging.

But Anne Tilston seemed less offended by his question than she had been by his previous offer of help. 'I've thought about it, of course. But this is our home. It always has been. I couldn't move my sisters now. It would be too disruptive.'

'I can understand that,' Murrain said, though he wasn't sure he really could. 'But it must be a tremendous burden.'

'These things are sent to try us.' Her tone made it sound more like a Biblical pronouncement than a familiar platitude. 'The Good Lord has a plan for us.'

If He has, Murrain thought, I wish He'd take the trouble to share the detail once in a while. Out loud he said, 'I was wondering whether you'd be able to spare me a few minutes this evening? Just to talk through a few things.'

'I'll need to get my sisters into bed before too long.'

'Just briefly. I'm afraid at some point tomorrow we'll have to interview you formally about your father and any information you might be able to give us about Mr Newland and the other victim—'

'I know nothing about them. I barely knew Mr Newland.' The abruptness in her tone suggested she wanted to move on from the subject. Which, in Murrain's experience, was usually the time to stick with it.

'You didn't have much contact with Mr Newland?'

'Not if I could help it. He wasn't up here much. Just the weekends. Our paths didn't cross very often.'

'It sounds as if you didn't much like him?' Murrain was trying to keep his tone light, conversational. There'd be plenty of opportunity to pursue this in their formal interview with Anne Tilston if it seemed worth exploring.

'As I say, I barely knew him. But I didn't entirely approve of his lifestyle.'

'His lifestyle?'

She hesitated, as if seeking an acceptable way to express her feelings. 'Don't get me wrong. I've nothing against – well, people like that. But he seemed to have a different young man with him every time he was here. I didn't think it was quite seemly. But no doubt I'm old-fashioned.'

Murrain regarded the woman standing before him. She must be only in her early-thirties, but she looked and behaved like someone much older. Not just her clothes and hairstyle, but her whole demeanour. He could easily envisage her peering out of the window, tutting her disapproval of Newland's behaviour. 'But you had no other problems with him? As a neighbour, I mean?'

There was a noticeable hesitation before she responded. 'Not problems as such. But there was the odd disagreement.'

'Disagreement?'

She shrugged, but shifted uncomfortably. 'I don't like to speak ill of the dead.'

'Any information you have may be pertinent to our enquiry.'

'I don't see how—'

'Anything you can tell us about Mr Newland may be helpful, however trivial or irrelevant it might seem. At the very least, it may provide us with an insight into Mr Newland's character or background.'

'I can see that. Well, he was a difficult man, Mr Newland. A difficult neighbour. As I say, I did my utmost to keep out of his way. But he seemed to want to make our lives difficult...' Her voice trailed off, as if she were reluctant to say more.

'In what ways?' Murrain gestured for her to take a seat at the kitchen table, lowering himself on to the chair beside her. He wanted to coax as much information out of her before she became too anxious to respond.

'It was little things. To start with, anyway. Little complaints about the state of our house, for example. I haven't had the time or the money to do the place up as I ought to. I know that, but it really wasn't any of his business. He reckoned we were spoiling the look of the village. I mean, he'd only been here five minutes—' She stopped and took a breath, as if conscious of the emotion welling up in her voice.

'What form did these complaints take?'

'Initially, it was just the odd passing comment if I happened to see him outside. Presented as a joke, you know? The sort of joke that's not really meant to be funny. But it gradually escalated. Notes pushed through the door. Even a complaint to the local council about one of our bushes that was supposedly intruding on to the road.'

'It sounds rather trivial.'

'Oh, it was. Very. I think it was mainly because he knew I disapproved of his lifestyle. His petty form of revenge.'

'Had you told him? That you disapproved of his lifestyle, I mean.'

'Not in so many words. I'd tried my best to be polite. But I suppose he must have realised what I thought.'

'I see.' Murrain could easily imagine how a neighbourly dispute might have escalated. He couldn't see that there was likely to be any obvious connection with Newland's death, though, unless Newland had been in the habit of antagonising more formidable characters than Anne Tilston. 'Anything more than that?'

'It was mostly just something and nothing. He complained once or twice that my car was blocking his access. It wasn't, of course. I'd just left it out on the road. It's a little narrow out there, but he wouldn't have had any difficulty getting past it. Then there was the thing about the churchyard—'

'The churchyard?'

'The church here. Well, you've seen it. There's no congregation up here now. Hasn't really been for years. There was a time, when I was a girl, when it used to be quite busy. Local farmers and suchlike used to come here rather than having to head down into town.'

She had paused again. This time, Murrain assumed, it had been the mention of her own childhood. He wondered whether Robert Tilston, with his hellfire and brimstone religious views, had been an active member of that congregation. Presumably so, though Murrain could recall no details from the trial about Tilston's religious practices.

'Anyway,' she went on after a moment, 'the Church have been talking about selling that building for years. They hold a token mass there once a fortnight. I go out of a sense of duty, but there've been times when I've been the only one there.' She gave an uneasy laugh. 'Just the vicar and me. Awkward for both of us.'

'I can see that. So where does Toby Newland fit into this?'

'That church had meant a lot to me.' She responded as if she hadn't heard his question. 'I'm the only one who goes in to take care of the place now. I don't have time to do much. A bit of dusting and polishing. I try to put out some fresh flowers before the services. Anyway, I ran a little bit of a campaign to try to prevent the Church selling the building. Wrote letters to the Bishop. Tried to get some local interest going, though frankly I was on a hiding to nothing. There's hardly anyone left in the village now. The cottages have mostly been turned into holiday homes or weekend places. Nobody was very interested. But I thought I ought to do my bit. Anyway, Toby Newland found out. At least, I assume that's what happened. I was out walking Dougie one day and Newland made a point of coming up to me. Told me I ought to know he'd written to the diocese enquiring about their plans for the church building and land, and saying that, if they were interested in selling it at some point in the future, he'd be keen to buy some of the land so he could expand his garden.'

'Did anything come of that?'

'To be honest, looking back, I doubt whether he'd even written the letter. He was just taunting me. He knew how much the church meant to me. I go in there for a little peace. Just to get away. He knew he'd touched a nerve. He kept it up for a while. Told me he'd had a response from the diocese saying that they were still considering their plans for the church, but that his interest was noted.'

'Did you speak to the diocese yourself?'

'I wrote a letter. Got a bland response from them, actually pretty much saying what Newland had said. That they hadn't yet made any decision, but they'd communicate with local residents at the appropriate time. I've heard nothing since so I assume they haven't progressed it. And Newland obviously got bored with the whole thing, presumably because I didn't gratify him with the response he'd hoped for.'

'Had you had any further run-ins with Mr Newland? In recent weeks?'

'Would it be significant if I had? I'm not sure why we're even discussing this.'

'I'm just interested in knowing what kind of man Mr Newland was. There's nothing we can do formally tonight, but any insights might be helpful. If you found him difficult to deal with, others might have found the same.'

'He certainly wasn't a man to ingratiate himself. I tried to avoid him as much as I could, but sometimes he seemed to make a point of being there. Outside. In the garden or doing something with his car. Always seemed to pick the moment when I was out walking Dougie.'

'Some people enjoy being provocative.'

'He certainly did. Though he didn't deserve – well, what happened to him.'

'I'm not sure anyone deserves something like that. Can I just ask you another couple of quick questions, while we're talking? I'm just trying to get everything clear in my own mind.'

'I really do have to get back to my sisters.'

'Just very quickly. I think you mentioned a younger brother—'

It took her only a moment to recompose her features, but Murrain had noted the surprised expression in her eyes. 'I don't think I did.' There was a note of finality in her tone.

'I must have misunderstood,' Murrain said, blandly. 'Or perhaps I picked it up from somewhere else. Am I right in thinking you had a younger brother?'

Anne Tilston was silent for what seemed like an age. 'There was a brother, yes. Bradley. He died when we were very young. He was barely a toddler.'

'I'm sorry, I was being insensitive. I didn't realise—'

'No, that's fine.' She seemed to have regained some composure now. 'It was a long time ago. My parents barely ever talked about him, and that just became how things were. I hardly remember him myself.'

'I shouldn't have mentioned it.'

'I'm not sure how you'd have found out about him, anyway. Or, again, why it's relevant.'

She was smart enough, Murrain thought. He could see he wasn't going to get any further with this conversational approach. If there was anything worth pursuing, he'd have to do it through the formal interview. 'It was just an idea I'd picked up from somewhere. I just wanted to be sure I hadn't overlooked something.'

'Nothing relevant. Bradley was hardly even part of this household. Now he's long gone.'

There was something odd about her words, Murrain felt. Some deeper meaning that he couldn't quite fathom. But he knew he couldn't push this any further. Nor could he easily raise the question of whether Anne Tilston had really been in the car with her sisters at the time of the accident. If there were any mysteries there, they'd have to wait till she was interviewed. Murrain hoped that by then he'd have been able to obtain some more reliable background information on the Tilstons.

'I'd better let you get on, then. Are you sure there's nothing I can do to help?'

'I'm sure.' Her tone suggested the very idea was absurd. 'Thank you, but I am very accustomed to coping with all this.'

'I know you let the Carters use your room down here. Are you still planning to sleep downstairs this evening?'

'There's a spare bed in my sisters' room. I sometimes sleep in there anyway, particularly if either of them seems to be going through a difficult time.'

'That's good. It's probably better if we all stick as closely together as we can. If there are any problems, we're just along the corridor.'

'That's very reassuring.' It was difficult to tell if there was any note of irony in her voice. 'I'm sure we're safe enough in here.'

'Let's hope so.' Somewhere in the depths of his mind, Murrain could feel that familiar sensitivity, the cold chill that told him the real danger, whatever it might be, had not receded. There was something waiting, and he had a sense that it might be something even closer than the killer outside.

'Let's hope so,' he repeated. He was conscious that this time it sounded almost like a prayer.

CHAPTER THIRTY-ONE

Murrain closed the kitchen door silently behind him, leaving Anne Tilston preparing her sisters' medication. He wasn't sure what he'd learned from his conversation with her. But he'd been struck by the surprise he'd seen in her eyes when he'd mentioned the brother. She'd regained her composure quickly enough, but there was something there she hadn't wanted to discuss.

He walked back down the hallway and stood by the front door, peering through the small window into the snow covered garden. He needed a few moments by himself before he returned to the rest of the team. The odd resonance triggered by his discussion with Anne Tilston was still humming in his brain. It was the same unease he'd felt earlier, but stronger now, more definite. He closed his eyes, willing his brain to provide a clearer understanding, to unveil to him what the sensation might mean.

'Still quiet out there?'

Murrain started, annoyed at allowing himself to be taken by surprise. Rob Carter was standing close behind him, gazing past him out into the darkness.

'I've left Liz trying to get the boys off,' Carter said. 'She's better at calming them down than I am. This is all a big adventure to them.'

'I can imagine.'

Carter pulled out a packet of cigarettes. 'Look, I know I'm a pain in the arse, but would you mind?'

Murrain repressed his initial instinct to tell Carter what to do with his cigarettes. Carter might be a self-obsessed idiot, but he was no doubt feeling the shock and stress of their situation as much as any of them. 'Okay. But I'll come out with you. I don't want anyone out there alone.'

'Thanks. I know I should give them up. But this doesn't quite feel the moment.'

Murrain opened the door and stepped out into the porch, moving aside so that Carter could follow him. The snow was still falling, less heavily than earlier. Carter moved to the edge of the porch and, with a theatrical sigh of relief, lit up a cigarette.

'Are your sons okay with all this, then?' Murrain asked.

'Like I say, it's just a game to them, really. That's how Liz is playing it, too.'

'Is she coping all right?'

'It's always hard to tell with Liz. She seems okay. But it's a real shock. It's not what you expect in a place like this.'

Murrain nodded, though an irrational part of him felt that Merestone was a place long haunted by black deeds. Even on a summer's day, the place would feel closed in on itself, clutching its secrets tight. 'Did you know Toby Newland well?'

'Just a neighbour. This was just a weekend place for him, so we didn't see him about much. He seemed pleasant enough. I can't imagine why anyone would wish him any harm.'

'I have the impression that not everyone was so positive about him?'

'You mean Anne Tilston, I'm guessing? She had her own reasons for disliking him. Or disapproving of him, anyway.'

'Because he was gay?'

'Mainly. And because he made no pretence about it. He liked to wind her up. He knew which buttons to press to get a reaction from her.'

'She told me he'd expressed interest in buying some of the church land if it became available.' Murrain pulled his jacket more tightly around his body, conscious of the chill of the night. His eyes were fixed on the road beyond the Tilston's garden, alert for any movement other than the swirling snow.

Carter laughed. 'I didn't know that. But it doesn't surprise me. She's obsessed with the church. The building, I mean, as well as the institution. Though she's a pretty committed God-botherer as well. A few months back, she tried to get us to sign some round-robin letter objecting to the closure of the church. I'm not sure what she expected to achieve. There's only a handful of houses up here now, and most of those are holiday lets or weekend places. I don't imagine the bishop will lose much sleep over anything we might think. Anyway, as far as I'm concerned, the sooner they sell it the better. It might get turned into something more useful. Something that brings a bit of life into the place.'

'What brought you up here?'

'God knows,' Carter said with feeling. 'Or, more accurately, Liz does. She always had this thing about moving to the country. We had a flat in Chorlton, which was getting too small for us, especially when number two son turned up. We couldn't really afford the size of place we wanted there, so we were looking to move further out. I hadn't really bargained on moving quite as far as this. But it was a great house for the price, and Liz fell in love with it. So here we are.'

'Must be a trek to work?'

'It's not bad, usually. And I could work at home more if the boss would let me. IT stuff, so I can be anywhere. Liz works as a teaching assistant at the boys' school, so that works okay. Might be more difficult when they go to secondary school, but we'll manage. We don't get many days like today, I'm glad to say.' He paused. 'The weather, I mean. Not the other stuff.'

'Do you know Anne Tilston well?'

'Again, just a neighbour. We see a bit more of her than we saw of Newland, obviously. But we're not exactly in and out of each other's houses. We see her walking the dog, but that's about it. It was ages before we even realised the two sisters were here, too. Liz tried to see if she needed any help from us, but she got pretty short shrift.'

Murrain glanced back into the hall to confirm that Anne Tilston had not emerged from the kitchen. 'She seems to be very self-sufficient.'

'She just seems a difficult character to me.'

'You've had your own run-ins with her?'

'I wouldn't put it as strongly as that. I don't think she was best pleased we weren't keen to sign her letter to the diocese. We've had the odd comment about the boys being noisy when they're playing outside. She can be a bit – well, brittle, I suppose. But then you think what she has to deal with here...'

'It can't be easy.'

'No, but she doesn't seem to want any help. Maybe pride, or maybe she just likes her privacy. I got the impression she'd have preferred not to have us all under her roof tonight.'

'Who can blame her? It's not the ideal situation for any of us. But I'd rather everyone was safe until we can get some back-up.'

'Let's hope things are looking better in the morning,' Carter said. 'I think we've all got a bit of cabin fever.' He followed Murrain's gaze out into the darkness. 'And you reckon he's still out there, whoever did this?'

"We have to assume so. Until we know different.'

'Jesus,' Carter said, as if the reality of this had only just struck him. 'Roll on the morning, then.'

Murrain watched as Carter flipped his used cigarette butt out into the snow, a tiny arc of orange light across the night. 'Amen to that. Let's get back inside, shall we?'

CHAPTER THIRTY-TWO

Joe Milton spent another half hour searching through the on-line files for any information on Robert Tilston or the Tilston sisters. There was little of value readily available, and no chance of accessing anything more until the records office opened the following morning. He moved on to a general internet search. There was plenty of stuff on Tilston's trial and conviction, but nothing that added anything of significance to what Wanstead had already told him. There were news reports of the sisters' traffic accident, but again little new other than confirmation that Anne Tilston had not been in the car with her sisters. He'd been able to find nothing about the younger brother, and little about Tilston's wife, other than a couple of cursory mentions in the trial coverage.

Finally, realising he was having difficulty concentrating on the screen in front of him, he fetched another cup of coffee and dialled Murrain's number. The phone was answered almost immediately. 'Joe?'

'Hi, Kenny. How's it going up there?'

'We're having a whale of a time. Much like you, I imagine.'

'It's party time here.'

'Anything to report?'

'Not a great deal. I've checked the files but there was little of interest. Then I had the bright idea of phoning Paul.'

'Hope you didn't disturb his evening of domestic bliss.'

'Not so's you'd notice. He'd have come back into work, given half a chance. He's probably the only man in the world who'd be envious of my situation.'

'What did Paul have to say about any of this?'

Milton repeated what Wanstead had told him. 'He seemed quite exercised by it all. I got the impression there was some bad blood between Paul and Robert Tilston.'

'Not like Paul to get exercised about anything. Though I've heard him being rude about Tilston before. Mind you, Paul takes his responsibilities seriously. He wouldn't have much time for any senior officer who didn't. Let alone one who behaved like Tilston did.'

'I'm sure you're right. It just felt – I don't know, more personal than that. It didn't feel like the usual Paul at all.'

'Intriguing,' Murrain said. 'Though, if it's Paul, there's probably less to it than meets the eye. He always reckons he's a man with hidden shallows. What he told you was interesting, too. About Anne Tilston not being in the car with her sisters.'

'I've confirmed that. Found several reports. She was due to go with them, but decided against it at the last minute. The newspapers all went big on the "miracle escape" line.'

'Yes, we've found a few reports of the accident, too. There doesn't seem to be any doubt. So why did she lie to me?'

'Guilt?' Milton suggested. 'Maybe one of those psychological things. Survivors' syndrome, or whatever they call it. She feels bad that she was the only one to escape unharmed, so she unconsciously rewrites history to put herself in the car.'

'It would have been even more of a miracle escape if she'd actually been in the car,' Murrain pointed out.

'Yes, but she wouldn't have been responsible for it. As it was, it was her own decision, her change of mind, that saved her.'

'You're wasted as a detective, Joe. Have you thought of taking up psychoanalysis?'

'Pretty much the same thing, I'd have thought.'

'Fair point. Odd that she would have said it to me, though. Given it's so easy to check.'

'Maybe she's come to believe it herself. We all tell ourselves the stories we want to hear.'

'Thank you, Dr Freud.'

'Paul said he recalled a mention of the brother during the trial, but knew nothing else about him. Thought the brother had died in some accident or other. No suggestion that Tilston was to blame, as far as he could recall.'

'They do seem to have been an unfortunately accident prone family. What about the mysterious Mrs Tilston?'

'Paul couldn't add anything, really. She seems a bit of a cypher.'

'This story just feels odder and odder. As if we've a whole selection of jigsaw pieces that make up part of a picture but half of them missing. And none of it seems to link to our bloody killer outside.'

'Wish there was more I could do,' Milton said, sincerely. 'You all holding up okay?'

'We seem to be. Everyone's pretty much resigned to their fate for tonight. Just hope things look better in the morning.'

'Jesus, I really hope so.' Through the window beside his desk, Milton could see the main A6, the trunk road through the centre of Stockport. It was a pure white strip, now unsullied by tyre-tracks. He couldn't recall ever seeing it like that before. The traffic had simply stopped – no cars, no buses running, no lorries heading through towards Manchester. From the news he'd looked at on-line, it looked as if the north west of England was the most affected by the snow, though coverage was widespread. At that moment, it felt as if nothing might ever move again. 'Fingers crossed,' he said to Murrain, but with no confidence that their hopes would be realised.

The team had all returned after eating and helping to clear up, leaving Anne Tilston and the Carters to their various tasks. After his exchange with Murrain outside, Rob Carter had left to check on Liz and the children. He seemed finally to have grasped the seriousness of their situation.

Bert Wallace was curled up on the sofa, still scrutinising her phone. She'd found a few more articles on

Tilston's trial and some reports of the sisters' accident, but nothing that added to what Milton had already told Murrain. Marie Donovan, Will Sparrow and Neil Ferbrache had rustled up a pack of playing cards from somewhere, and were engrossed in some game Murrain didn't recognise.

He sat down at the table with them, shaking his head when Donovan asked if he wanted to join in. Neil Ferbrache was scrutinising his hand of cards with a seriousness that suggested he might have bet his livelihood on the outcome of the game.

'You've been around in the force a long time, Neil—' Murrain said.

'Thanks for reminding me,' Ferbrache said. 'We staff types don't get your retirement perks, or I'd have been off long ago.'

'You aware of any particular bad blood between Paul Wanstead and Robert Tilston?'

'Can't imagine Tilston was even aware that Paul existed. He was only a junior copper when Tilston went down. Why?'

'Joe just had a conversation with Paul about Tilston. Said he seemed unexpectedly wound up by the topic.'

'Nobody had a good word for the bugger. Not just after he was convicted, either. He'd clawed his way up the greasy pole, right enough, but he hadn't left many friends in his wake.'

'That's how I remember it. Just wondered why Paul would have been particularly worked up about it. Not like him.'

'He can be a stubborn so-and-so when he wants to be. If Tilston had got on the wrong side of him, he wouldn't forget. Paul would be one to serve his revenge cold.'

'I don't doubt that. Just wondered how Tilston might have trodden on Paul's toes in the first place. Paul might be stubborn, but he's not one to get worked up about nothing.'

'So maybe Tilston stepped on him without realising. He never seemed to bother how many bodies he left behind him. Figuratively and literally, if that's not in bad taste.'

Murrain felt a sudden pain in the front of his brain, an intensifying of the sensation he'd felt earlier, the loose connection momentarily sparked into life. An image. Figures. Two figures, he thought, one standing, the other lying on – what? A table? A bench? Not a bed, he thought. Too high for that.

He could make out nothing more. The figures were little more than silhouettes, their features invisible. He could discern nothing of the background or setting. He had no sense of whether the figures were moving or still. No understanding of what the image might be telling him. As quickly as it had appeared, he had lost it. The pain had gone, and the image, if it had ever been there, had dissolved.

'You okay, Kenny?' Ferbrache was looking at him with concern.

'Fine. I think.'

'The usual?'

'The usual. And, again as usual, something and nothing.'

'More something than nothing, from the look on your face.'

'Maybe. Who knows? Not me, certainly.' But there was something there, Murrain thought. Something that meant something, even if he hadn't a clue what it might be.

He pulled out his mobile phone and stared thoughtfully at the screen. Then he thumbed through his list of contacts and found Paul Wanstead's mobile number. He thought it best not to call Wanstead's home number because – from the little glimpses that Wanstead allowed them of his domestic existence – it was probable that Helena Wanstead would already have retired for the night, early as it was.

The call went straight to voice mail, suggesting either that the line was engaged or that Wanstead had turned off the phone. Either seemed unlikely. Wanstead, in his usual punctilious way, used the phone exclusively for police business and almost never turned it off. Perhaps Joe Milton had called him back on that number for some reason.

Murrain wondered whether to leave a message. But, in truth, he had no idea what to say. He wasn't even sure what he'd have said if Wanstead had answered. No doubt he'd just have burbled something about Robert Tilston, in the hope that Wanstead would cast some light on whatever had inspired his animosity towards Tilston. But he didn't see how he could ask the direct question. Wanstead was a notoriously private man, even though Murrain had worked with him over many years. If he wanted to tell you something, he would, eventually and in his own distinctive way. If he didn't, nothing would drag it from him.

Murrain gave it another ten minutes, watching the others continue their incomprehensible card game. Then he dialled Wanstead again, expecting that this time the call would be taken. But again there was only Wanstead's bland voicemail message.

Murrain cut the call and dropped the phone on to the table. It would have to wait till the morning, he thought. Like everything else in this bloody case.

CHAPTER THIRTY-THREE

Paul Wanstead had returned to the living room where his wife Helena was watching some television cooking show. 'Work?' she said.

'Just Joe. He was after a bit of information. Nothing important.'

'But worth disturbing your evening for?'

They'd had some variation on this conversation pretty much every night for years. Probably most nights since they'd been married, Wanstead thought. It was always partly light-hearted, but only ever partly. Helena knew what she'd married in Paul Wanstead, and she mostly accepted it. But she always reminded him her acceptance had limits. She might have to share her marriage with Wanstead's job, but she had no intention of letting the job always come first. Wanstead tried to play to the unarticulated rules they seemed to have agreed between them. Mostly, he succeeded. 'It was only a five minute phone call. He's stuck in the office.'

'Ten minutes. And you wish you were stuck there with him.'

'I don't—'

She smiled. 'Don't lie to me, Paul Wanstead. I know you too well after all these years. Is there something big on?' That was another of their unspoken rules. They never discussed any detail of the investigations Wanstead might be involved in, not even anonymously. He preferred not to tell her and she, in all honesty, didn't really want to know. But she did want to know if he was under particular pressure or stress.

'Maybe the start of a couple of things. I'll have a better idea once this bloody snow clears.'

She gestured towards the television. 'Should be better tomorrow, according to the forecast. Snowfalls should stop overnight, and the temperature's warmer tomorrow, so it shouldn't last too long.'

'Then we'll get the bloody floods.'

'A policeman's lot is not a happy one,' she intoned.

'Too bloody right.' Wanstead settled himself beside her to watch the rest of the programme.

Just ten minutes later, Helena Wanstead declared she was ready for bed. She kissed her husband lightly on the forehead, and left him to it. It was still relatively early, but this was another part of their marital routine. Helena Wanstead was an 'early to bed, early to rise' type, at her best in the early mornings. Her husband, by contrast, was something of an insomniac, reluctant to go to bed until well after midnight but quite often awake even before his wife. They'd long ago come to an arrangement about that. If he was late coming to bed, or if he felt the need to get up during the night, she was unconcerned, as long as he managed not to disturb her. She knew she'd find him watching some overnight television or reading a book, so mostly she was content simply to sleep on.

Wanstead waited until she was upstairs, hearing the clunk of the bedroom door closing behind her. There was little chance of her emerging again before the morning. Shutting the living room door silently behind him, he crossed the hallway to the small table near the front door. Because they tended to work different hours and because Helena Wanstead was reluctant to disturb her husband at the office, they left a notepad there so they could leave notes for each other.

Wanstead scribbled: 'Something unexpected turned up. Had to head back into the office.' She'd no doubt assume he'd lied about his earlier telephone conversation with Joe Milton and had been intending to head back all along. That would definitely constitute a breach of the marital rules, but there wasn't much he could do about it.

He pulled on his heavy waterproof and boots. Outside, the snow was still falling, but less heavily than before. The air was warmer too, the snow close to sleet. Not that that would help him tonight. But it might augur well for the morning.

He tramped down the snow-covered drive and unlocked the car. Wanstead was the kind of cautious individual who drove a four-by-four just because he might need to use it on a night like this. There'd been one or two previous instances when he'd had to head in on police business in bad weather, although nothing like this. He had no confidence the car would get him to his destination tonight, but he needed to try.

He made his way back out on to the main road safely enough. Very few others were choosing to venture out this evening. The residential roads through the estate had been undisturbed until his own tyres cut through the snow. Some vehicles had passed on the main road, but not enough to clear the surface.

He chose his route through the town carefully, avoiding all but the gentlest of hills, conscious of the spots where his or other vehicles were most likely to become stranded. The town itself was more deserted than he'd seen it. Many of the restaurants and pubs looked as if they'd closed early for the night, lacking custom or staff. There were a few people out on the streets, mainly young people trudging back through the snow, heads bowed against the chill wind. There were no other moving vehicles – even the gritters were being deployed exclusively on the motorways.

His circuitous route added another mile or so to his journey, but he eventually found himself heading out through the suburbs on the east side of town, up to where the flatter urban landscape gave way to the edges of the Pennines. So far, he'd done pretty well, keeping his speed low without losing traction, maintaining a high gear. There'd been one or two moments when he thought he might lose control, and others where he'd suspected that even a slight slope might have been sufficient to defeat the car. But he'd made it as far as he'd hoped, to the point where the main road rose more steeply towards the hills.

He turned off the main road, taking the B road up towards Merestone, and managed another five or six hundred metres into the thickening woodland. He was an experienced driver, with police training, but it took all his skill to hold the road and keep the vehicle moving. The car felt always on the point of skidding, wheels barely holding.

Then, as he'd known he would, he reached the point where no more progress was possible. He tried reversing and pushing on, but gained only another metre or two, tyres spinning helplessly. After manoeuvring the car off the road, he turned off the engine and sat back to take a deep breath.

He'd done better than he'd feared, but he was still a mile or more from Merestone, the route steeply uphill through the thick snow. But that was only what he'd expected. He was wearing warm clothes, a thick weatherproof coat and heavy walking boots. He was as well prepared as he could be.

He locked the car behind him. With only the briefest look back, he trudged up the hillside, unknowingly following almost the same route as the man who, the previous evening, had made his way up this road towards his own fate in the churchyard.

CHAPTER THIRTY-FOUR

Murrain had felt the energy drain from the room as the evening went on. The card game became increasingly desultory until the participants finally called it a night. Bert Wallace was curled up on one of the sofas, ostensibly still searching on the internet but her head beginning to nod. Will Sparrow was convulsed by repetitive yawns, his substantial frame stretched out in a manner that suggested his movements might eventually prove too much for his wooden dining chair. Neil Ferbrache had dropped his head on to the table, looking as if he might already be asleep.

Only Marie Donovan seemed relatively sprightly. She'd found a handful of books on one of the shelves and was leafing through them.

'Anything interesting?' Murrain asked.

'Not really. Couple of volumes of famous trials, ironically enough. Tilston's not being one of them. Few old crime novels...' She held up the books to show Murrain. 'P D James. Reginald Hill. Seems to have liked police procedurals.'

'Busman's holiday, then. I usually just get irritated spotting the errors. I assume these were Robert Tilston's?'

'Assume so. The trials ones have his name in the front. Looks like they were presented to him as a speaker at some conference. Don't know about the detective ones.'

'Will give you something to read in the wee small hours of the morning, anyway.'

'I'll need something. Can't imagine I'm going to get much sleep. How do we want to organise things, anyway? I'm assuming none of us is going to get a bed for the night.'

'I'd rather we were all down here overnight. Limits the sleeping options, though.' There were two small sofas, though probably only Bert Wallace would be able to stretch out full length on either of them. 'To be honest, I don't think I'm going to be sleeping, so I'd suggest that the four of you take turns to get what rest you can.'

'I'll just stick with the caffeine to get me through the night. If Bert, Will and Neil want to take advantage of the sofas, that's fine by me.' As if illustrating her point, she walked over to the tray of tea and coffee Anne Tilston had left for them. 'Anybody else want one?'

Murrain nodded his thanks. Ferbrache opened his eyes and said: 'I'll have one, thanks. Won't try to sleep yet in case that blow to the head did more damage than it seems. I'll leave the sofas to Bert and Will. Mind you, I reserve the right to turf either one of them off if I'm feeling suitably knackered later.'

'Fair enough,' Wallace said. 'In which case, I'll decline the kind offer of coffee in favour of trying to get some rest.' True to her word, she kicked off her shoes, lay back on the sofa and closed her eyes. 'Just carry on,' she said. 'I could sleep in the middle of Piccadilly Station.'

'That's what I call a gift,' Ferbrache said. 'I can't even get to sleep in my own bed, most nights.'

'I'm the same,' Will Sparrow said. 'No matter how knackered I'm feeling. I'll stick with the caffeine for the moment.'

'If every one of you's jumping on the bandwagon, I'll need to get some more water for the kettle,' Donovan said. 'Anne Tilston won't mind me using the kitchen, will she?'

'Don't imagine so. We've done our best to keep out of her hair.' Murrain was feeling weary himself, and he didn't imagine that the coffee would do much to reinvigorate him. At the same time, sleep felt nowhere near imminent. He'd had similar feelings before – nights when the recurrent echoes in his brain kept sleep away.

'Kenny?'

Marie Donovan, who had embarked on her quest for water, had stuck her head back round the door and was gesturing towards him.

'What is it?'

'I think you'd better come and have a look. Something a bit – odd.'

He followed her back into the kitchen. She pointed to the back door. 'There.'

It took him a moment to work out what she was showing him. Then he realised. The two lockable bolts on the door had been drawn back.

Murrain's first thought was Rob Carter, though he couldn't imagine how Carter might have got hold of the key to the bolts.

'The even odder thing,' Donovan said, 'is that the door itself is still locked.' She gave a pull on the handle to demonstrate. 'Why would anyone draw back the bolts but leave it locked?'

'Are we sure there's no-one out there?'

'If there is they must have locked themselves out or been locked out deliberately. The door's deadlocked. I couldn't see a key around.'

'The key's here,' a voice said from behind them. 'If it's any of your business.'

Anne Tilston was standing in the kitchen doorway, a bunch of household keys in her hand. He couldn't immediately read her expression. She looked displeased, certainly, but also slightly embarrassed, as if caught out in a misdemeanour.

'It's only my business because I'm concerned about the security of the house.' Murrain allowed a little iciness to creep into his tone. 'I don't want to interfere with your domestic arrangements any more than I have to. But I do need to ensure we're all as safe as we can be.'

She nodded, though her face suggested she was still in no mood to be conciliatory. 'The door's still locked, and it's been unbolted only for a few minutes. It would have been less, but I had to go and check on my sisters.' She walked past Murrain and Donovan with the keys in her hand but, instead of rebolting the door as Murrain had expected, she inserted the mortice lock key and opened the door.

Murrain exchanged a glance with Donovan, but for the moment decided not to intervene. He watched bemused as Anne Tilston peered into the night and whistled. There was silence for a moment. Through the doorway, Murrain could see the snow was still falling, though less furiously than before. A moment later, there was a scuffling and panting from somewhere at the far end of the garden.

He tensed, feeling the same sudden pain in his temples he'd felt earlier. Then he saw a dark shape racing across the pale white of the garden towards them.

'Dougie!' Anne Tilston called.

The dog swerved across the lawn, as if about to race off in the opposite direction, then turned and ran, still panting, back into the kitchen, pausing momentarily to shake off the snow. Anne Tilston closed and locked the door, sliding the bolts firmly back into place. Her expression suggested she was expecting a challenge.

'What was I supposed to do? He needs to go out. I wasn't about to risk walking him myself. He's well trained. He comes when I whistle.'

'You weren't worried about him?'

'Dougie can look after himself. I wouldn't give much for the chances of anyone who tried to harm him.'

Murrain looked at the small, if enthusiastic dog, but decided there was no point in arguing. 'If you say so. But if you need to open the door again tonight, please let us know. Simply for your own safety. I'd much rather be safe than sorry.'

'I'm sure you know best.' Her tone implied that this was highly unlikely. 'I don't have any intentions of opening that door again before morning. Is there anything else you need for tonight?' She looked pointedly around the kitchen.

'We were just getting some water for the kettle,' Donovan said. 'Other than that, I think we're fine. Thank you.'

'In that case, I'll say goodnight. Let's hope that things are easier in the morning.'

'Let's hope so,' Murrain agreed.

Donovan filled the kettle and followed Murrain back through into the study. Wallace was lying on her back on the sofa, apparently asleep. Sparrow and Ferbrache had started another card game, though neither looked fully engaged.

'Much ado about nothing, I suppose,' Donovan said. 'Sorry about that.'

Murrain was frowning. 'I suppose. And I can see why she wanted to let the dog outside. It's just—'

'What?'

'Part of it's just – well, you know, my usual stuff...' Murrain lowered his head. He still found it difficult to raise the topic with anyone but Eloise. 'There was a moment, just as the dog appeared, when I felt something. Something that felt important.'

'Something about the dog, you mean?' It was impossible to tell if there was any scepticism in her tone.

'Just something. About that moment. But that wasn't the only thing.'

'Go on.'

'You saw when the dog swerved across the lawn? I thought it was going to go back, not come in.'

'I noticed that, But that's just dogs, isn't it?'

'Maybe. But there were footprints on the lawn. At that point. They were barely visible in the dark because more snow had fallen. But they were there. Someone had walked up the lawn and then had walked away again.'

'Our killer?'

'I assume so. But there was also a line of the dog's pawprints leading out to that spot and then a lot of scuffling of the snow. As if the dog had run out to greet someone.'

'Or drive someone away, maybe?'

'I'm not sure I really buy the idea of Dougie as a guard dog. But it's a possibility. It was difficult to make out much just from the marks in the snow. But to me it just looked like something else.'

'Such as?' There was definite scepticism in her tone now, he thought, though she was doing her best to conceal it.

'It just looked like the sort of movements a dog would make if it was going to greet someone it knew. Someone it knew very well.'

CHAPTER THIRTY-FIVE

Paul Wanstead was already beginning to feel exhausted. The road was steeper than he'd realised, and the thick snow made walking much more difficult than usual. He had to bow his head against the stiff wind that rattled through the woodland to the east. Even the silence was unnerving. Apart from the crunch of his own footsteps and the background wash of the wind, the night was dead, the usual noises muffled by the thick covering of snow.

He still had little real idea how far he'd got to go. The distance to Merestone could be no more than a couple of miles at most. Perhaps a forty minute walk in normal circumstances. But these were not normal circumstances, and Wanstead was conscious he was making very slow progress.

He'd been here before, of course, on that fool's errand. But that had been years before and on a bright summer's day. At night, draped in this coat of snow, the landscape bore no resemblance to anything he remembered. It felt simply eerie, the wooded hillside stretching away above and below him, the unblemished white road ahead of him, the single trail of his own footprints behind.

He used his flashlight sparingly, partly to preserve the batteries and partly because he wanted to avoid any unnecessary warning of his approach. His expectation was that his quarry would have taken shelter long ago, but nothing about this was predictable.

If his previous visit had been a fool's errand, then what was this? It was quite probable he was wrong, that he'd misjudged the situation. That he had taken the risk of coming out for no good reason. But if he was right, the journey was only the smallest part of the risk.

He trudged on as long as he was able, then paused to take a rest. He briefly turned on the flashlight and shone the beam around him, double-checking he hadn't strayed from the road. He'd imagined that keeping to the route would be straightforward, but he'd already been almost fooled by a sharp bend in the road or a sudden shift in its direction. For the most part, the slope down from the road was relatively gentle. But in a few places the land fell away more sharply. On one sharp bend he'd encountered an all-terrain van, possibly a police vehicle, abandoned above one of those steeper drops. The driver had clearly recognised the dangers of trying to navigate this road on a night like this. Wanstead could only hope the driver had found refuge and that this in turn indicated that the village was close at hand.

He turned off the flashlight. His eyes had become well-adjusted to the darkness and, despite the brief illumination from the torchlight, it took him only a few moments to re-accustom himself to the night. Wanstead was becoming more cautious as he approached Merestone. It was safer to assume the worst. Ensure he was the one who had the advantage, the benefit of surprise. If he was right.

There was still no sign of the lights of Merestone, but he must finally be drawing close by now. He remembered from that previous visit that the appearance of the village had surprised him, the scattering of buildings and the church suddenly visible as he rounded the final bend.

He checked in his pocket for his mobile phone. He'd turned it off as he'd left the house for almost superstitious reasons. He'd felt that, if he'd left the phone turned on, someone would have called him – maybe Murrain, maybe another call from Joe Milton, perhaps even Helena if for some unfathomable reason she'd broken the habit of a lifetime and returned downstairs.

If any of those had called, it would have been enough to prevent him going through with this. Enough to make him pause and reflect on what he was doing. Enough to make him see sense. It wouldn't have taken much. There had even been one or two points on the drive over when he'd been tempted to stop, turn round, head back home.

But he'd pressed on, and now he was almost there.

When he reached the village, he'd turn the phone back on. Make sure he had contact, the potential for back up. Murrain and his other colleagues were already here. Assuming there was any signal in this godforsaken spot, he could call them at any moment. He could put a stop to all of this.

He would do that, he told himself. Of course he would do that. He needed to do this properly. Do it by the book. So in the end he would make that call.

But not just yet.

CHAPTER THIRTY-SIX

Joe Milton had been experimenting with pulling together two office chairs to make a makeshift bed. He was on the point of abandoning the idea, having decided that the resulting surface would be even more uncomfortable and considerably less stable than the floor, when his mobile phone rang again. Murrain.

'Kenny?'

'Hi, Joe. Sorry to mither you again.'

'No worries. What can I do for you?'

'I was just wondering whether you'd spoken to Paul again?'

'Since I spoke to you? No. Why?'

'It's just that I've been trying to call his mobile. It's been either engaged or switched off for the last hour or so.'

'Not like Paul to keep it switched off. And I can't think who else he'd be talking to on his police line at this time.'

'That's what I thought. I was a bit concerned, after what you'd said.'

'About the way he talked about Tilston, you mean? It felt a bit out of character, but nothing to worry about, I'd have thought. Maybe he's got some problem with his phone.'

'I know. I'm being stupid. It's probably because I'm going slowly insane cooped up in this place. But when Paul starts behaving out of character, it does concern me. He's the most predictable man I know.'

Milton hesitated, knowing that Murrain might react badly to his next question. 'Is this another of your feelings, Kenny?'

There was an equivalent pause at the other end of the line before Murrain said: 'It might be. I'm not sure. But, yes, something.'

'Have you tried calling his home number?'

'God, no. He always tells me that Helena's in bed by ten. From what he's told me, disturbing her would be more dangerous than disturbing Eloise once she's hit the sack. And even I wouldn't dare do that. We've already had an unnecessary panic up here about an errant smoker and a bloody dog. I don't want to risk causing any more trouble.'

'I won't ask. Sounds like you're having more fun than I am, anyway.' Milton looked around him at the bleak office. 'I can't even find a decent place to bed down for the night.'

'There are some nice sofas in the Chief Officers' suite,' Murrain offered. 'But I suspect they wouldn't thank you for dossing down on them.'

'I'll see how desperate I get. Whether it's worth the wrath of the Chief's PA.'

'Rather you than me. I'd rather stick with our crazed killer.'

'Sorry I can't help you with Paul.'

'No problem. It was just on the off chance you'd spoken to him. I'm sure I'm worrying about nothing.'

'He'll be tucked up snugly with the long-suffering Helena,' Milton agreed. 'It's all right for some.'

Wanstead paused for the third or fourth time to recover his breath. The backs of his calves were aching from constantly pushing down into the snow. His shoulders were strained from his hunched stance against the driving wind and snow. The road was steeper than he remembered, the surface treacherous even under his sturdy walking boots.

He'd been telling himself for the last ten or fifteen minutes that the village must be around the next bend, but each time he'd been disappointed. He was almost beginning to think he'd missed his way, that he'd overlooked a junction in the road somewhere below, and had managed to leave Merestone far behind him. If so, he really was in deep trouble.

He hesitated, wondering whether to turn back. But if he really was lost, he reasoned, he might be better continuing in the hope of finding shelter. He'd passed nothing on the way up, and there must be surely be other houses or buildings nearby, even if he'd somehow by-passed Merestone.

In the end, Merestone appeared in the same way it had the last time he'd travelled up here, unexpectedly visible as he rounded yet another bend, the small cluster of buildings looming so close he couldn't imagine how he hadn't spotted them before. Tonight, visibility was down to only fifteen or twenty metres, but the illusion had been the same on the bright summer's day when he'd arrived here previously. Then he'd been driving, so the sudden appearance of the village had been even more startling.

The village didn't appear to have changed much in the intervening years. It was still a tiny place, barely even a hamlet, a few residential buildings huddled in the shade of the incongruous church as if seeking its protection. Perhaps they'd felt the need for that when these cottages were built. As was more than evident tonight, this was a hostile environment in winter. Even when the weather was less extreme, this area could easily become inaccessible. As Wanstead recalled from his days as a beat officer, it took relatively little snow to render some of the smaller Pennine routes impassable.

Wanstead wondered about the incomers who had bought places up here for the glorious summer views over the Goyt valley. Were nights like this a price worth paying for that, or did they regret their decision as the winter weather set in?

He trudged the final few metres up the hillside until he was standing in front of the Tilstons' house. He was tense now, his senses alert for any movement. It would be frustrating to be caught out so close to his objective.

The Tilstons' house looked little different, too. A little shabbier, the garden more overgrown. But otherwise unchanged. Nothing much could have been done with the place since Robert Tilston's imprisonment. There were lights showing behind some of the curtains. Kenny and the gang would be in one of those rooms, and that offered him some reassurance.

He pulled out his mobile. He was tempted, just for a moment, not to turn it on after all. Even now someone might call him, some random call about nothing, but enough to deflect him from his task.

Sure enough, there was a voicemail message waiting for him. From Kenny Murrain. The smart thing to do would be to return the call, tell Murrain exactly where he was. To seek shelter in there with the rest of them, rather than going through with this.

But he knew he wouldn't do that. If he did, he'd have to explain to Murrain what had brought him up here. Murrain would have to stop him, make sure he had nothing to do with this case. He'd have to do everything by the book. That was Murrain's way. Usually, it was Wanstead's way, too. But he had no confidence it would help him uncover the truth that had eluded him for so long.

He didn't fool himself his own approach would necessarily be any more productive. But it was all he had. He'd tried playing it straight, and that had got him nowhere. If his instincts were right, he had one shot at this and he needed to make it count. If he failed, he'd have lost nothing.

Except, he added to himself, as he turned to complete the last few metres of his journey, possibly his reputation, his career, even his life.

CHAPTER THIRTY-SEVEN

'I think it's finally bloody stopping.'

Joe Milton looked up in surprise. He hadn't been asleep, he told himself, just resting his head on the desk for a few moments. But somehow Marty Winston had come into the office without him noticing. 'Sorry?'

Winston was carrying two mugs of coffee. He pushed one across the desk towards Milton, and dumped himself down on the seat opposite. 'You look as if you need perking up. Consume some caffeine.'

'I need something. Ideally to get back home.'

'We could all do with that. Still, as I say, it looks as if it might finally be stopping.'

Milton pushed himself to his feet and walked over to the window. The main road outside was eerily empty, still covered with unblemished snow. It felt like the middle of the night, though it was barely after ten. But the snow had indeed stopped. 'Earlier than forecast?'

'A bit. It might start again, of course. But I had a peek outside, and it looks as if the really heavy clouds have passed over. Even a few patches of clear sky up there. Forecast reckons the temperature's going to rise a bit overnight, so hopefully we can get some of the roads cleared first thing and get things moving again.'

'And that of course will set off a whole new set of problems for us.'

'It's being cheerful that keeps you going, is it?' Winston himself was sounding much chirpier than earlier.

'People often comment on my naturally optimistic disposition, now you come to mention it. But, no, you're obviously right. It's felt as if we've been paralysed all night. It'll be a relief to get things going.'

'Tell me about it. I've been going quietly crazy. Been doing some phoning round, partly just to pester any of my colleagues who managed to make it home tonight. Looks like I've managed to round up some resources to kick off a proper manhunt for this Merestone killer as soon as conditions allow us to get into the area. The warnings went out on the news earlier in the evenings. That's resulted in a few calls, but there've been no reliable sightings.'

'Kenny reckons the killer's probably still sheltered away up there somewhere.'

'I had a chat with him earlier. He was obviously feeling bad about not being able to do anything tonight. I told him to stay put. Even with the four of them up there, it feels too much of a risk to go after someone like this until we can be sure of getting some back-up to them.'

'Don't imagine he took much persuading. Kenny's an assiduous cop, but he's not a fool. Even just trying to carry out a search on a night like this would be risky. There must be dozens of places to shelter up there if you know the terrain.'

'Anyway, we've now got the back-up teams identified and ready to be mustered first thing. As soon as the weather improves we can get people up there. Even get the chopper deployed. I'll feel much more comfortable once we've got this bastard. Whatever the story behind it, it sounds a nasty piece of business.'

'That's what intrigues me, though,' Milton said. 'What is the story behind it? I mean, is this just a random killing, or were those two killed for a reason? And where does Tilston fit in? It's a bloody odd coincidence.'

'I guess we'll find out when we catch the bugger. I'm not going to waste time speculating. As for Tilston, Christ knows. He was before my time in GMP, but I get the impression he was the type to attract bad news.'

'Not in recent years, supposedly. Though Paul Wanstead's not convinced.'

'I don't know much about the story. I mean, I remember it at the time. Not really the sort of story you could ignore if you were a copper. Even on the other side of the Pennines. I think we were just grateful he wasn't one of ours. We had our own share of bad apples.' Winston had spent the earlier part of his career with South Yorkshire Police. 'So what's Tilston been up to in recent years?'

'Keeping his head down, mostly, as far as I know. There was some talk of charity work. Stuff to do with the church, I think. But very low key.'

'He was always a man of God. I do remember that. Though quite what sort of God he worshipped, I dread to think. Not one I want much to do with.' Winston paused, clearly thinking. 'So what does Paul think?'

'This was just on the basis of a quick telephone chat with him earlier. He seems to have something of a bee in his bonnet about Tilston.'

Winston raised an eyebrow. 'Paul doesn't strike me as the kind to get worked up about anything.'

'Mr Unflappable,' Milton agreed. 'There seems to have been some bad blood between the two of them. Paul apparently caught Tilston out in some minor expenses fiddle. Or, maybe more to the point, trying to bully some poor admin assistant into ignoring his expenses fiddle. Tilston took it badly, and Paul's career never quite recovered. That's the way Paul tells it, anyway.'

'Might explain why someone of Paul's calibre is still a sergeant, I suppose. Though I always assumed that that was because he was happy doing what he does.'

'I think he is. Though that doesn't mean he's not had ambitions to do more.'

'That would certainly give him a reason to resent Tilston. I'm just surprised at him still nursing a grudge after all this time. He doesn't seem the type. You say he thought that Tilston might not have turned over a complete new leaf, though? Did he have any reason to think that?'

'He just thought that Tilston was the type who doesn't change.'

'Some people do, though, don't they? Sometimes the people you least expect. Maybe Tilston finally found a different God.'

'Anything's possible, I suppose.'

Winston swallowed the last dregs of his coffee. 'I'll leave you to your beauty sleep, then. Are you still planning to stay the night here?'

'I don't really see an alternative. I'm just trying to work out if there's anywhere I can crash out. What about you?'

'Same. I did have the bright idea of trying the hotel at the station. I thought they might have some cancellations because of the weather. But on the contrary it's filled to the rafters – passengers stranded after the trains stopped running. I don't think I can be arsed to walk any further.'

'Have you found somewhere to sleep, then?'

Winston frowned, his face reddening slightly as if he'd been caught out. 'Don't tell anyone. But I was wondering about the sofas in the Chief Officers' suite.'

CHAPTER THIRTY-EIGHT

'How's it looking?' Murrain asked.

Marie Donovan had her head between the closed curtains, peering out. 'It's definitely letting up. I think it might even have stopped. Nothing like it was, anyway.'

'I'm just praying that things improve over night. Marty Winston texted me to say he's got some resource together to get things moving with chummy out there, as soon as they're able to get them here.'

'I hope that's not long. The thought of chummy, as you call him, being out there gives me the creeps.'

'Me too,' Murrain agreed. 'I don't like the idea of not being able to do anything about it. It feels as if we're not doing our job.'

'Our job isn't to head out on a wild goose chase, leaving members of the public at risk, without proper risk assessment and back up.' Donovan was echoing the words that Murrain had used earlier when she'd suggested trying to track down the killer.

'Of course that's the right answer. It's even what Marty Winston said to me, minus a few choice expletives. It's just it's not what any copper ever wants to hear. If someone gets hurt or worse, because we've failed to take action…'

'You'll feel just as bad as you would if someone, including one of your own team, got hurt or worse because you *did* take some action. But, for the moment, that looks like the less risky option.'

'The frustrating thing is that he's probably still close at hand. He'll wait till first light before he tries to make a break for it,' Murrain said. 'We just have to hope we can get some resource in place before he gets away.'

'As long as we can stop him before he harms anyone else.'

'We don't know whether he's likely to harm anyone else. This could be random, or there could be some reason why Newland and his associate were chosen. We don't know anything.'

'From what you said about the injuries, it didn't sound like a professional hit,' Donovan said. 'Trust me on that one.'

'I bow to your expertise.' There was no irony in Murrain's tone. He knew enough about Marie Donovan's operational background not to question her judgement on such matters. 'But it could be something personal. In any case, we have to be concerned about anyone who can kill like that.'

He stopped at the sound of a soft tapping on the door of the study. Murrain raised a quizzical eyebrow to Donovan as the door opened and Rob Carter peered into the room. 'Sorry. I didn't know if you'd be asleep. It's taken us until now to get the kids off.'

Marie Donovan gestured towards Bert Wallace, who was now curled up on the sofa, her back to the room. 'Some of us have managed it. The rest of us, not so much.'

'Something we can do for you?' Murrain asked, pointedly.

Carter was looking uncharacteristically awkward. 'I think there's something you should maybe see.'

'What sort of thing?'

'I'm not— Well, just let me show you. I don't know if I'm making something out of nothing, and if it's even my business. But I thought you ought to see it.'

Murrain glanced at Donovan, who could offer only a shrug. 'Okay, show me.'

He followed Carter down the hallway to the bottom of the stairs. As Carter placed his foot on the bottom step, Murrain said, 'What are you doing?'

'It's upstairs. What I want to show you.'

'Did Anne Tilston give you permission to go upstairs?'

Carter looked uncomfortable. 'Not as such—'

'Then I think we'd better not go up there, don't you? We're already imposing enough without trampling over the whole house.'

'I was looking to see if there was some kind of bedside light we could borrow. Anne had said she was off to sleep in the room with her sisters down here, so I didn't want to disturb her. I didn't think she'd mind if I just borrowed something from upstairs.' The tone was that of a small child talking himself out of trouble.

'Even so, I don't we should be taking the liberty of going up there again.'

Carter hesitated. 'It's your decision. But you ought to see this. In the circumstances.'

He was clearly a man accustomed to wheedling his own way, Murrain thought. 'Just tell me.'

'I think there might be someone else living here. Someone Anne Tilston hasn't told us about. A man.'

There was silence for a moment, as Murrain absorbed this. 'Okay,' he said. 'Lead on.'

The light upstairs was turned off, but there was sufficient light from the ground floor for Murrain to make out four doors leading off a narrow landing. Bedrooms and a bathroom, he presumed.

Carter turned the old-fashioned Bakelite handle on the nearest door. He reached into the room and turned on the light. Murrain peered past him.

It was a bedroom, as Murrain had assumed. There was a large double bed, a slightly shabby-looking dressing table with a mottled mirror, and a heavy oak wardrobe which Murrain assumed was either Victorian or Edwardian. Otherwise, the room was sparsely decorated, with no pictures on the walls, bare varnished wooden floorboards, and, alongside the bed, a threadbare rug.

The wardrobe doors were open. The clothes inside, including a suit hanging on the inside of one of the doors, were all male. On the dressing table, there was a can of shaving foam and a hand razor. A shirt and a pair of trousers were strewn across the bed, again both male clothing. The bed itself was unmade, an old-fashioned quilt pulled untidily back.

Murrain's first thought was that Anne Tilston had maintained the room as a shrine to her father, in the way that bereaved parents sometimes leave their dead children's rooms untouched. He and Eloise had almost fallen into that trap – and Murrain was clear, in his head if not his heart, that it was a trap – until one weekend Eloise had unilaterally decided to have a ruthless clear out. He'd been angry with her initially, but quickly realised she was right. They couldn't continue to fetishise their dead son. They had to move on.

But, on second glance, this didn't look like that at all. This looked like a room occupied by a living person. The shaving equipment and other toiletries on the dressing table, the discarded clothes thrown casually across the bed. Those were not what you'd find in a shrine, however casual. They were the leavings of a living person.

He took a step forward. A pair of black leather shoes sat on the floor at the bottom of the bed. On the far side of the bed, half protruding from beneath the mattress, he could see a battered looking suitcase, with a leather ID tag fixed to the handle. Murrain crouched down and turned over the tag.

There was an address which offered nothing more than a flat number, a street name and a Manchester postcode. From memory, Murrain thought the address was in Withington or that vicinity, but the street name meant nothing to him.

But, above the address, there was a name which meant much more.

Robert Tilston.

Perhaps he'd been right after all, then. Perhaps this room had been kept unchanged by the Tilston sisters. It seemed odd, given the way Anne Tilston had talked about her father. But people's motives were often unfathomable. Perhaps, after Tilston's trial and conviction, the sisters had felt unable to touch the room. After the sisters' accident, it would no doubt have been a low priority for Anne Tilston.

Murrain could imagine how the years might have drifted by, this room left to gather dust.

That was part of it, though. Murrain straightened and ran a finger across the surface of the dressing table. The room hadn't been left to gather dust, or no more than the rest of the house. Although he hadn't initially registered it consciously, that was part of what made the room feel lived-in. The air didn't have the stale feel of a space left closed up and unused. If there was a scent in here, it was a human one and recent.

'What do you think?' Rob Carter's voice was scarcely above a whisper.

'I don't know what to make of it.' The ever-present buzzing in the back of his brain had grown more forceful since they'd entered the room. It was like voices now, a demonic choir muttering some truth outside the range of his hearing. But close at hand, ominous.

He moved back towards the door, but paused as he passed the wardrobe. Tossed into the bottom, next to another pair of shoes, was a folded newspaper. A tabloid. The Daily Mail.

Murrain had half-expected it to be an old copy, left there from years before. But it wasn't. It was dated only a few days before.

If this was some sort of shrine, he thought, it was the oddest he'd ever come across.

'I don't understand,' Carter said. 'If there's someone else living here, why didn't Anne Tilston tell us?'

'Perhaps because they're not still living here,' Murrain said. 'I think we'd better leave this and head back downstairs.' The murmuring in his head was growing louder and most insistent. It was rhythmic and repetitive, telling him something that he could almost understand.

He followed Carter out of the room. Without turning on the landing light, he led the way down to the ground floor.

A figure was standing at the bottom of the stairs. Anne Tilston gazing up at them, her face caught in the light from the hallway. Murrain could almost read her changing expression. At first, he thought, something close to fear, then puzzlement and finally anger. Genuine anger, he thought. Not just the irritation you might expect from someone whose hospitality has been abused. There was a cold fury in her eyes.

'I heard movements,' she said. 'The sound of footsteps upstairs. I thought – well, you can imagine what I thought.'

'Of course,' Murrain said, trying to keep his voice as emollient as possible. 'I apologise—' He wondered for a moment about holding back the truth, perhaps simply saying he'd wanted to check the upper floors.

Behind him, though, Carter had already interrupted. 'Who's living up there? Who's in that room?'

Anne Tilston's face was blank and unreadable, but the fury in her eyes had intensified. When she spoke, her voice was monotone and icy. 'I think the two of you owe me an explanation.'

Murrain took a breath, content to allow the silence to build. Whatever was going on here, he had no intention of being intimidated by Anne Tilston. He descended the last two steps to the hallway so that he was standing immediately in front of her. Then, his voice soft and calm, he said, 'I'm sorry, Ms Tilston. But I think you're the one with some explaining to do.'

CHAPTER THIRTY-NINE

As he entered the churchyard, Paul Wanstead looked around him, still alert for any movement. The wind had dropped, leaving the night eerily quiet. The graveyard itself was thick with unblemished snow, the graves shapeless mounds in the pale light from the streetlights outside. If anyone had been here, their footprints were already concealed by the fallen snow.

There were patches of clear sky above now, fragments of constellations visible between the drifting clouds. The night was colder than ever, but it felt as if the snow might finally have passed.

The dark mass of the church loomed above him. There had never really been a village of any size here as far as Wanstead knew, and he had no idea why a building like this should have been erected on such a remote spot. No doubt someone had had their devout reasons.

The main doors of the church were, as he'd expected, firmly locked. He imagined that, these days, the place would be opened only for the infrequent services held here. It could be only a matter of time before the building and grounds were sold, though Wanstead found it hard to imagine who might want to buy it.

He made his way round to the side of the church. Perhaps his instincts had been wrong, and he really was here on a fool's errand. His decision to come here tonight had little to do with reason. Intuition. Copper's gut. Whatever you wanted to call it. Voices in the head, in Kenny Murrain's case, though Wanstead didn't think he'd reached that point yet.

As he'd hoped, there was another door to the side of the church which presumably led into the vestry. Even if he were right, he had no grounds for supposing this wouldn't also be locked, perhaps even bolted from the inside. That might be what you would do if you were seeking sanctuary, however unholy.

The cast iron handle was cold to his touch and turned only with difficulty, grinding noisily in its socket. Any hope he'd had of concealing his arrival had now surely gone. But that probably mattered little. The advantage of surprise would have been short-lived and limited. The only risk was that he might be prevented from doing or saying what he needed to.

The interior of the church felt almost colder than the night outside, and the silence even more intense. Wanstead waited, his back to the door, allowing his eyes to grow re-accustomed to the darkness. Eventually he was able to make out the room's overall shape and the bulky shadows that represented items of furniture. A table, a couple of wooden chairs, a large cupboard filling one wall. Ahead of him, a door into the main body of the church.

Wanstead made his way to the door, feeling for the handle. This time, it turned easily and silently. He pushed open the door, listening intently. The quality of the silence felt different, and he was conscious of stepping into a much larger space. He moved to one side and stood with his back to the stone wall, looking around him. The large stained-glass windows allowed in some light from the streetlights, and he could see more here than in the vestry. The church interior was much as he had expected – rows of wooden pews, the altar visible at the end of the nave, the walls lined with the disapproving stone effigies of once-important local dignitaries. Close at hand, there was a table strewn with leaflets optimistically set out for churchgoers or visitors.

At first, the church seemed even more silent than the night outside. Then he detected something else. Something soft and rhythmic. Breathing that was not his own.

His back pressed against the wall, trying to keep his voice steady, Wanstead called, 'Where are you?'

At first, there was no response, no change to the almost silence. Then Wanstead detected a movement, a shifting of shadows, in the first few rows of the pews. He remained motionless, his eyes fixed on that point, determined not to speak again until there was a response.

He heard the sound of a throat being cleared and a hoarse voice said, 'Who is that?'

'Wanstead. Paul Wanstead. You remember me.' It wasn't a question.

There was another silence. Then the voice said, with a note of puzzlement, 'What are you doing here?'

'I'm here to see you. Why else would I be here?'

Again, there was no immediate response. There was another cough before the voice said, 'I haven't seen you for a while.'

Wanstead knew exactly how long, almost to the day. 'About twenty years. There or thereabouts.'

'A lot's happened since then.'

'But nothing has changed,' Wanstead said. 'You haven't changed. Not really.'

'I—' The voice stopped. 'Will you come closer? I won't hurt you.'

Wanstead found himself laughing, though with no obvious humour. 'No. You won't hurt me. Not any more. You've hurt me all you can.' He walked forward slowly, his eyes still fixed on the point where he'd seen movement.

There was a flash of light. Wanstead blinked, annoyed at having allowed himself to be taken by surprise. For a second, all he could see was the drifting of crimson shapes across his vision. When his sight cleared, the light was still there. A flashlight held by a figure in one of the pews. 'I'm here.'

Wanstead sat at the end of the pew, then slid along until he was close to the seated figure. He hadn't been sure what to expect after all this time, but it wasn't this.

The man's face was lined and haggard, his cheeks poorly shaven. His eyes flickered up and stared at Wanstead. The pupils seemed unnaturally bright, but with a blankness behind them. 'Who did you say you were?'

'Paul Wanstead. You remember. Hayley's brother.'

'Hayley.' He spoke the name almost, but not quite, as a question. 'Where is Hayley?'

Wanstead was silent for a moment. 'She's nearby.'

'That's good,' the man said. 'I've been missing her.'

'When did you last see her?'

The man frowned, clearly puzzled at his own inability to answer the question. 'Not – long ago. Yesterday, maybe.'

Yesterday, Wanstead thought. All our bloody yesterdays. 'How was she?'

The man thought for a moment. 'Not happy. I don't think she was happy.'

'No,' Wanstead agreed. 'I don't imagine she was.' His instincts had been partly right, then, though he'd expected nothing like this. He could see it made sense. It explained at least something about what had happened here. He was only just beginning to piece together the sequence of events, but this was another part of the story. 'Did she know what you did?'

The man was silent again, the same puzzled expression on his face. 'I think so. She told me what to do. She told me to do it.'

Wanstead took a breath. No, she didn't, you bastard, he thought. You did it all by yourself. Don't you dare to try to say that. But then another thought struck him. 'When did she tell you to do it?'

Another long silence. The man was staring blankly into the dark, his bright eyes unnervingly piercing.

'When did she tell you?' Wanstead asked again.

'Yesterday,' the man said. 'Before I did it. She told me. She's been helping me.'

'What did she tell you?'

'What they did. What they got up to. Why I had to do something about them.' The man's voice was just a whisper in the silence of the church. His eyes were fixed on some point in the darkness, as if he were staring at something Wanstead couldn't see.

'Where was this?'

237

'In the house. I saw her in the house.'

'Your house?'

'Yes, of course my house.' The man sounded uncertain again now, as if he'd been caught out in some half truth.

'Where were the children? Did you see the children there?'

The man's gaze switched to Wanstead, the eyes brighter than ever in the torchlight, the expression even more baffled than before. 'The children?'

'The girls. Did you see the girls?'

'I – I must have done. I don't know. I must have done.' The man dropped his head, as if suddenly exhausted. 'I must have done.'

'You must have. Perhaps they were out playing?'

'Playing?' The man stopped, thinking. 'Yes, playing. That'll be it.'

'Did she tell you why you needed to do it?'

The man's expression had changed again. Wanstead would have been hard-pressed to describe it. Passionate. Zealous. Obsessive, perhaps. A man locked into his own fervour, rather than someone given instruction. 'They were unclean. I was doing God's work. I've always done God's work.'

Wanstead heard a movement behind him and twisted to peer into the gloom. The sound had been barely discernible and there was nothing further. Perhaps a mouse or some other night-dweller. The man was murmuring some words under his breath. 'Hayley,' Wanstead said. 'Was that the Lord's work?'

The murmuring had shaped itself into what sounded like a prayer or incantation, the sound rhythmic, the words unintelligible. Then the man stopped abruptly. 'The Lord giveth and the Lord taketh away.' It wasn't clear whether this was intended as an answer to Wanstead's question.

'What about Bradley? Was that the Lord's work too?'

The sharpness had vanished again from the man's eyes. For a moment, they had looked purposeful, focused. Now they were blank again. 'It's all the Lord's work,' he said, in a tone that suggested he was talking to someone other than Wanstead. 'It's all the Lord's work. The Lord's work, the Lord's work...' The last words were a half sing-song, as if they were the beginning of a nursery rhyme.

There was another sound from the rear of the nave. Again, something only just detectable. A place like this would be full of noises, Wanstead told himself. The shifting of old timbers, scuttling of church mice, bats literally in the belfry.

'Has Hayley told you to do it before?'

The blank expression cleared for a moment, and the man peered closely at Wanstead. 'Hayley's dead. Hayley's been dead for years. Didn't they tell you?'

Wanstead nodded. Suddenly, unexpectedly, he had been given the confirmation he had been seeking all these years. Not in a way that would have any substance in a court of law, or even would necessarily persuade anyone else. But enough for him. Enough for him to know it was true. Not that he had ever really doubted it, however much he might have wished otherwise. But he'd wanted to hear this man say it. 'No,' he said. 'No, they didn't tell me. Nobody told me.'

'Somebody should have told you,' the man said, earnestly. 'Hayley should have told you, at least.'

Wanstead realised the moment of lucidity, if that's what it had really been, had already passed. But, in his own mind, he had no question that what the man had just told him was true. Hayley was dead. She'd died a long time before.

He had all he needed now. It wasn't something he could ever use, and it seemed unlikely the man in front of him would ever be fit to be charged or convicted. But it was what Wanstead had come here for.

'Shall I take you back to the house now? You don't need to stay out here.' The haggard elderly man looked anything but dangerous, though Wanstead knew that that must be deceptive. Just as the lucidity had faded like the sun behind a cloud, so the calmness and passivity might unexpectedly be replaced by something else. What might trigger that change, there was no way of knowing.

He should call Murrain now, get the team over here before anything changed. Wanstead began to reach into his pocket, trying to move gently to avoid any risk of provoking the man.

Then he heard the sound again, louder and more definite this time. A movement at the rear of the nave. Something moving along the ground, a scraping. Louder and more insistent than anything likely to be made by a church mouse.

This time, the man had heard the sound too. His over-bright eyes twitched and his gaze flickered in its direction. 'Hayley?'

The note of hope in his tone was almost enough to ignite Wanstead's anger, but he swallowed his instinctive response. 'Not Hayley. Whatever it is.'

The man had lost interest again. His eyes were as blank as before and he was staring at nothing. Wanstead shuffled back along the pew. 'I'll go and see what's making the noise.'

The man nodded, then his eyes once again regained focus. 'That's why I'm here. That's why I have to stay. That's what she told me.'

The sound was growing louder and more definite. Something moving, or trying to move, across the stone floor. And something else. Almost like a voice. A low moaning. 'Why do you have to stay?'

'To keep her. Until it's time.'

'Keep who?'

But the man's interest had dissipated again. He was humming a tune which Wanstead half recognised. Some hit from the 1980s, but he couldn't pin down what.

Wanstead had reached the end of pew. Feeling his way along the rows of pews, he made his way slowly to the rear of the church. There were three large stained glass windows at this end of the building, and a faint light entered from the streetlights. Even so, the space at the rear of the nave was nothing more than a mass of shadows.

He pulled out the flashlight and shone it across the floor.

At first, he thought there was nothing there. Just the worn stone flags, a couple of empty vases presumably used when there was a service here, an old table. Then the beam of light reached the far wall, and he saw it.

'Dear God—'

He had no time to say anything more, as the hands reaching from behind tightened on his throat.

CHAPTER FORTY

'I don't think it's any of your business,' Anne Tilston said again.

She looked a different woman, Murrain thought. The earlier assurance had vanished, replaced by a cowering, anxious demeanour. Her arms were wrapped tightly round her body as if to protect herself from an impending blow. Even so, she'd so far offered Murrain nothing in the way of an answer to his questions.

He'd sent Rob Carter back to join his wife and children, judging that this was better handled more discreetly. Then he'd ushered Anne Tilston into the kitchen and sat them both down, head to head, over the kitchen table, hoping they could remain undisturbed. At first, Anne Tilston had been her usual self, angry, icily controlled, firmly occupying any available moral high ground.

It was only when Murrain had asked again about the bedroom upstairs that her manner changed.

'Which bedroom?'

'You know which bedroom, Ms Tilston. The first room at the top of the stairs. It appears to be occupied. That's what Mr Carter was referring to.'

'I don't know what you're talking about.'

'You do. It appears to be occupied by a male. Judging from the clothes and other items in there. I'm wondering who this person is and why you didn't choose to tell us about them. In the circumstances.'

Murrain could almost read her thought processes from her expression. He could see she was wondering whether she could bluff her way out of this without offering him any meaningful explanation. 'The clothes were my father's.'

'You're telling me they've been there since your father left?'

'Why not? I couldn't bring myself to change anything.'

'That's not true, is it, Ms Tilston? There's someone living in that room. Someone's been occupying it very recently. There's even a newspaper in the wardrobe from just a few days ago.'

'I don't know about that.'

'Why would there be a recent newspaper in a room you've supposedly left untouched for years?'

'This is none of your business.'

'My business is to protect the people living in this house. I can't do that if you're not being honest with me.'

She was silent for so long Murrain had almost begun to think she wouldn't respond. She was still curled up on the chair as if expecting to be physically beaten. 'I have been honest. About everything important.'

'I think that has to be for me to judge,' Murrain said. 'Go on.'

'My father. Robert Tilston.'

It was Murrain's turn to offer no response. His silence, though, was tactical, knowing that eventually Anne Tilston would feel impelled to fill it.

'You're right,' she said. 'He was living here.'

'Since when?'

'For a few months. He contacted me. He needed help.'

'You told us you'd had no contact with him. You gave us the impression you wanted no contact with him. Why did that change?'

'He needed help. He was our father.' The last two words sounded, momentarily, as if she were invoking a deity.

Murrain leaned back in his chair, watching her intently. Her head was down, as if she were deliberately avoiding catching his eye. Her body was still hunched, arms wrapped round her frail body. 'Why did he need help?'

For the first time she looked up, her expression suggesting she was challenging him to refute what she was saying. 'He was suffering from dementia. Early-onset Alzheimer's. He said the signs had been there for some time. He'd initially found he was having short-term memory problems. Hadn't worried at first, but had spoken to his GP during a routine check-up. Diagnosis was that it was dementia and progressing quickly. When he contacted me, it had got significantly worse.'

'I'm sorry.'

'Sympathy doesn't help very much,' she said, bluntly. 'At that point, he could still more or less look after himself. But he was worried he wouldn't be able to for much longer. He had no-one else to turn to.'

'So you brought him here?'

'I went and collected him. The doctors had been right. He's deteriorated rapidly especially over the last couple of months. For the last few weeks, he mostly had no idea who I was. I think, half the time, he didn't even know who *he* was. He could remember things from years ago, and quite often thought he was back there. Kept asking where the children were. I suppose it was a blessing in a way. It took him back to – well, back to before everything happened.'

'Happier days?' Murrain offered.

'If you like,' she said, in a voice that suggested she very much didn't. 'But, yes, he was up there in that room. I'd been thinking about bringing him down into one of the downstairs rooms. He was prone to wandering about at night, He'd wake up in the small hours and I'd hear him clattering around. When I heard your footsteps up there today—'

'I'm sorry,' Murrain said, for the second time. 'We shouldn't have gone up there without checking with you first.'

'I don't suppose it really matters. I wanted to tell you the truth. I would have done once you interviewed me properly.' Her tone was unnaturally neutral, and Murrain wasn't sure whether he believed her. Though it was difficult to see how she could have concealed this for very long.

'So why didn't you at first?'

'I don't know. I suppose partly because I felt responsible for his death. As I say, he had a tendency to wander about the house at night. My main worry was that he might fall down the stairs, though he seemed to have an uncanny ability to navigate around the place. Probably because his mind had slipped back to when he first lived here. But I never thought he'd manage to get outside.'

'You kept the doors locked at night? From the inside, I mean.'

'Of course. The back door was locked and bolted, and the front door's locked with a deadlock. I still don't know how he managed to get out there. Again, he must have been more aware than he seemed. There's a spare set of keys to the back door in a wall cabinet in the kitchen. The back door set of keys is missing, so I'm guessing he must have got hold of it somehow. It's probably still in his pocket.'

'Did you realise he was missing? Before you went out yesterday, I mean.'

'I'd have called the police then, if I'd known. He normally sleeps late these days, so I usually take him a coffee around nine-thirty if there's no sign. I was up early yesterday, so I thought I'd take Dougie for his morning walk and perhaps get myself some breakfast when I got back. He hadn't surfaced before I went out, but, as I say, that was usual for him. I didn't think there was any cause for alarm.'

'I still don't understand why you didn't just tell us the truth from the start. We could have ended up wasting considerable police time investigating how and why he'd ended up here.'

'I know.' She was looking more relaxed now, Murrain thought, as if she'd overcome some barrier that had been troubling her. Perhaps it was just because she'd finally told him the truth. Perhaps she'd been wanting to find a way to do that. But it didn't quite feel like that. It felt as if there was still something more, something that even now she wasn't saying. It was more as if she was relieved to have persuaded him to accept her story. 'I don't know why I did that. As I say, it was partly my own embarrassment and, well, self-reproach that I'd allowed this to happen.'

'We'll need to investigate the full circumstances. But I don't imagine that anyone will consider you culpable.'

'Anyone but me, you mean?'

'You can't blame yourself. You've more than enough on your plate. Did social services provide help with your father?'

'Not so far. I'd considered involving them if things became too bad. But you know how difficult it is to get support these days. They'd have made us jump through endless hoops. Tests and assessments. That was why I've never pursued it with my sisters. I didn't want to put him through all that.'

'It must have been a shock when you found him.'

'I didn't know what to do. I'm sorry. That's when I came up with the stupid story about not having seen him for years. I don't know what I was thinking.'

Neither do I, Murrain thought. People could behave in the most irrational ways in the face of unexpected bereavement. He'd had more than enough experience of that over the years, usually when breaking the news to some distraught parent or partner. Maybe that was what had happened here. Anne Tilston had been worried that she'd be held responsible for her father's death – morally if not legally – and had concocted a story to protect herself. He couldn't imagine how she coped with the stress of looking after her father as well as her two sisters. It was more responsibility that any individual should be expected to bear.

But it struck him now what an oddly private world Anne Tilston inhabited. Hidden away in this desolate corner of the Pennines. According to the Carters, she'd largely kept out of the way of the few neighbours, despite her supposed run-ins with Toby Newland. She hadn't mentioned her sisters until she was forced to. Then, for whatever reason, she'd been trying to conceal the fact that her father had been living upstairs. It was the life of someone who didn't want anyone to intrude more than she could help.

That had also been Robert Tilston's preference, he recalled. After the trial, the press had devoted pages to speculating how a senior police officer could have concealed his predilections and behaviour for so long. Tilston had kept his professional and private lives completely separate. Everyone had wondered why he'd chosen to live up here rather than in one of the Cheshire towns favoured by his senior colleagues. The answer had been that, up here, no-one knew him. There'd been even fewer neighbours in those days, and there had been nobody to observe his comings and goings. It seemed as if Anne Tilston had inherited this disposition from her father.

'We'll need to go through this properly when we interview you formally,' Murrain said.

'He died from natural causes. Hypothermia, I assume. I don't see why you have to interview me at all. What else is there to say, now I've told you the truth?'

It was a startling question from someone who, for whatever reason, had been lying to him until only a few minutes ago. 'Until we've completed the post mortem, we still have to treat this as a sudden and unexplained death.'

'Hardly unexplained.'

'Nevertheless, we have to follow the procedure. I'm sure you appreciate that.'

'If you say so.'

'I'm afraid I do.'

She pushed herself up from the table, clearly indicating that as far as she was concerned the discussion was at an end. 'I'll get myself back to bed, then. I hope you won't have need to disturb me again tonight.' Her demeanour had changed yet again. The anxiety and sense of submission had again been replaced by something closer to her usual frosty assurance. It was as if she'd overcome some challenge, Murrain thought. As if, perhaps, she'd won some conflict with him that he hadn't even been aware he was fighting.

'I hope so too,' he said, as he watched her leave the room.

The buzzing in his brain had not lessened while she'd been talking. If anything, that choir of inhuman voices had grown stronger, if no more comprehensible. There was something wrong, he thought. Something wrong with this picture. Something wrong with her story.

Something, he thought, even beyond the fact that he hadn't believed a bloody word of it.

CHAPTER FORTY-ONE

The hands had crushed Wanstead's throat so suddenly and inexorably that he'd expected unconsciousness to follow almost immediately. His response had been instinctive rather than rational, his hands trying to prise the fingers away from his flesh then struggling vainly to push backwards against his assailant.

The release came by accident rather than design. He stumbled forward, pulling his attacker with him. The grip loosened for no more than an instant, but it was sufficient for him to get a grip on the tightening hands on his throat, dragging them loose. He twisted his body and threw a hefty punch at his assailant's midriff.

Wanstead wasn't one for much physical activity these days, but in his youth he'd been a keen amateur boxer, representing the force on a number of occasions. His strength and fitness weren't what they had been, but he knew how to land a blow. He heard his attacker gasp and fall backwards, stumbling on to the stone floor.

Still partly off balance, Wanstead reached out for him, but the other figure had already staggered back to his feet. He was now a couple of metres away from Wanstead, no more than a bulky shape in the darkness. His panting sounded almost animalistic, a guttural sound close to a snarl. Yet this was the same man who, only minutes before, had been sitting peaceably among the pews.

The man was moving forward again, a hunched shadow in the darkness. Then Wanstead saw something glint in the faint light. He glimpsed it only momentarily, but had little doubt what he'd seen. A knife. Presumably the same knife that had been used on Toby Newland and the other as yet unidentified man.

To his left, Wanstead could hear that same shuffling sound, the rasp of an object against the stone floor. He knew he should draw the man away from that end of the nave, provide what little protection he could. But none of that would matter if Wanstead couldn't find some means of defending himself first.

He looked around frantically in the darkness, trying to identify anything he could use to fend off an attack. There was nothing. Wanstead was cursing himself. In the car he had his police baton and a hefty flashlight which could double as a weapon. In his desire not to burden himself on his trek up here, he'd brought only the pocket torch.

The man was standing motionless no more than a couple of metres away. Wanstead considered what chance he had of making a break past him back into the body of the nave. If he did that, he'd have to draw the man with him, luring him away from the rear of the church.

As before, he kept his movements slow and gentle, trying to do nothing that would provoke an immediate response. He drew out his torch and then, preparing to make a bolt towards the centre of the church, he shone the beam full into the man's face, with the intention of momentarily blinding him.

But what he saw there made him pause. He'd expected the man's expression to be manic or furious, but there was nothing more than fear. Fear and loss. The bewildered gaze of a man who no longer even knew where he was. As Wanstead stared at him, the man raised his hands and stumbled back into the church, disappearing into the darkness.

Wanstead's first thought was to follow. But he had two more urgent tasks first. He pulled out his mobile phone and thumbed Murrain's number. The call was answered almost immediately.

'Paul? Something wrong?'
'You always know, don't you, Kenny?'
'What is it? Are you at home?'
'Not exactly. It's a long story, but I'm in the church.'
'Church?'
'The church at Merestone. About five hundred metres from you.'

There was a silence, which was the sound of Murrain absorbing this. 'What the hell are you doing there? For that matter, how the hell did you get there?'

'Like I say, long story. But here I am. And I need you over here to help me. Your killer's here.'

'Christ, Paul. What the hell are you doing?'

'It doesn't matter. I'll explain everything. But I need you all over here—' Wanstead stopped, his mind still working through everything he knew and had witnessed. 'No, you'd better leave someone there, just in case. But I need the rest of you over here.'

'We're already on our way, Paul. But take care. Don't take any unnecessary risks.'

'I think that ship's already sailed. Depending on what you mean by unnecessary. And you take care. I'm not sure where the killer actually is. He'll be somewhere in the church or its immediate vicinity. I'm not sure he's actually dangerous, but he'll be – well, let's say unpredictable. Handle him carefully if you find him. He's bewildered and scared out of his wits. You'll need to come round to the door at the rear. It's open.'

'Tell me about it. Hang on the line, Paul, and we'll be with you.'

'Sure thing.'

Even so, Wanstead slipped the phone back into his coat pocket, knowing he'd need both hands for what he had to do next. He'd already left it longer than he'd intended. He could hope only he wasn't too late.

CHAPTER FORTY-TWO

'Wanstead? Paul Wanstead?'
'The one and only,' Murrain said.
'What the hell's Paul doing up here?'
'You know,' Murrain said, 'the very same question had occurred to me.'

He and Marie Donovan were hurrying along the snow-covered road towards the church, Will Sparrow puffing along in their wake. As they reached the churchyard gate, Murrain held out his hand to stop Donovan and Sparrow. 'We need to be careful now. Paul reckoned the killer was somewhere in the vicinity of the church. Move slowly and keep alert.'

Ahead of them, there was a line of footprints in the snow leading in the same direction. Presumably the trail Wanstead had left on his arrival. As they approached the church, the prints became more confused, overlain by a second set made by someone apparently leaving the church. Murrain shone his flashlight along the prints, following the trail behind a row of ancient-looking gravestones.

It took him a moment to spot the figure crouched on the ground behind the stones. At first, he thought it was nothing more than a pile of earth, a tarpaulin flapping softly in the chill breeze. Then he saw it was human, a body slumped on the ground, its head twitching as it followed their progress.

As he grew closer, Murrain saw that there was a knife – a large, slightly curved gardening instrument of some kind – held loosely in the figure's left hand. The figure raised its head and gazed blankly at them. It was a man, Murrain now saw. Elderly, haggard, unshaven, dressed in a battered brown raincoat.

'Do you want to give me that?' Murrain gestured towards the knife.

The man looked at the blade as if he had forgotten that it was there. Then he tossed it, without force, in Murrain's direction. Murrain took a step back, allowing it to fall into the thick snow. He pulled on one of the fine plastic gloves he always carried and carefully picked up the knife. 'Anyone think to bring an evidence bag?'

For once, it was Will Sparrow who came up with the goods, producing a roll of sealable bags from inside his coat. Murrain dropped the knife inside, then sealed the bag and handed it to Sparrow. 'You'd better get it labelled. I assume that's our murder weapon.'

He looked more closely at the figure cowering in front of them. This was the man who'd put the fear of god into them all. The man who'd had them hiding behind locked doors.

The man who had savagely hacked two people to death.

Wanstead had said the man was scared out of his wits. If so, Murrain thought, he seemed to have left his wits far behind. He looked as if he had no idea where he was or what he might be doing there.

Murrain helped the man to his feet. Now that he was close, he could smell a rich, intense stench. He shone his torch across the man's clothing. It was caked with dried blood.

'You going to impress us even more by producing a set of cuffs, Will?' Murrain asked.

'Don't know about Will, but I can,' Donovan said. 'You never know when they might be useful at parties,' she added, catching Will Sparrow's expression. 'Truth is, I've had more than enough experiences that make me want to ensure I can look after myself if I need to.'

Murrain turned the man around, pulled back his arms and snapped on the cuffs. The man gave no response, other than to twist his head to gaze uncomprehendingly at Murrain.

'What's wrong with him?' Sparrow asked. 'Looks like he's on something.'

'Maybe,' Murrain said. 'No smell of alcohol. Maybe drugs.'

'I don't think it's that,' Donovan said. 'I've seen that blank look before. My late partner. In the weeks before he died.'

Murrain nodded. 'Let's see what Paul's got to tell us.' He led them across to the rear door of the church, which was standing open. They entered the vestry, Sparrow and Donovan easing the man along with them. He showed no resistance, but needed coaxing to take each step.

Murrain clicked the light-switch, but to no effect. The mains power was presumably turned off when the church wasn't in use. Holding his torch steady, he made his way through the next door into the main body of the church.

'Paul?'

'Over here. Just by the main doors.'

Murrain shone his torch across the row of pews, and finally pinpointed Wanstead in the far corner. He was crouched over something in the corner of the nave. It was only when Murrain reached the back of the pews and entered the space before the main doors that he realised what it was.

'Christ.'

'We're in the right place for it,' Wanstead agreed. 'Let's hope he's prepared to lend us a hand.'

The figure was bound up tight with plastic cords, a thick band of tape around the mouth. At first Murrain couldn't make out whether the figure was male or female. Then he realised it was a woman, a young woman.

She was alive and conscious, her eyes staring terrified into the semi-darkness. Her body rasped across the stone floor as she struggled with her bonds. Wanstead was doing the same, desperately trying to free the net of cords wrapped tightly around her body. 'You got a knife or anything?'

Murrain pulled out the Swiss Army Knife that Eloise had bought him for his birthday a year or two before. It had been an obscure joke on her part, given that Murrain was hardly the outdoors type. It was enough to meet the current need, though. Wanstead snapped open the blade and sawed at the plastic ropes.

It took him only a few minutes to loosen the cords to the point where he could begin to unravel them. 'Sorry,' he said to the woman, sounding genuinely apologetic. 'Want to get you out of this as quickly as we can. Hope I'm not being too rough.' As if prompted by his own words, he reached up and cut gently at the tape wrapped around her mouth. 'Christ, sorry. Should have done that first. Not thinking straight...' He was talking gently, the voice of man offering calm and reassurance.

As he finally pulled off the gag, the woman let out a deep breath. For a moment, Murrain thought she might vomit, but she simply sucked in a deep mouthful of the chill air. As Wanstead cut away at the ropes, she said, 'Oh, thank God...Thank God...'

It took Wanstead several more minutes to release her. They tried to help her to her feet, but her legs collapsed under her. Murrain and Sparrow half carried her across to the pews, helping her sit awkwardly in a corner.

'Police.' Murrain held his warrant card in front of her. 'You're safe now. We'll need to ask you some questions. But not yet. We'll get you out of here to somewhere more comfortable. Take your time. Take some deep breaths. Try to relax.' Sparrow, ever resourceful, had produced a bottle of water which he handed over to the woman. She took it gratefully, and tipped it back into her mouth, heedless of the water dripping down her cheeks.

'I think you need to tell us what's going on, Paul,' Murrain said. Wanstead was standing watching them. 'And don't start by telling me it's a long story.'

'I think,' Wanstead said, 'that what you're witnessing here is the last act in a Greek tragedy.'

'And what's your role in this? The chorus?'

'Maybe,' Wanstead said. 'Though I'd have liked to have played a more active part.'

'So who's the tragic hero?' Murrain took the bottle from the woman, who had almost emptied it.

'I don't think hero is the right word. But the central figure, the one who caused all this, is the man standing over there.' He gestured towards the figure still standing motionless beside Marie Donovan, his head bowed, his body shaking slightly as if he were weeping.

'And who the hell is he?'

'That poor bugger,' Wanstead said, his own eyes filling with tears, 'is none other than your old friend and mine. That bastard Robert Tilston.'

CHAPTER FORTY-THREE

'Tilston? It can't be Robert Tilston,' Murrain said. 'Tilston's dead. His body's in the back of the bloody car outside.' But he could already feel that incessant buzzing in his head resolving itself into something calmer, something more resonant. As if finally some meaning was beginning to emerge.

'That's what I thought,' Wanstead said. 'That's what I couldn't understand. Then I realised. I thought back over what you and Joe had told me about it. Tilston's body had been identified by his next of kin. Anne Tilston. You had only her word that the body out there was who she said it was.'

Murrain was trying to compute what Wanstead was saying. If it had been anyone else telling him this, he'd have concluded they'd lost the plot. 'You're saying that Anne Tilston lied to us.'

'That's exactly what I'm telling you.'

It wasn't so far-fetched, Murrain supposed. After all, he knew Anne Tilston had already lied to him once. There was no reason to think the lie might not have gone much further. 'So who's the body outside?'

'I'll come to that.' Wanstead had the air of someone who'd waited a long time to tell his story and wanted do it properly. 'But it's not Robert Tilston.'

'She couldn't have expected to get away with it. We'd have identified the body in due course. At the post mortem or afterwards.'

'Would we?' Wanstead said. 'I'm not sure how rational or planned Anne Tilston's actions were. I suspect she might have just done it on the spur of the moment. But I don't know she wouldn't have got away with it, if she'd kept up the lie. She'd confirmed his identity as his next of kin. We'd have had no reason to doubt her word. Unless there'd been some major disparity between the body and what we knew of Robert Tilston, we'd probably never have thought to question it. Tilston had no living relatives other than his daughters – two of whom aren't in a position to offer us their views – and as far as we know no close friends. I think she could easily have got away with it.'

'But why would she even have tried?'

'If you'll forgive the expression, Kenny, that really is a long story. I'll tell it to you in full, but if the young lady here is feeling up to it, I think we ought to get back to the house. Talking of Anne Tilston, I'm getting an uncomfortable feeling.'

When they'd first arrived here, Murrain thought, it felt as if he'd encountered a Paul Wanstead he'd never seen before. A more active, impetuous figure than the one they were used to in the office. Now the familiar Wanstead was back – understated, cautious, doing things very precisely but at his own pace. It was frustrating but it was also, he had to admit, mildly reassuring.

'Okay, Paul. We'll do it your way.' He looked down at the woman. 'Are you feeling up to moving?'

The woman hadn't spoken again since her initial words, but Murrain had thought it best not to press her at the moment. When they were back in the Tilstons' house, he could get her something to eat and drink. Then he'd see whether he could get some basic information from her before giving her a chance to sleep. He didn't even know her name, let alone why or how she'd ended up in the church.

But he shared Wanstead's discomfort about what was happening. His mind felt calmer following the revelation about Robert Tilston's identity, but other thoughts had almost immediately arisen to fill any mental vacuum, like black clouds drifting back into a briefly empty sky.

If anyone had asked him to describe it, he couldn't have said much more than that he had a bad feeling. A stirring of unease under his flesh. The voices in his head were still there, telling him it was time to move. That something was still wrong. Or that whatever had been wrong before had not yet been fully resolved.

It took them longer than he'd hoped to get back to the Tilstons' house. The young woman could still barely walk, and had to be half carried much of the way by Murrain and Sparrow. Donovan and Wanstead were taking care of Robert Tilston who could walk with assistance but required constant prompting to make any progress. Wanstead himself was limping, his ageing limbs feeling the effects of his struggle up the hill. They constituted a pretty motley band, Murrain thought.

The snow-covered ground remained hard going, difficult to negotiate and treacherous underfoot. The sky was now largely clear, heavy with winter stars. There was still an icy breeze blowing in from the valley, but it felt to Murrain as if the temperature was rising.

Back at the house, he fumbled with the keys he'd borrowed from inside the front door. He'd initially decided not to disturb Anne Tilston before leaving, on the assumption that they wouldn't be away long and he was leaving Bert Wallace behind in case anything occurred in their absence. In the event, she'd appeared in the hallway just as they were departing, her expression suggesting outrage at being disturbed yet again.

Murrain had offered her little in the way of explanation. He'd told her only that they wanted to check out something in the church. Her expression had been surprise and then, he thought now, something more than surprise. He hadn't stopped to wonder why.

He was only just beginning to process properly what Wanstead had said. If the man with them really was Robert Tilston, his daughter knew full well that he was alive. That meant she'd probably been sheltering him since their arrival. He thought back to the unbolted back door and the incident with the dog, and wondered whether Anne Tilston had already been out to provide her father with food.

Countless questions led on from that. Not least about the deaths of Newland and the second man. The identity of the dead man in the churchyard, and of the young woman apparently being held in the church. None of this made sense to Murrain, and his mind was still struggling to come to grips with it.

At the moment all that seemed relatively unimportant. From the moment he'd arrived back at the house, his unease had been growing. The endless voices in his head, which had calmed briefly back in the church, were rising again, their soundless chanting like a drumbeat of warning. Something felt wrong. Desperately wrong.

He exchanged a glance with Wanstead. He could see that Wanstead was feeling the same, though presumably his reasons were more straightforward.

Murrain finally succeeded in engaging the key. He pushed open the door and stepped inside.

At first, everything seemed unchanged. The house was silent, the lights in the hallway lit as he'd left them. He paused, listening. Nothing.

He took another step into the gloomy hallway. Now he could see the full length of the corridor to what lay at the far end.

A figure prone on the ground. A female figure, dressed in plain black trousers and a black shirt.

Bert Wallace.

Murrain hurried along the hallway, his senses alert for any other movement or sound. He crouched down next to Wallace's motionless body and pressed his fingers against her neck. There was fresh blood in her hair, a trickle of red running down her cheek.

Donovan was crouching beside him, her face ashen. 'How is she?'

'Alive. There's a pulse. Quite a strong one. She seems to be breathing okay. Let's get her into the recovery position.' He gestured for the others to make their way past into the study they'd been occupying earlier. 'Best if you're all out of the way. We don't know what's going on here.'

Sparrow and Wanstead led Tilston and the young woman into the study. Tilston's expression was still blank, showing no signs of recognising the house or the room that had once been his own study. The woman looked shell-shocked, confused, as if she had no idea what was happening around her. Join the club, Murrain thought.

As Donovan and Murrain finished manoeuvring Wallace into position, her eyes flickered open. She gazed uncertainly up at them, then her vision focussed. 'Where's Ferby?'

The question had already begun to occur to Murrain, along with a host of others. 'I don't know. What happened?' The straight question felt brutal given Wallace's condition, but Murrain was increasingly feeling there was no time to waste.

'I don't know. Ferby had gone into the kitchen to get some more water. I heard a noise. Some kind of disturbance out in the hallway. I came out to see what was going on and then something – someone hit me. They must have been waiting outside the door.'

'How are you feeling?'

'Very sore bloody head. Bit woozy. Not too bad, though, considering.'

'Think you can sit up?'

'I think so.' With help from Donovan, Wallace eased herself up to a sitting position. She looked past Murrain into the study, where the slumped figure of Robert Tilston had been placed on the sofa, Sparrow standing over him. The young woman was sitting on one of the dining chairs, being tended by Paul Wanstead. 'What the hell's going on? What the hell's Paul doing here.'

'I wish I knew.' Murrain was about to say more when something made him pause. The inarticulate vocal drumming was still pounding in his head, but there was something more overlaying it. An endless wail, faint but piercing. The cry of a child in torment, he thought, not knowing where the thought had come from. He looked up at Donovan. 'Did you hear something?'

She shook her head, looking down at him curiously. 'No. This place is as silent as—'

But then they both heard it. A high-pitched scream. A child bewildered and terrified. From inside the room where the Carters had been sleeping.

It could be nothing, Murrain told himself. The sound of a child waking from a bad dream. But his heart was already telling him this was the opposite. This was the sound of a child waking into a nightmare.

'What do you want to do?' Donovan had lowered her voice.

'I don't think we've any choice. We have to go in.' He'd been here too often, he thought, entering a room with no real idea what was waiting on the other side. He was concerned less about the risk to himself than what response his entry might provoke. But there was no way of knowing, and if a child was in danger they couldn't wait to find out.

Gesturing for Donovan to stand behind him, he moved forward and silently turned the door-handle. He pushed open the door as gently as possible, tense in the face of whatever might be inside.

Even so, the scene in the room was heart-stopping. The room was in semi-darkness, the only light coming from a small bedside lamp. The same lamp that Rob Carter had presumably brought down from his earlier expedition upstairs, Murrain thought irrelevantly.

The Carters themselves were gathered in one corner, the two parents sitting on one of the beds, with one of their sons between them. Neil Ferbrache was on the floor beside them, staring hard at Murrain as if trying to impart some telepathic message.

Anne Tilston was sitting away from the rest of the group, stooped forward in an old rocking chair. The chair was battered, but had once been painted in bright colours as if for a nursery or a child's bedroom.

The second child was curled up on Anne Tilston's lap. At first glance, the scene looked maternal. Then Murrain realised the child was terrified, his reddened eyes staring fearfully at the woman holding him.

The woman holding the barrel of a revolver to the child's temple.

Anne Tilston had looked up at Murrain's entrance but looked untroubled by his presence. Murrain himself took a breath, conscious now of the reaction that might have been triggered by his opening of the door.

'Anne,' he said, gently. 'Put down the gun. Let the boy go back to his parents.' He was racking his brains to remember the two boys' names. Jack and Ben, he thought. But he had no idea which was which.

Anne Tilston shook her head sadly. 'I can't do that. Bad boys have to be taught a lesson. Bradley knew that.'

There was something chilling about the way she spoke the last three words. The child on Anne Tilston's lap was silent, frozen with fear, but the child in Murrain's head was still screaming, a lost soul forever in the far distance.

'He's done nothing wrong.' Murrain's voice was soft. Unthreatening. 'Let him go.'

'He's disruptive. Noisy. Bradley was always like that.'

'Just put down the gun, Anne.'

She finally looked up at Murrain. 'This is our house. We do what we like here. Who are you to tell us different?'

'I'm a police officer, Anne. I'm here to help you.'

'My father was a police officer,' she said, as if rebutting Murrain's point.

'I know that.' He wondered whether to tell her that her father was waiting in the next room, but he wanted to do nothing to disturb the equilibrium. Not until she no longer had the gun in her possession. 'Is that his gun? He wouldn't want you to be handling it.'

She looked puzzled. 'He's always let me play with it. Ever since I was small.'

It was quite possible, Murrain thought, that the gun wasn't even loaded. It looked like a police revolver, though he had no idea how Tilston had managed to retain it after leaving the force. Tilston had always made his own rules.

He decided to risk a step forward, keeping his movements slow and unthreatening. 'Just give it to me, Anne. You don't want anyone to get hurt.'

Her puzzlement had been replaced by a smile. 'I don't care about people getting hurt. I've never cared about people getting hurt. I just want to protect my father. I just want time to get him away from here. Get him somewhere safe. Where I can take care of him.'

'He's here, Anne. Put the gun down and I'll take you to him.'

'I need the gun. Then you'll keep us safe.' She looked down at the boy. 'In any case, he needs to be punished.'

Murrain heard an intake of breath from Liz Carter. He hoped that neither she nor her husband would be tempted to do anything unexpected. The last thing they needed was for Rob Carter to try to play the hero.

'He's done nothing wrong, Anne. Look, keep the gun for now if you want to, but let me have the boy. You don't really want to hurt him.'

He could feel her hesitate for a moment as if almost persuaded by what he was saying. 'He's been bad. Disruptive. Just like Bradley was.'

Murrain could sense something happening behind him, but he didn't dare to take his eyes off Anne Tilston. There was a noise of some kind from the study, a raised voice. He prayed the others could keep control of whatever was going on. 'He's just a small boy, Anne. He means no harm. Send him over to me.'

He had no idea whether he was getting through to her or not. The commotion behind him was growing louder. The raised voice was one he didn't recognise, though he could hear Marie Donovan and Bert Wallace saying something.

'Anne, please let me have the boy—'

He was pushed forcibly to one side, and turned to see Robert Tilston behind him in the doorway, Paul Wanstead and Will Sparrow trying to hold him back. He looked a different figure from the person Murrain had seen in the church. He was gaunt and his face remained unshaven, but he no longer seemed frail and submissive. This was the Robert Tilston Murrain half remembered from all those years before, the hammer of God jabbing his finger at the television cameras as he spat out his denunciation of some supposedly degenerate group.

'Hayley! What are you doing? I've told you never to touch my gun. If the boy needs disciplining, that's my job. I've told you you're too soft with him. He can twist you round his little finger.'

Anne was looking up at him, startled, her expression suggesting she was as baffled by this intervention as Murrain was.

Wanstead and Sparrow were grasping Tilston's arms, but he pushed them off as if they were scarcely there and walked further into the room. 'Give me the gun, Hayley. I've told you before don't mess with things you don't understand. If anyone here needs discipline, it's you, and not for the first time.'

He reached out to take the gun from his daughter. She was staring up at him, both of them oblivious to the fact that the boy was now screaming in terror. Murrain started to move forward, conscious that on the other side of the room Rob Carter was doing the same.

'Mr Tilston—'

He never finished the sentence. Anne Tilston's arm had twitched involuntarily at her father's looming approach, and with no warning the gun went off.

CHAPTER FORTY-FOUR

The silence after the gunshot was almost as shocking as the noise itself.

Murrain had closed his eyes momentarily in response to the explosion. He reopened them to see Anne Tilston still sitting on the rocking chair, the pistol held loosely in her hand. Her face was white, her eyes blank as if unable to take in the enormity of what she was seeing.

The Carter boy had taken advantage of the brief confusion to wriggle free and had already run over to his mother, who was clutching him as if never intending to let him free.

Robert Tilston was face down in front of Murrain, a pool of red spreading slowly from beneath his chest.

Murrain took the gun from Anne Tilston's hand, holding it as carefully as he could. It would be important to preserve the evidence, but that was far from his top priority at this moment. Wanstead, characteristically, had already produced an evidence bag from somewhere and was holding it out. Murrain dropped the gun inside and nodded his thanks.

He crouched down and took Tilston's hand, checking for any sign of a pulse. There was nothing, but he'd never really doubted Tilston was dead. He looked up and nodded to Liz Carter. 'Take your boys next door. We'll deal with everything here.' Easy enough to say, he thought. The sounds in his head had changed in quality since the gunshot, but they were still there, pounding away, and somewhere there was still the sound of screaming.

Anne Tilston was sitting in the rocking chair, motionless, looking as if she might never be capable of moving again. The other members of Murrain's team had shuffled in and were standing awkwardly, as if waiting instructions.

Murrain turned to Wanstead. 'Okay, Paul. We're sitting, or at least standing, comfortably. I think it's time for you to tell us your story.'

Wanstead was silent for a moment, as if reluctant or unable to begin. Finally, he gestured to Anne Tilston. 'Anne can tell the story better than anyone. Remember me, Anne?'

She looked up, her eyes still glazed, and stared uncomprehendingly at Wanstead.

'You remember, Anne. Uncle Paul. You remember Uncle Paul.' There was an uncharacteristic note of bitterness in Wanstead's tone.

'Uncle Paul.' There was no understanding in Anne Tilston's voice. She sounded like an automaton, Murrain thought.

'Uncle Paul,' Wanstead said again. 'Your mother's brother. Hayley's brother.'

'Hayley?' Murrain remembered the words Robert Tilston had spoken as he'd entered the room.

'Aye, Hayley. My elder sister. The late wife of the now equally late Robert Tilston.'

'Tilston was your brother in law?'

'I never exactly boasted about it. Don't think most people even knew,' Wanstead said. 'I'd tried to warn Hayley he was an utter bastard, but she just told me to bugger off. He was a man on the way up, and she wouldn't hear a bloody word against him. She paid for that, right enough.'

'You said late wife? Not just missing. You know that for sure?'

'I've always known it. I came here once to challenge him about it, but he laughed in my face. Then he screwed my career. Now Tilston's gone, Anne here is the only one who can really confirm it, if she's ever in a state to do so. That was why I came on this wild goose chase tonight. When I heard what was happening up here, I had a feeling things would end up like this.'

'A feeling?' Murrain was still wrestling with his own feelings. The child was still there, somewhere in the depths of his mind. No longer screaming, but whispering truths Murrain couldn't begin to comprehend.

'Not like your feelings, maybe. Copper's gut.'

'You knew Tilston was still alive?'

'I didn't know anything. But the two killings. They were Tilston, right enough. Either he'd returned from the grave – and frankly I wouldn't put it past the bugger even now – or he wasn't dead. Not yet.' He gestured towards Tilston's body. 'But this was always where it was heading.'

'So you came all the way up here for what? To make him tell you that Hayley was dead?'

'That's about the size of it. I wanted to hear it from him. Even when he was convicted, he never admitted anything more than GBH. I thought tonight he might be far enough gone not to care any more.'

'And was he?'

'He was too far gone, really. Much more than I'd expected. But in the end he said it. He told me she was dead. Not a confession that would stand up in court. But enough for me.'

'I'm sorry,' Murrain said.

Donovan had been watching the exchange with a bemused expression. 'I'm not sure I'm following this. Are you saying Tilston killed your sister?'

Wanstead gestured to Anne Tilston. She had dropped her head again and seemed oblivious to anyone else's presence. 'Like I say, Anne's now the only one who can confirm any of this. But Hayley was bullied and beaten by Tilston from the day she married him, and probably before. He treated all the family the same. All except little Anne herself. The only one he loved. I dread to think how he treated her.' He paused, as if unsure how to continue. 'I'm pretty sure he killed Bradley. It was supposedly an accident, a fall on the hillside here. Fractured his skull. But Tilston saw Bradley as a disruptive kid. Trouble. Whatever really happened to Bradley, it was no accident. Hayley swore it had been a fall, gave Tilston an alibi. Reckoned he'd not even been in the house when it happened. There was no evidence either way, and no reason for anyone outside the family to start throwing accusations at a senior police officer. A good Christian pillar of the community.' He spat out the last words.

'But you don't know for sure he killed Bradley,' Murrain pointed out.

Wanstead stared at Murrain for a moment. 'No, you're right. That was the way he did things. But they all knew what he'd done. Hayley. The daughters. They were too afraid to challenge him. And when Hayley finally did—'

'You're saying he killed Hayley too?'

'I know he did. She's buried somewhere in the bloody churchyard. Somewhere not far from where you found Vic Perry's body.'

Murrain could still hear all the voices in his head and then, momentarily, there had been an image. A bedroom. The bedroom in Toby Newland's house where they'd found the second knifed body. 'Vic Perry?'

'Perry lived in one of the cottages along the road, all those years ago. I'm guessing it was the same cottage where you found the body. It was much less gentrified in those days. Perry was a builder. One man band, but did okay for himself. Worked mainly for the local farmers around these parts. Did some work on the house here.' He paused. 'And started an affair with Hayley. I suspect she was attracted to him because he was actually kind to her.'

Murrain was watching Anne Tilston as he listened. She still had her head bowed down, but he had a sense she was following Wanstead's story. Something about the tension in her shoulders suggested she was taking in every word he said.

'I don't know what happened after that exactly,' Wanstead went on. 'Maybe Hayley threatened to tell the truth about Bradley's death. Maybe Tilston simply found out about the affair. Tilston reckoned she'd simply walked out one day, left without a note or any kind of forwarding details. He was pretty much just taken at his word. He revealed she'd been having an affair, so the police spent more time interviewing and investigating Perry than they did Tilston. Perry had a criminal record. Nothing major. A couple of burglaries when he was younger. He'd avoided prison, but only just. Enough for the police to have him pegged as a wrong 'un, anyway, with a bit of prompting from Tilston. There was no evidence against him and the investigation was dropped, but it provided the deflection that Tilston needed. In the end, they accepted Tilston's claim that the affair had given her a taste for freedom, and she'd just decided to take it.'

'What about Perry?'

'He threw some accusations at Tilston, but most people thought that, if anything, that just proved his guilt. Why else would you make those kinds of accusations against a man like Robert Tilston. Even though the police didn't pursue the investigation, there were a lot round here who thought there was no smoke without fire. Perry couldn't get any work and was made to feel pretty unwelcome. Went off down south somewhere, and as far as I know didn't return. Until yesterday.'

'The mysterious man in the graveyard. You think that was him? So what brought him back?'

'I've kept in touch with Perry off and on over the years. Not closely, you know. But the odd e-mail exchange, social media. Christmas cards. The usual bonding over a suspected murder. Like I say, I'd had my own shot at challenging Tilston and that's the real reason my card was marked in the force. Tilston had made it bloody clear that if I pursued it, he'd find some serious disciplinary offence to pin on me. He'd done the same to Perry, apparently. Told him he'd find a way of fitting him up on some serious charge. Serious enough, with his record, to get him sent down. Perry had rebuilt his life down south. He couldn't afford to take the risk.'

'But this must have all changed when Tilston was convicted?' This was from Marie Donovan, standing behind Murrain.

'Yes and no. Yes, in that Tilston's word no longer counted for anything. No, in that by then no-one was really interested. They had enough to put Tilston away. The force just wanted to put a lid on the whole thing. No-one was interested in opening up any more cans of worms. I tried.' Wanstead sounded weary, as if everything – not just his journey tonight, but the previous twenty or more years – had finally caught up with him.

'And Perry?'

'Perry was dying. Pancreatic cancer. No more than weeks left, they'd said. He'd been trying to make contact with Tilston. He wanted to have one last go at making Tilston confess. Like me, he just wanted to hear the truth. But I don't know how he worked out that Tilston was living here—'

'He didn't.'

The intervention was unexpected, and it took Murrain a moment to work out who had spoken the words. Anne Tilston had raised her head and was staring fixedly at Wanstead. 'You all think you're smart. You're not fit to lick my father's boots.'

Wanstead looked as if he was about to respond, but Murrain signalled for him to remain quiet.

'Perry had been pestering my father for months. My father was – unwell, though he was as strong as he'd ever been. But he was declining and I didn't know how long he'd have. I didn't want him wasting it with scum like that. So I invited Perry up here, supposedly for a last meeting with my father. I thought if he came here, we could find a way of dealing with him. Maybe pay him off or something. I'd been expecting him today. I don't know why he came last night. Maybe just knew from the forecast that he wouldn't get here if he left it any longer. Perhaps he just wanted to make a dramatic arrival at first light. Catch us by surprise. Instead, he just sat out there and died.' She was laughing to herself now, as if she'd told the funniest joke imaginable.

Murrain watched her, thinking about what she'd just said. Maybe it was true. But Ferbrache had thought Perry had died from the effects of some toxin. Perhaps Perry had preferred just to make the gesture. To die next to the woman he'd loved. 'I still don't understand why you said Perry was your father.'

'It was a spur of the moment thing. He was pretty much the same age. He even looked a little like father. That was probably why mother was attracted to him—' She hesitated, as if she'd inadvertently stumbled into unwelcome territory. 'I knew father didn't have long to live himself. I thought if I persuaded you he'd already died, everyone would leave him alone in his last days.'

She's the insane one, Murrain thought. She seems icily rational, but there's something terrifying squirming not far from the surface. In his head, he could hear the child screaming again, as if from far below ground. He took a breath, wanting to control his voice. 'What was wrong with your father?'

'A form of dementia. As I told you, a very aggressive form of dementia.'

'What did it do to him?'

She stopped and looked up at him, as if suddenly aware of what he was asking. 'At first, it seemed to make him young again. Not physically, though he's—' She paused again. 'He was in good shape for his age. But at first the illness made him more disinhibited. It was as if it took him back to the man he'd been.'

The man who'd been convicted of serious assaults and had perhaps committed much worse crimes, Murrain thought. 'The woman we found in the church?'

She was staring at him now, defying him to judge her. 'It was what father used to do before his illness. He did it differently then. He was good at it, even at his age. He'd approach them in bars. Flatter them. Get to know them.

Sometimes just in – well, a fatherly way. Sometimes more straightforward. It depended on how they responded.'

He must have told you all this, Murrain thought. His own daughter. But then Tilston's relationship with Anne and her sisters was another question. 'And then?'

'Then he got tired of them. He'd dispose of them. He always disposed of them. Except me. I was the only one he loved.'

I was the only one he loved, Murrain thought. Not Charlotte or Emily. Only Anne. The only one he hadn't disposed of. Struggling to keep his voice calm, he asked, 'And after his illness?'

'He couldn't do that anymore, not in the last few months. But his appetites were the same. So he made me help. I didn't want to, but I could never disobey him. It was more random. We just used to pick them up off the streets around Manchester. Father knew how to handle them. How to get them into the back of the car. How to deal with them. Then we'd bring them here until he was tired of them. He always wanted the same kind of woman. Women who were like me when I was younger.' She paused, thinking. 'Not just women, though it was women since he became ill. He was worried that men might be too strong for him. But he liked young men too. They were like the son he never had.'

Murrain exchanged a glance with Wanstead. Perhaps, if his wife had been having an affair, Tilston had never even believed Bradley was his own.

It felt as if all the air had been sucked from the room. Wanstead's eyes were blank. Donovan was ashen, her expression suggesting she couldn't believe what she was hearing. Murrain had nothing but questions – how many? what had happened to them? – but there would be time for those later.

'What about Toby Newland?' he asked, instead. 'And the other man?'

Anne Tilston shook her head, as if he was bothering her about some trivial point. 'That was unfortunate. I told him

Perry was back. I didn't get chance to explain properly. He went over to the house where Perry had lived—'

'And killed the man he found there.'

She nodded. 'Newland arrived just as he was leaving. Saw what had happened.' She paused. 'Father was still a strong man.' She spoke with the air of a proud daughter. 'He dragged Newland down the hill, telling him to keep quiet. But Newland wouldn't. So he had no choice, really, did he?'

Her voice was as chillingly calm as when Murrain had first met her. She looked up at him, and he could see nothing in her eyes. 'That's it,' she said. 'That's the story.'

Murrain stared back at her, unable to offer any response. Deep in his head, the child was still screaming. And slowly, moment by moment, other voices were rising to join the same unholy chorus.

CHAPTER FORTY-FIVE

'You look like death warmed up.'

Those had been Joe Milton's first words after Murrain had opened the front door to him. 'You don't look too hot yourself,' he responded.

Not the sparkliest of repartee, Murrain thought, but he was grateful for anything that felt like normality after the previous twenty-four hours. He and the team had sat up for the rest of the night. Keeping watch over Anne Tilston and tending to the Carters and the young woman.

The young woman who, it had turned out, was the missing Kirsty Bennett.

'Jesus, you're joking,' Joe Milton had said when Murrain had phoned to tell him.

'Trust me, Joe, I'm in no mood for jokes. It's Bennett all right. She's not in a great state. She's spent most of the time tied up and has been fed the absolute minimum. But she's okay and able to tell us what happened. She was just grabbed, dragged into the back of a car, somewhere near Stockport Station.'

'I'm just glad I didn't go and break the news to her parents,' Milton said. 'Though it raises the question of who our body is.'

'One of Tilston's previous victims, I'm guessing. We don't know how many of them there are, or how they usually – disposed of them, to use Anne Tilston's choice phrase. That's all stuff we'll have to get from her if we can.' Murrain's mind was already contemplating the pile of missing persons files sitting in his cupboard. Perhaps some of those could now be closed. Perhaps.

To his relief, the snow had not returned overnight and the temperature had continued to rise. By first light, snow was already slipping from the trees and rooftops, and there was a constant dripping from the gutters. Murrain had been on the phone to Marty Winston overnight, telling him he could call off the manhunt. The main priority now was just to get them out of what Murrain was increasingly beginning to think of as a literally godforsaken place.

In the end, Winston had somehow managed to commandeer a snow plough, and by mid-morning the narrow road up to Merestone had been sufficiently cleared to allow access to a car carrying Winston and Milton, closely followed by a pair of ambulances. The first ambulance had taken Bennett, along with Bert Wallace and Neil Ferbrache. The second had taken the two disabled sisters who would shortly be in the care of Social Services. Murrain had no idea how that particular situation would be resolved.

That left the police to deal with Anne Tilston and the three bodies. The final task had been to persuade Ferbrache it really was safe for him to leave his precious van and equipment with them.

'I'll get Will to drive the van back for you, Neil,' Murrain had said, though that prospect hadn't seemed to do much to allay Ferbrache's concerns.

After the ambulances had departed, Murrain stood on the doorstep of the Tilstons' house with Winston and Wanstead, watching Marie Donovan and Joe Milton leading Anne Tilston down to one of the police vehicles.

'Not the most romantic of moments,' Wanstead observed. 'But I bet those two are pleased to see each other.'

'I'm guessing that won't be high in their priorities, given the night we've had,' Murrain said.

'You think? Tell you what, after the night I've had, I'll be glad to get back to Helena.'

'Well, there's a first,' Murrain said. 'You'll have some explaining to do there, as well.'

'She knows all about the history with Hayley. I wouldn't say she's actively encouraged my obsessions – in fact, I think her exact words were "just bloody well leave it, Paul" – but she understands. If nothing else, I've laid a few ghosts now.'

'I hope so,' Murrain agreed. 'Though I reckon there's a lot about this we'll never know for certain. Not unless Anne Tilston's really prepared to spill the beans.'

'She seems to have been forthcoming enough last night, from what you've told me,' Winston said.

'Maybe,' Murrain said. 'She wanted to prove she knew more than we did. She wanted to boast about her father. She was still in shock from Tilston's death and her part in it. That's what worries me, I suppose. Anne Tilston's a psychopath maybe, but there's something chillingly calculating about whatever she does. It sounds like she might have played a part in inciting Newland's murder, maybe because he was gay or maybe because she resented his interest in buying the church. Apart from anything else, she wouldn't have wanted any risk of her mother's remains being discovered. Then there's the question of her sisters' supposed accident. She's her father's daughter, right enough. So I just wonder whether her shooting of Tilston was entirely accidental, or whether she wasn't sorry to silence him.'

'The man was suffering from dementia,' Winston said. 'Nobody was going to rely on anything he might say.'

'No, but that's my point. He was in and out of lucidity. He might have said anything, including revealing things that Anne Tilston might have preferred not to talk about.'

'Such as what?'

Murrain could still hear the chorus of lost voices in his head, calmer now, but endlessly seeking his attention. Perhaps he always would. 'Perhaps that Anne Tilston had always been more in control of all this than she wanted us to think. Perhaps that Tilston had never acted entirely alone. Perhaps not even with Bradley or with Paul's sister. Perhaps she'd always wanted Tilston to herself.'

Wanstead was staring at him. Winston, on the other hand, was looking bored and restless. 'You've had a long night, Kenny,' Winston said. 'You need some rest. Let's get you away from here.'

Murrain nodded, getting the message. There'd be time enough later, he thought, to worry about what those voices in his head were really saying. He took one last look back at the gloomy house and wondered what other secrets might still be concealed in its walls. 'You're right. Let's get out of here. I need to meet the real world again. I feel as if I've been away much too long.'

Printed in Great Britain
by Amazon